PRESS RELATIONS

Recent Titles by Elisabeth McNeill from Severn House

A BOMBAY AFFAIR
THE SEND-OFF
THE GOLDEN DAYS
UNFORGETTABLE
THE LAST COCKTAIL PARTY

DUSTY LETTERS
MONEY TROUBLES
TURN BACK TIME

THE EDINBURGH MYSTERIES

HOT NEWS
PRESS RELATIONS

PRESS
RELATIONS

Elisabeth McNeill

This first world edition published in Great Britain 2003 by
SEVERN HOUSE PUBLISHERS LTD of
9–15 High Street, Sutton, Surrey SM1 1DF.
This first world edition published in the USA 2003 by
SEVERN HOUSE PUBLISHERS INC of
595 Madison Avenue, New York, N.Y. 10022.

British Library Cataloguing in Publication Data

McNeill, Elisabeth
    Press relations
    1. Woman journalists - Scotland - Edinburgh - Fiction
    2. Investigative reporting - Scotland - Edinburgh - Fiction
    3. Murder - Investigation - Scotland - Edinburgh - Fiction
    4. Detective and mystery stories
    I. Title
    823.9'14 [F]

    ISBN 0-7278-6002-X

Typeset by Palimpsest Book Production Ltd.,
Polmont, Stirlingshire, Scotland.
Printed and bound in Great Britain by
MPG Books Ltd., Bodmin, Cornwall.

You cannot hope
to bribe or twist,
thank God! the
British Journalist.
But, seeing what
The man will do
unbribed, there's
no occasion to.

Humbert Wolfe,
'Over the Fire', 1930

One

It was nine forty-five. With trembling hands Patricia removed the cover from her typewriter and, smoothing down her fashionably full skirt and stiff petticoats, settled at her desk.

The skirt belled round her legs like the head of a flower but she took no pleasure in it. Her throat ached with the effort of biting back tears and a pulse throbbed in her forehead.

The Chief Subeditor, who sat at the desk facing hers, looked up and said, without smiling, 'What exactly are you intending to do today, Miss Aitken?'

I was thinking of throwing myself in the Thames. What would the reaction ~~would~~ *be if she said that*, she wondered?

Probably only: 'Make sure you do it in your lunch hour and not in the magazine's time.'

She had no intention of drowning herself, of course, but she wanted to lean over the desk and say to the heavily made-up harridan, 'I'm miserable. I hate all of you and I hate this place. I want to go home.'

Home was Edinburgh and the chaos of the *Evening Dispatch* office where, at the moment, her friends would be doing the rewrites and drinking cups of ghastly orange-coloured canteen tea. She missed them badly – she even missed the tea.

In the office of *Women's World*, where she now worked, there were no mould-growing teacups abandoned on the desks, no ashtrays overflowing with butt-ends, no empty gin bottles in the waste-paper baskets.

The women who worked beside her were obsessively

tidy. The deputy sub rested her coffee cup on a white lace doily, and the others displayed framed photographs of their nearest and dearest on their desks alongside vases of flowers, which were thrown out before they began to wilt. A phalanx of green plants in pots were arranged beside the double windows, grabbing for the grey London light.

In a high, falsely confident voice, Patricia said, 'I went to the Happy Homes exhibition yesterday and I'm writing about it now. Then I'll tidy up that article about the secrets of a successful marriage.'

'Tidy it up?' queried the chief sub, Imogen Parker. Patricia had been told to address her as Miss Parker as first names were never used in the office. Even after five months, she could not get used to hearing herself referred to as Miss Aitken.

'Yes, Miss Parker. I want to make it more readable, and give it a bit of oomph,' she said.

'Re-*ally*?' Miss Parker said, emphasizing the word in a supercilious drawl. 'The contributor who sent in that piece is one of our most respected writers. Please don't spoil her work. "Oomph", as you call it, isn't quite our style.'

Patricia said nothing, but straightened her back and stared with loathing round the office. Framed copies of the magazine's most recent covers were hanging on the walls and all featured close-up portraits of wholesome-looking, smiling young women with magnificent teeth and gleaming hair; the sort of girls that Hugh called 'good breeding material'.

Hugh. Thinking of him made her heart ache.

Lowering her head, she went back to work, feeling out of place in every way. The other four women in the room were wearing hats, for all were about to go out on social engagements. Many of the *Women's World* staff were recruited because of their society connections, and did not allow their journalistic duties to constrict their social lives.

Miss Parker's hat was the most eye-catching because it was black velvet, circled by primroses and finished off with a natty half veil. Patricia looked at the nodding primroses with loathing and her mind went back to the sartorial choices of the staff in her Edinburgh newspaper office: Rosa, her great friend and fellow reporter, in a brass buttoned pea jacket and tartan trousers; Alan, the Australian theatre critic and obscure poet, in crummy tweeds, asleep with his head on his typewriter; Mike, the ambitious, wannabe Fleet Street reporter, with his carefully combed coiffure and horrible suits; Lawrie, the paper's racing tipster, in an unravelling sweater and corduroy trousers.

She missed them, how she missed them. Tears pricked her eyes again, but she knew the best cure for her misery was work.

Rolling a sheet of paper into the carriage of her typewriter, she smoothed out and started to read the manuscript of the article about successful marriage. As she expected, it was a gushing tirade of clichés.

If you want to have a long and lasting marriage, there are some basic rules you must always observe:

RULE ONE: When hubby returns from a hard slog at the office, NEVER start telling him about your problems the moment he steps into the house, no matter how fraught your own day might have been.

RULE TWO: No matter how tiring your own day, do your hair, refresh your make-up, put on a clean dress before he comes home, have his favourite evening drink and his newspaper by his chair and his slippers on the hearth.

RULE THREE: Smile, give him a loving kiss, and keep the kiddies quiet. A husband who comes home to a tranquil home and an uncomplaining wife will never stray!

She thought the advice was rubbish, but didn't dare change a word of the copy, only bent her head and concentrated on putting in the necessary subediting instructions for the printers before sending it on its way.

It made her feel guilty to be disseminating such advice

to the magazine's readers. Did none of the women editing magazines like this feel like traitors to their own sex? Did they never wonder why the divorce rate was rising? Did none of them think that their average reader might have higher aspirations than to be forced into domestic slavery?

She fought against a strong desire to tear up the copy and scream out loud, 'This is shit, shit, shit!' That would make them sit up but Miss Parker was pulling on long black gloves in preparation for an expensive lunch with a fashion designer who wanted her clothes to feature in the magazine.

The Art Editor was painting her fingernails.

The Agony Aunt was reading a paperback novel beneath the edge of her desk.

And the society column's resident debutante, Miss Pembroke-Grey, was languidly phoning someone she addressed as 'sweetie'. It was obvious that 'sweetie' was cancelling their lunch date and the debutante surveyed her colleagues as she hung up. When her eye fell on Patricia, she got up and came across to say, 'I've been meaning to ask you, Miss Aitken, are you related to the Beaverbrooks?'

Patricia looked blank. 'I'm afraid not,' she said, forgetting that Lord Beaverbrook's surname was Aitken.

Miss Pembroke-Grey was obviously disappointed. 'Oh! Or perhaps the Aitkens of Strathdon? They have a lovely house up there in Scotland – a shooting lodge. My brother went to school – at Eton – with their eldest son.'

Patricia wondered if she should admit that this Miss Aitken's father drove a lorry for an Edinburgh brewery, but she only shook her head, and said, 'Sorry, no relation.' The admission meant she lost any chance of having lunch with Miss Pembroke-Grey, who stalked off alone, adjusting her little hat with a languid hand.

When they had all gone, Patricia began to eat an apple and read a letter she brought out of her handbag. It was from Hugh, and had arrived at her lodgings in St John's Wood that morning. He wrote one letter to every four or

4

five of hers, and today's was even shorter than usual, only one page covered with his spidery-looking writing.

There was no way he could visit her in London, he said. He had a lot on in Edinburgh. There was a very good reception in the Arts Club last night and he was going to dinner with Maitland Crewe, his friend, at the weekend because Maitland wanted him to meet his wife Sonya's cousin, an American who had come over to study at Edinburgh University.

'You must get it into your head that I'm not eager to get married. I won't make good husband material,' he wrote.

This filled her with panic, as it was meant to. When she'd come to London, she'd hoped he would rush after her, or at least plead with her to come back. Before she left Edinburgh, they were occasionally sleeping together, with great success, she thought, and he'd reacted badly when she decided to take the job in London.

Once away, the ambition that used to burn in her was dampened down by her love and longing for him. It would not be easy to give up her chance of advancement, and a wage of fifteen pounds a week on a highly respected women's magazine. She'd thought that staying in London, might have brought him to the point of proposing. The gamble hadn't worked.

She felt as if the reference to the cousin in his letter was written with emphasis. What if he found someone else? He was an attractive man, and if this woman was an academic, he might be seduced by her learning. Some of those highbrow women were incredibly immoral. Terror of losing him made the palms of her hands sweat.

She asked herself, *What's more important? My career or my life?* Her answer decided her: she could not live without him.

Members of the magazine staff were not allowed to use the office telephones for personal calls, though, when the editor was out, they all did. Patricia walked across to where two black receivers squatted like frogs on a shelf, and lifted the first one. First of all, she dictated a telegram to Hugh:

AM LEAVING MY JOB STOP COMING HOME TO MARRY YOU STOP LOVE YOU STOP DON'T ARGUE STOP PATRICIA.

Then she gave the operator the number for the newsroom of the *Evening Dispatch*.

Lawrie, who was lurking in one of the newspaper's phone boxes, phoning bets to his bookie, answered at the second ring.

'Is Rosa there?' asked Patricia.

'Yeah, is that you, Patricia? Good to hear you. How's the smoke?' he said, recognizing her voice.

'It's awful. Get me Rosa,' she said. Her voice sounded sharp and anxious; she was afraid one of the other women in her office would come back.

'OK, OK, keep your hair on,' he said. She heard him calling out, 'Hey Rosa, Patricia's on the line, acting like a prima donna.'

When Rosa arrived she sounded breathless. 'Patricia! How are you? It's good of you to phone. We all miss you. The girl Jack hired in your place is awful. When are you coming back?' That last question was meant to be a joke for it was said with a laugh.

'That's what I'm calling about. Would you think I'd gone mad if I gave up this job?' Patricia asked urgently.

Rosa's voice became guarded as if she didn't want to be held responsible for giving bad advice. 'That depends,' she said.

'Well, I am mad. And if I stay here, I'll get even madder. I hate it. And I miss Hugh.' Her voice cracked when she pronounced his name.

Rosa said nothing.

'Are you still there?' asked Patricia, looking over her shoulder at the office door.

'Yes, I'm here. I'm thinking. I hope you're not giving up your job because of *him*. You've got a great opportunity there, you know,' said Rosa who cherished hopes of her friend becoming the editor of a prestigious glossy – perhaps even of *Vogue*.

Patricia hissed, 'I *hate* it here. You've no idea how awful it is. They wear their hats in the office.'

'Hats? Really? My God, you'd better come home, but *not* because of Hugh,' laughed Rosa.

'But this *is* because of him. I'm going to marry him as soon as possible and I want you to be my bridesmaid,' Patricia told her.

Two

R osa opened the door of the phone box and looked for someone to tell about Patricia's call.

What a mistake to give up a chance of the big time for Hugh Maling, she was thinking.

Lawrie had disappeared to the canteen and Mike was sitting with his head in his hands. Facing him was Barry, the show business writer Jack had brought in to fill the place of Alan, the Australian poet. Barry had been a stage comedian whose career peaked when he topped the bill at the London Palladium, but fame went to his head. He took to drink, profligate spending and serial marriage, and was on his uppers, bankrupt and trying to escape from his last marriage to an oversexed blonde film actress, when his old friend Jack, Editor of the *Dispatch*, rescued him and offered him a job as a columnist in Edinburgh. Jack was a Good Samaritan to a lot of hopeless cases. Barry did not know Patricia, however, because she had been gone before he joined the paper, so he'd be no help.

Hilda, Patricia's replacement as a reporter, was standing in front of Old Bob's desk with a notebook in her hand. The seams of her lisle stockings were absolutely straight but her sensible skirt was baggy round the bum. *When she's middle-aged she'll be plump – probably very plump*, thought Rosa nastily, and dismissed her as a confidante because she didn't know Patricia either.

Hilda was foisted on Jack by the powers above, and, because she was boringly pedestrian, he studiously ignored her, but Old Bob, the Chief Reporter, who liked to keep in with the management, favoured her. She was the sort of undemanding employee that he could patronize and send off to report on page-filling events like championship dog shows, from which she returned with meticulous lists of prize winners, but no unusual stories or insights.

'She wouldn't know a story if it sat up and bit her,' was Mike's sour verdict on the latest recruit.

Rosa particularly disliked Hilda because she could not help comparing her with Patricia, whom she sorely missed.

No two people could be more different. Patricia was glamorous; Hilda wore rimless glasses with squared-off edges that looked sharp enough to be used as an offensive weapon. Patricia had unerring dress sense; Hilda dressed in flat-heeled shoes and neatly tailored grey or brown tweed suits. Hilda used no make-up, not even lipstick, because it upset her skin, so she was not annoyed when Harriet, the Women's Page Editor, refused to share out to the other girls free samples sent to her by cosmetic companies.

Patricia was sharp tongued and funny; Hilda was humourless and never joined in with the other reporters when they were moaning about their employers or assignments. Patricia was a rebel; Hilda was on the side of the management and refused to exaggerate her expenses righteously putting in weekly claims for sums like three shillings and two pence halfpenny, while the others filed demands for two or three pounds. Hilda lived at home in a detached villa in Colinton with people she referred to as 'Mummy' and 'Daddy'.

Patricia was racy; Hilda blushed and ran to hide in the women's lavatory when Jack started using his favourite Anglo-Saxon curses. Patricia and Rosa enjoyed themselves during their time off; Hilda did not drink, and would not set foot in a pub. Hilda did not smoke. Hilda went to church every Sunday. Hilda thought it was low class to go dancing at the Plaza or the Palais.

Patricia was clever, a star; Hilda's prose was as heavy as half-risen dough, so heavy it was impossible to work out why Jack had taken her on to the staff. Then, one day, she let slip about her father being on the newspaper's board of directors.

9

Mentally comparing Hilda with Patricia made Rosa sigh heavily and caused Mike to ask, 'What's up with you, Makepeace? Has somebody stolen your last shilling?'

He was sitting up now, groaning loudly like a man in agony. He'd been out drinking last night and was hungover. Rosa walked across to him and said, 'Something *is* wrong. That was Patricia on the phone. She's coming back.'

He looked up with a spark of interest in his eyes. Rosa suspected he'd always yearned for Patricia but didn't have the nerve to come out and say so.

'To work with us again?' he asked hopefully but Rosa shook her head, 'I don't think so. She's going to marry Hugh Maling and they don't let married women work here.'

Mike groaned, 'Marrying Maling? She's nuts. He's a snobby bastard.'

'I know that, you know that, but she doesn't,' said Rosa. 'She's asked me to be her bridesmaid.'

He shook his head. 'I don't envy you the job. You'll have to be polite to Maling.'

She laughed. 'Don't bet on it.'

When Lawrie came back from the canteen with Tony – another reporter on the team, who, despite being a minster's son, was the office's finest and most enthusiastic dancer at the Palais on a Saturday night – they were told the news and echoed Rosa's opinion that Patricia was giving up a brilliant chance to throw herself away on a far from brilliant marriage. Lawrie was the least concerned.

He grinned and said, 'It's not such a tragedy. Don't forget, there's always divorce. Our Patricia's probably starting on an interesting matrimonial career.'

Rosa could not hide her disapproval of this attitude. Divorce was unknown in her family or among their friends.

'That's a terrible thing to say about people who haven't even got married yet,' she protested.

'You're a petit bourgeois, almost as bad as Hilda,' said Lawrie.

She bristled, highly insulted by the comparison. 'I am not, but I don't know anybody who's divorced . . .'

'You do. You know Barry – he's been married three times – and you know me.'

She stared at him. 'You?' This was new. He was always talking about his mistresses but she'd never heard of a wife.

'Yes, I was divorced when I was twenty-five. The marriage lasted a year and a half. I'm getting married again in a couple of months.'

'My goodness, how old *are* you now?' asked Tony.

'I'm twenty-nine. Mark my words, Patricia'll be in the divorce courts pretty soon, maybe within a year,' said Lawrie.

The rest of the afternoon was quiet. Rosa was on the calls, ringing round the police, fire brigade and ambulance service every hour, but nothing was happening in the city. As a result, Mike, who considered himself chief crime reporter, had nothing special to do either, so they were left alone in the office, playing noughts and crosses with each other, when the other reporters began drifting off on their various assignments.

When she'd done the calls at two o'clock and still come up with nothing, Rosa slumped down in her chair and said to Mike, 'How I wish something interesting would happen!'

At that point, as if on cue, the office door opened and a stranger walked in. Normally visitors were brought along by a copy boy, but this man was on his own. The old doorman must have decided he was harmless. He certainly looked very innocuous, a bit like a dejected beagle.

'Is this the *Dispatch* newsroom?' he asked.

Mike and Rosa nodded in unison.

'I have an appointment, but I'm early. Is the editor in?' said the stranger.

Mike looked at Rosa and the thought flashed between them that this was another of the candidates for a vacant reporting job that had been advertised in the *United King-dom Press Gazette*. Hopeful candidates had been trooping through the office all week but nobody had been taken on yet.

'He's in the pub. He'll be back in half an hour,' said Mike, looking at the office clock.

'Can I wait?' was the next question.

They chorused, 'Sure, sit down.'

Before they had time to quiz the visitor, however, Jack, the Editor, and Gil, his deputy, came breezing in, full of bonhomie from three double gins in their favourite hostelry, Jinglin' Geordie's.

The newcomer stood up and said something to Jack who shook his hand and ushered him towards his private office. They were not out of earshot when Mike hissed in his penetrating Newcastle accent, 'Get a load of that sweater!'

The stranger heard the comment and flushed as he walked across the newsroom floor.

Rosa followed Mike's disapproving stare, which was making the embarrassed object of his scrutiny stumble and almost fall, and saw that beneath his unbuttoned sports jacket, he wore a garishly coloured V-necked jersey, knitted in a jagged rib design.

'It's a Fair Isle jumper. They used to be very fashionable. My granny bought me one when I was a kid,' Rosa whispered, trying to quieten Mike down.

'Yeah, when you were a *kid*! I bet that one was hand-knitted by his mother,' was his even louder, scornful reply.

They turned in their swivel chairs to watch as Jack and the stranger disappeared into the editor's private sanctum. Then Mike called across to Gil, the Deputy Editor, 'Who the hell is that dopey-looking git?'

'He's been called in for an interview,' said Gil laconically. So, they were right.

Mike laughed. 'He hasn't a chance! Jack'll never hire him.'

'What makes you arrive at that intemperate conclusion?' asked Gil, who always spoke as if he was making a speech.

'The jumper. He's a milksop. Only a mother's boy would go out looking like that.'

Mike was highly critical of other people's wardrobes, and dressed in the height of street fashion, favouring suits made of glossy fabric with wide-shouldered, long jackets that tapered tightly over his hips, and drainpipe trousers that ended in ankle-hugging turn-ups over shoes with thick crepe soles. To finish off this Teddy Boy appearance, he teased his black hair into an upward turning curl in the middle of his forehead and carefully combed it into a 'duck's arse' overlap at the back.

'It's unseasonably chilly today. Maybe he's wearing that woollen jumper because he is sensitive to the cold,' suggested Gil, who was also a snappy dresser, but more in the style of a 1940s bandleader or a gangster, because he favoured double breasted suits with wide lapels and built-up shoulders.

Mike snorted in scorn, rolling his eyes like a shying horse as he turned to Rosa for support. 'You think he looks soft too, don't you?'

She shrugged indifferently. This applicant would probably disappear like all the other would-be reporters who'd paraded through the office recently, and it wouldn't matter to Rosa if he turned up wearing a tiger skin, for he was not her type. A pale face and soulful eyes were never going to make her heart beat faster. Why couldn't Jack hire someone who looked like Robert Mitchum or Burt Lancaster? The chap in the Fair Isle sweater was more in the Stan Laurel or Buster Keaton league.

Because Hilda had not come up to scratch, Jack was still interviewing replacements for Patricia, who was sorely missed both by the newspaper and especially by Rosa. They had been close friends, listening to each other's problems, giving advice, sharing confidences, discussing men, and gossiping over lunches in the Chinese restaurant near the University.

When Patricia's ambition took her off to work on a magazine in London, Rosa was left badly in need of a new friend. When she thought about Patricia's plan for coming back, her spirits rose and she began to feel more cheerful. Even if Patricia married Maling, perhaps everything could go back to being as it was before.

Three

J ack screwed up his eyes as he re-read the neatly typed letter of application which his secretary took out of a filing cabinet and put in his hand. Vanity made him refuse to wear spectacles; he had a theory that if you started wearing the damned things, you were doomed to wear them forever. Every morning, he rinsed his eyes in cold water and rolled them around in a series of frightening-looking exercises as recommended in *Better Eyesight Without Glasses* by an American called Dr Bates, but so far it wasn't working and Jack was losing faith in the doctor.

After a few seconds of struggling to get the letter into focus, he succeeded in deciphering what it said and remembered that he'd decided to interview this fellow because he described himself as 'indefatigable in pursuit of a story'.

Suppressing a smile, he said, 'I like your style.'

The young man reddened and shifted from foot to foot.

'Your writing style, I mean. You write well,' said Jack hurriedly, hoping the lad didn't think he was admiring his clothes. That sweater was hard to take and the man inside it was equally unimpressive. He looked more like a junior bank clerk than a reporter.

'Thank you,' said the job applicant.

'It reminds me of someone,' said Jack, looking back at the letter of application. Few of its sentences were more than six words long, few paragraphs longer than two lines.

'I'm a great admirer of Cassandra. I try to write like him,' the young man said eagerly.

Jack brightened. This was more like the thing. 'You mean

15

the *Daily Mirror*'s Cassandra? Bill Connor? I know him. He's a great journalist.'

'Yes, I read everything he writes. I'm modelling my style on his.'

Jack grinned. 'Really? You're aiming high. How old are you?'

'I'm twenty-six.' It was an exaggeration because he was not yet twenty-four.

'You look younger. Your name's Rutland, isn't it? What's your first name? You've only put your initials down here,' said Jack.

The young man visibly swallowed as he took more liberties with the truth. 'My name's – er – Charles L. Rutland . . .'

Jack noticed the swallowing and wondered why such an ordinary name could cause embarrassment, but, in fact, the applicant's real name was Cedric and the *L* stood for Lancelot.

His mother named her only child after characters from a historical novel she was reading during her pregnancy. At home he was called 'Our Cedric' or, even worse, 'Ceddy'.

He hated his name. When he was at school or doing his National Service at a base camp on Dartmoor, Cedric endured hellish ragging, and he was determined that, if he succeeded in getting this job and leaving home, he'd become more dignified, someone in the William Connor mould.

'And where have you been working, Charlie?' the Editor asked.

He did not see himself as Charlie either, but smiled and said, 'On a weekly paper in Salford, my home town.' There, in fact, he was copy boy, filing clerk and tea maker, and the only writing he did was occasionally composing captions for photographs of local dignitaries, all standing in line and grinning at the camera.

But he yearned for fame and, in the hope of learning his craft by osmosis, obsessively read the national dailies, especially the *Daily Mirror*. At home he sat in his bedroom rewriting his own newspaper's stories in the staccato style of the *Mirror*'s columnist, Cassandra.

When he saw an advertisement in the *United Kingdom Press Gazette* for an enterprising reporter to work on the Edinburgh's *Evening Dispatch*, he painfully composed a letter of application, weighing every word. Finally he read the letter aloud to himself in a sonorous voice he imagined to be like Connor's, and sent it off. He was delirious with delight when a reply came back inviting him to attend for an interview.

Now the fearsome-looking editor was asking him the question he dreaded. 'You can type, and do Pitman's, can't you?'

In fact, though Charles did not know it, this was an irrelevant question because Jack didn't really care at all if his reporters typed fast and wrote speedy shorthand. The journalists he most admired, and wanted on his staff, were word spinners, not technicians.

Verbatim shorthand writers, who sat in the courts taking down every word and transcribing them without giving them any personality, were two a penny. He was looking for reporters who could give a story that special spin to make it jump off the page.

Charles only typed with two fingers and was teaching himself Pitman's out of a textbook, but he lied nobly and said, 'Oh *yes!*'

'Have you brought some cuttings with you?' was Jack's next, and also dreaded, question.

No story had ever been published with Charles's byline on it, but he gathered himself together enough to say brightly, 'I brought the carbon copy of my most recent story.'

In fact it was a Salford newspaper piece, originally done by someone else, but rewritten and embellished by Charles with more colourful details. Dressing stories up was not difficult for him because he had a very fertile imagination. When he started what his mother called his 'daydreaming', he even surprised himself by the ideas that came into his head.

Carbon copies of stories were not the sort of thing on which Jack put much store. He was about to show this applicant the door, but something about Charles intrigued him so he took the proffered sheet of paper and began to read it.

After a few moments he looked up with sharpened interest in his eyes.

'Did this one-legged guy really catch a bank robber?' he asked.

'Yes. He threw himself at the masked robber. All the money, £2,000, was recovered,' said Charles. In fact, in the original Stockport story, a passer-by, with a bandage on his ankle, had rugby tackled a 16-year-old youth who'd grabbed a bag of coins from a local greengrocer carrying his takings to a local bank. Twenty-five pounds and ten shillings had been recovered in full and the would-be thief put on probation.

'Did he get a reward?' asked Jack.

'The man who owned the money gave him £100. With his reward he bought a better false leg,' lied Charles.

The words came out so swiftly and smoothly, they astonished even him.

'Christ,' gasped Jack. 'That's a national story. But it never made the nationals, did it?'

'It was never picked up and our editor doesn't permit us to sell our stories on to other outlets,' said Charles piously.

'Then he's a bloody amateur, and it's no wonder he's stuck in Salford,' said Jack.

The story about the one-legged hero swung the balance in Charles's favour. Purely on instinct, Jack decided to take a chance on him.

'I'll give you a month's trial. Seven pounds a week plus expenses. Start next Monday at eight a.m. If you don't suit, you're out,' the Editor said.

Of course it was all right. If Jack had offered Charles two pounds a week and said he was to work in a windowless cell, he would have jumped at the job, but he managed to contain his jubilation enough to say, 'That sounds quite satisfactory, sir.'

From childhood Mrs Rutland's only child had lived more in imagination than in actuality. His mother read him to sleep in his cradle with fairy stories; in school he sat dreaming at his desk, driving teachers to gibbering rage by his ability to be present in body but not in mind. Friends of his parents, seeing him as a teenager wandering like a lost soul through the streets and along the canal banks near his home, shook their heads and said that the Rutlands' boy wasn't right in the head.

He knew he was a social misfit, but books were his friends, his treasure and solace. When he read John Buchan, he became so involved that, during his walks to and from school, he thought he was being chased over heather-covered moorlands. Graduating to Ernest Hemingway he took to expanding his chest and sticking out his chin so fiercely when he collected his father's evening paper from the corner shop that the old lady behind its counter became quite afraid of him.

His next literary enthusiasm was Scott Fitzgerald who made him so distracted that his father, who preferred the Hemingway mode, worried in case his son was turning 'limp-wristed', and started taking him to pubs and wrestling matches in the hope of toughening him up. Charles hated the wrestling and took secret revenge by mentally composing conversations about it with his most lasting idol, the *Daily Mirror* columnist William Connor, who, he was sure, would loathe the heaving, sweating spectacle as much as he did.

Connor was a good hater, as the Salford lad discovered when he first chanced on Cassandra's diatribe against Christmas cards. From that time he was a committed fan and talked his mother into taking the *Daily Mirror* every day instead of her preferred *Daily Express*.

At the breakfast table, his parents were forced to listen as he read out extracts from Cassandra's latest pieces in tones of awed reverence.

When Stalin died in 1953, Charles treated them to a

spirited delivery of Cassandra's tribute to the Russian leader: 'He died in his bed . . . No assassin ever succeeded in pulling a single whisker out of his pock-marked face; no gunman ever nicked him with so much as an air gun pellet . . .' He wept over Cassandra's diatribe against the hanging of Ruth Ellis in July 1955. Sobbing, he read the recurring lines:

**IF YOU READ THIS BEFORE NINE O'CLOCK THIS MORNING . . .
IF YOU READ THIS AFTER NINE O'CLOCK . . .
IF YOU READ THESE WORDS OF MINE AT MIDDAY . . .**

They reduced him to such a violence of emotion that his mother insisted he take a day off work.

'You must stop reading that man. You're too sensitive for the sort of thing he writes,' she protested.

As soon as Jack offered him a trial on the *Dispatch*, he felt the blood pulsing in his ears. He wanted to jump up and down with his arms in the air, but managed to restrain himself enough to run along the corridor to the back door and down the steps of Fleshmarket Close.

He loved animals but he was so excited he didn't pause to gaze at a trio of black and white puppies frolicking in the window of the pet shop opposite the newspaper's back door. He ran headlong down the steps two at a time, dashed into Waverley Station and ended up, flushed with exertion and excitement, in front of his mother, who was sitting patiently on a wooden bench beside the bookstall with a big brown holdall on the pavement by her feet.

Her face lit up when she saw him.

'Ceddy dear, you shouldn't be running about like that with your asthma, and especially without looking where you're going. You could get yourself run over by one of those taxis. I've been watching them. They're *trying* to run people down,' she said.

'I got the job, Mum,' he cried.

'Of course you did. I never doubted it. The moment that

20

editor laid eyes on you, he'd realize you're a good, hard working boy,' she said.

Before she could say anything else, he rushed on: 'At seven pounds a week! Now I have to find a place to live. Do you have those addresses Mrs Reilly gave you?'

She nodded. 'Yes, there's one in Broughton Street. I bought a town map at the bookstall and it isn't far away.'

'Let's go then,' he said, hoisting her to her feet, and lifting her bag at the same time.

They toiled up the lung-bursting Waverley Steps to Princes Street, where they consulted the map and headed north, crossing over to Leith Walk and joining crowds of people hurrying down the hill. The Broughton Street address was near the top of the street but, when Mrs Rutland saw the rundown district and the grimy front door of the house, which was even shabbier than the battered doors of its neighbours, she shook her head.

'This won't do. It doesn't look like a respectable neighbourhood to me. We might be poor but we're respectable. I'm not going in there and neither are you. The other address sounds much better. At least it's a prettier name.'

The second lodging house was in Mayfield Road. Once again the map was consulted and a passer-by told them to take a tram up the Bridges. Its Irish conductor said he'd tell them when they got to Mayfield Road and they sat patiently on the top deck, staring down into the city streets.

As they rattled along, Charles's mother passed him sandwiches out of her bag and urged him, 'Eat. Keep your strength up.'

He ate.

Number 14 Mayfield Road was more to her liking than Broughton Street. It was a large, grey stone mansion, set back behind a narrow, shrub filled garden, and dignified by two imposing pillars at the front door. In its heyday it housed a prosperous, middle-class family and was very different to any house the Rutlands had ever occupied for they lived in a street of workers' terraces with outdoor lavatories. Men parked their pushbikes in the backyards and nothing green ever grew there.

A notice on the house's front door said 'Vacancies' and the woman who answered their knock suited the grimly respectable facade for her body seemed to be encased in a corset of steel. Her grey hair was parted in the middle and scraped back into a tight bun.

When Mrs Rutland said she was looking for lodgings for her son, the woman stared at Charles without a smile and said, 'My name's Mrs Mackay and I own this house. He's not a medical student is he? I don't take them any more, not after the last time. Eyeballs in the sofa – *human* eyeballs!'

Charles paled, but his mother rushed to defend him against the charge of being a medical student. 'Oh *no*, my son is about to take up a position with the *Evening Dispatch*,' she boasted.

'As what?' asked Mrs Mackay.

'As a journalist,' was the proud reply.

'I don't take them either. They're worse than medicals.' Mrs Mackay regarded Charles as if he was about to sprout horns, and was just closing the door when his mother protested again, 'But he's not like the rest of them. He's delicate and a very respectable boy – he doesn't drink, never stays out late, and goes to church. It was our minister's wife who gave us your address . . .'

'What's her name?' asked the landlady, slightly mollified by Charles's virtues.

'Mrs Reilly. She's the wife of our Methodist minister in Salford.'

There was even more softening of Mrs Mackay's features as she said, 'Mrs Reilly is my second cousin.'

At last they were admitted, and within fifteen minutes Charles agreed to rent a back bedroom at two pounds and fifteen shillings a week with breakfast thrown in. He left his first week's rent in advance and walked back to the station with his mother.

On the way home in the train to Manchester, she exulted over the spacious glory of his new digs, but as evening drew in, she became tearful. Wiping her eyes, she said, 'Oh my dear, how am I going to manage without you? You're my baby, and very special.'

At last she fell asleep with her head resting on his shoulders while he sat dreaming of the brilliant future that lay before him. But, as the sooty suburbs of Manchester came into view, the magnitude of the step he was about to take struck him – especially because he'd lied so enormously about his credentials and capabilities.

Would he manage to acquire some expertise before he was rumbled?

Terror gripped his stomach, starting up dyspeptic pains, and he groped in his pocket for a Rennie's tablet, which he sucked in desperation.

Four

*M*y *career is finished*, Rosa said to herself as she drove her little grey Morris Minor car back from the office to her lodgings in Northumberland Street on the evening of the day Charles Rutland was hired.

It seemed to her that Jack had only taken on another reporter because he'd lost faith in her. A few months ago, she'd peaked when she broke the Boyle story – and almost her own neck – uncovering Police Sergeant Boyle as the manic murderer of two girls. She had been all over the front pages then, with her byline printed in large letters, but Boyle was now shut up for life in Carstairs Prison for the criminally insane and her story died a natural death. The only person who seemed to remember him was Rosa herself who often woke up in the middle of the night, shivering with terror because she had been dreaming about the night that he tried to kill her.

Since then, she had to admit, her output consisted of mundane and boring reports, uninspiring interviews, or falsely flattering accounts of trailing around after various members of the royal family where her perceived function as a woman journalist was to write descriptions of the royal ladies' clothes.

If some maniac assassinated the Queen, Rosa thought, *she would only be expected to describe what the royal dress looked like covered with gore.* Her dreams of becoming a hard news reporter were disappearing fast.

There is no kind of person more sensitive of their ability and reputation than a newspaper reporter. They live from one big story to the next, boosting their egos with the size of their bylines. If there are no bylines, they deflate like pricked balloons.

Rosa tried to be modest and sensible, but she was as egotistical as Mike. It was no comfort to realize that, tonight, Mike would be suffering the same torments of jealous apprehension. Like her, he would be wondering why Jack had hired such an unlikely looking reporter. He had to be good. What was he good at? Was he better than anybody else?

Jack still treated her with guarded admiration but she knew that if she did not come up with another good story soon, he would finally relegate her to the ranks of the no-hopers. She dreaded ending up like Hilda, going out day after day to report on flower shows, or the meetings of charities presided over by rigidly correct Edinburgh ladies.

'I need a big story,' she moaned aloud but there was no one to listen. What made her misery worse was the inescapable fact that, not only was her career going nowhere, but her love life was also non-existent.

She still felt pangs of pain at the memory of the philandering car salesman Iain, who, after sweet-talking her for a long time, went off and married the daughter of a rich town councillor – a good career move if anything ever was. She dreaded bumping into him and his picture-book pretty wife at the civic functions she was detailed to cover, because she was sure that before long, Iain too would manage to get himself elected to the City Council.

She had one devoted admirer left however: the faithful Dr Roddy Barton who she met while they were both at university. *But I don't love Roddy*, she thought. Being with him didn't make her pulse race or her gut lurch; she didn't fantasize about him when she lay in bed at night.

He was away doing his National Service in Cyprus but wrote regularly, telling her of his undying love and asking her to marry him. She replied with chatty letters, ignoring his proposals. She did not want to lose his friendship because she liked him a lot, admired his steely character, and absolute rectitude, but admiration wasn't love and she needed passion. She wanted the sweet fervour of counting the hours till she met some special man; she longed for the physical thrill of looking at him, of wanting to touch him and longing for him to touch her.

Damn you, Iain, she thought, *You've broken my heart. I'll become a sour old maid like my great aunt Fanny because of you.*

She could not reconcile herself to being manipulative enough to marry Roddy without loving him, though she knew he would make an admirable husband. At her lowest moments she dreaded that, one day, when her spirits hit rock bottom, she might give in and settle for him out of sheer desperation. That scenario, a loveless marriage of convenience, made her miserable even to think about it. It was almost as bad as spinsterhood.

Everybody else in the world seemed capable of finding love, even in unexpected places. A few months ago lovely Grace Kelly married the uninspiring Prince Rainier of Monaco, and recently it was announced that Marilyn Monroe was marrying the playwright Arthur Miller, who would not set many female hearts beating fast as far as appearance went. Even Patricia, with her love for the nauseating Hugh, was better off emotionally than Rosa.

Am I aiming too high? Don't most people settle for the best they can get? Why do I think I'll be lucky enough to find the perfect man? I've read too many novels, she thought as she parked in front of her landlady's house.

Mrs Ross, who had grown very maternal towards Rosa since the Boyle affair, was waiting for her. As soon as she heard Rosa's key in the door, she shot out of the sitting room with her huge ginger cat Oliver in her arms.

'The doctor phoned,' she carolled.

Rosa nodded and said, 'Did he?' In fact she knew perfectly well that Roddy phoned every week on Monday nights at eight p.m. and was as punctual as the one o'clock gun that fired from the castle ramparts every lunch time. Sometimes, like tonight, because she knew he'd be phoning, she deliberately stayed out till past eight. Perhaps if he played hard to get, she'd treat him less cavalierly.

'I told him I was sure you were held up because you were on a story. He's phoning back in an hour,' said Mrs Ross.

'Did you tell him about your chest infection?' Rosa asked. Mrs Ross took every opportunity to check out her ailments with Roddy who was invariably polite and helpful with suggestions for treatment.

'I did, and he said to use Vicks Rub and put lavender oil on my pillow at night,' said Mrs Ross.

'Have you got any lavender oil?' asked Rosa.

'Not tonight, but I'll get some tomorrow. I've got lots of lavender sachets among my bed linen though. Do you think it would work if I emptied them all into a pillow case and slept on that?' asked Mrs Ross.

'It can't do any harm,' Rosa told her, but she was thinking, *Maybe I should try to find some potion to put under my pillow to bring me love.*

'I've something else to tell you, dear,' said Mrs Ross. 'Mrs Neil next door has a runaway couple staying with her. They're hoping to get married and she thinks the girl is from a very rich family, like that Patina business. Maybe you could write a story about them.'

Rosa leaned over the banister and asked, 'Do you mean *Patino*, the millionaire's daughter who married Jimmy Goldsmith a couple of years ago?'

'Yes, and then died having her baby, poor thing.'

Rosa stepped back downstairs. Since Jimmy Goldsmith and Isabel Patino had eloped to Scotland against her father's wishes nearly three years ago, there had been a rush of young couples coming over the border to marry.

In Scotland, girls could marry younger without parental consent and a couple only had to fulfil a certified fourteen days' residence in the country before presenting themselves at a registrar's office for a civil marriage.

Rosa had already done three stories about runaway weddings. Why did something tell her this one was different? Perhaps her reporter's instinct was not dead after all.

'Will they talk to me?' she asked, and Mrs Ross nodded eagerly. She had obviously been setting the interview up for Rosa. It even seemed that Oliver nodded too and winked one of his golden eyes like a co-conspirator.

The neighbour, Mrs Neil, was a very refined army widow, who took in paying guests to defray the expense of living in Edinburgh's New Town. Her house was furnished with impressive antiques, and she was even more fussy than Mrs Ross about the sort of people she allowed into her establishment, which was far from being an ordinary lodging house. Her prices, for one thing, were almost as high as the room rate for Edinburgh's top class hotel, The George, and she behaved as if guests were lucky to be allowed over her doorstep.

Mrs Ross was bursting with information about the runaways. 'They've taken Mrs Neil's first floor for three weeks. Two bedrooms, so they've very proper. Of course, Mrs Neil wouldn't have taken them in if they weren't.'

Though the two women had lived in adjacent houses for forty years, drank coffee together every morning and knew everything about each other, neither of them ever used the other's first name. It was doubtful if they even knew them. They were 'Mrs Ross' and 'Mrs Neil' and maintained their association on a formal basis that suited them both.

'Three weeks are more than enough to get a marriage licence,' said Rosa.

Mrs Ross nodded. 'Yes, they know that. They're lovely people apparently. The girl has the most wonderful clothes – she arrived in a mink coat that goes right down to the ground. Mrs Neil is enjoying the whole thing.'

'Where have they come from?' Rosa asked. A runaway bride in a floor length mink really interested her.

'They're American. Why don't you go next door and speak to them? I told Mrs Neil you might.' Mrs Ross, who at first regarded Rosa's job with deep suspicion, now relished having a newspaper reporter as a lodger and was always avid for details of her latest stories.

28

'You'll be asking for tip-off money next,' Rosa joked as she headed for the front door.

Mrs Neil's lodgers were sitting in an overfurnished first floor drawing room where the furniture was solid Georgian pieces: a red sofa with a high back and drop ends tied up with thick looped ropes of silken cord; three deep armchairs; a fine Pembroke table; a grandfather clock with a painted face; a bow-fronted bookcase filled with leather-covered volumes; a partner's desk in the window, and red, blue and brown Turkish carpets on the floor.

A Scandinavian-blonde girl was nestling on the sofa with her feet tucked under her, and a slightly older, dark-haired man lay back in one of the chairs with his feet on a camel saddle. They seemed pleased to have a visitor when Mrs Neil showed Rosa in.

'Hi,' she said. 'I heard you're hoping to get married in Edinburgh. I'm a newspaper reporter and we've run several stories about runaway couples. Perhaps we can help you with advice and that sort of thing.'

They reacted as she hoped they would. It never failed to amaze her how eager people were to co-opt the press to their side in any dilemma.

'Gee, how wonderful. We heard it's easy to get married in Scotland but we don't know how to go about it really,' gasped the girl, who was blonde and beautiful with the sort of spectacular glitter to her skin, teeth and hair that American girls seemed to have in abundance.

It must be their food, thought Rosa. *All that milk.*

The man was more cautious. 'Oh honey, we do know. We just don't know where the registry offices are,' he said.

As he stood up, Rosa saw that, unlike the girl, he seemed underfed and shabby. In fact, he strongly resembled the crooner Frank Sinatra, because, though he was skinny and slightly reptilian, he oozed sexuality.

His eyes darted all over her face as if he was sizing her up, but she maintained her professional attitude and smiled back at him. There was something about him that reminded her of Iain, the same blatant maleness that showed he rated women by their bedworthiness.

'I can tell you about that because, as I said, I've done several runaway marriage stories, and here they're called *registrar's* offices,' she mildly corrected him.

He stuck out his hand and said, 'Then we'll pick your brains. I'm Jake Rosario.'

She took the hand and replied, 'I'm Rosa Makepeace.'

'Makepeace!' squealed the girl. 'What a lovely name. I'm Mary Lou Carter and I am very pleased to meet you. Jake and I were just wondering how we are going to pass the time in Edin-burry. There doesn't seem to be a lot happening here.'

'It's only spring,' said Rosa, apologizing for the city. 'If you want to be here when the place comes alive you have to visit during the Festival. Then it buzzes, it really does.'

'When's that?' asked Jake.

'August.'

'We're in no great hurry really, but I hope we're out of here by then. Exactly how long do we have to stay before we can get a marriage licence?' he said. His accent was sharper and harder than the girl's. Though she spoke with a soft drawl that made Rosa think of magnolias and pillared mansions like the houses in *Gone With The Wind*, he sounded like Jimmy Cagney.

Rosa explained, 'The notice of your intention to marry has to be displayed in a registrar's office window for fourteen clear days before a licence can be issued. That gives members of the public time to object if they have any legal grounds for doing so.'

The couple looked at each other. 'Fourteen days,' said Jake.

'You could be married in two weeks and a day's time if you lodge your application tomorrow,' Rosa told him.

'And what about grounds for objection?' he asked.

'Providing both of the people contracting to marry are over sixteen, and neither of them are married already, there isn't any problem,' said Rosa.

'But what if someone objects?' asked Mary Lou.

'If their objection has a legal basis, usually involving the question of age or marital status, you won't get a licence until the objection is investigated,' said Rosa.

'There's no question of any objections. We're not breaking the law in Scotland,' Jake said firmly.

The girl added, 'It's my uncle – when he finds out he'll make an awful fuss. I'd really like to go back and get married in New York if it was possible.'

'We can't because he'd try to talk you out of it,' Jake told her.

Mary Lou, gazing at her lover with rapt attention, sighed as she said, 'Aw honey, as if anybody in the world could stop me marrying you.'

He walked across the floor and hugged her. 'I love you too, baby,' he said.

Rosa coughed to break them up and asked Mary Lou, 'Why should your uncle stop the wedding if you're not under age?'

'I'm nineteen and it's legal to marry here at that age, isn't it? Jake's certainly old enough. He's twenty-eight. My uncle can't stop us legally but he's sure going to try. I think he might even try to snatch me,' said the girl.

'Snatch you?' Rosa was surprised. This story was developing fast.

'Yeah, grab me, rush me out of the country and back home to the States.'

'But that *would* be illegal.'

Jake laughed bitterly. 'That won't stop Joe Daniels.'

'Is that her uncle?' asked Rosa.

'It sure is and he's my trustee too. That's what this is all about. He doesn't want my money to slip out of his hands. I have an allowance at the moment but I come into my full inheritance when I'm twenty-one, or when I marry. Uncle Joe would like to marry me off to my cousin, his son. He wouldn't object to me marrying *him* at nineteen, but he sure objects to Jake,' said the ingenuous Mary Lou.

'Why?' asked Rosa.

31

Interrupting each other all the time, the couple told her that Mary Lou was an orphan with an uncle for her guardian, and he was against the marriage.

'He thinks Jake's after my money. It's all tied up in trusts and things like that but my parents, who were killed in an air accident ten years ago, left a will saying I could have control of it when I reached twenty-one or *when I marry*. That's where the trouble comes in with my uncle, but Jake's not a fortune-hunter,' said Mary Lou, holding her lover's hand.

'Is it a lot of money?' asked Rosa.

They nodded.

'It's a fortune. Millions,' Jake told her. There was an air of satisfaction about him . . . and no wonder.

'Millions?' Rosa repeated, thinking, *This* is *another Goldsmith-Patino case over again.*

'Mary Lou's father was the heir to a textile manufacturing company – one of the biggest in the Southern States. Her mother inherited railroad money. When they died, her mother's brother became her guardian,' Jake explained.

'But her uncle must be a rich man himself. Surely he won't want to keep his niece's money?' said Rosa.

'Have you ever met a rich guy who doesn't want more?' asked Jake.

'I don't know many rich guys,' laughed Rosa.

'It's not just money, it's class too,' interrupted Mary Lou. 'Jake's not Ivy League. He was working as a clerk in my uncle's office in New York when I went up there last fall to drop off some packages. I took one look at him and I was gone. He wasn't like any other guy I'd ever met. It was love at first sight – just like that, BOOM!' She snapped her fingers so loudly that Rosa jumped.

The couple looked at each other and hugged again.

It was obviously time for Rosa to go. She got up and said, 'Can I write a piece about you and bring a photographer along to take your picture? You're not breaking any laws here and a story could get people on your side, especially if Mary Lou's uncle makes trouble.'

'Sure, we'd welcome the publicity. We don't mind speaking to the newspapers, do we honey? We've nothing to hide,' said Mary Lou.

Jake nodded, but less enthusiastically, and asked Rosa, 'Is a photograph necessary? I'm a bit superstitious. I'd prefer if the first picture we have taken in little old Edinburgh is of our wedding.'

Rosa shook her head and said firmly, 'We need a picture. Our editor won't run the story without it, but if you like, we'll do a romantic, arty one – perhaps of the pair of you from the back, walking in a park or going along the street hand in hand – something like that.'

Mary Lou's face showed disappointment when it seemed press coverage might be denied her. 'Don't worry, Jake,' she said.

But he still frowned. 'Which paper do you write for?' he asked Rosa. She told him that she worked on an evening newspaper that circulated in and around Edinburgh.

'A local paper?' he asked. When she nodded, he said, 'I guess that's all right then. We don't want Daniels to find us through national publicity.'

'If you're frightened about being tracked down, we needn't give your address. I'll speak to my editor and if he decides to run the story, we'll keep your whereabouts secret,' said Rosa. That seemed to satisfy him.

Back in her own lodgings, she was told that Roddy had phoned again. Mrs Ross, who loved speaking to him, gushed, 'I told him about the couple next door. He said he'll be home on leave in a month and perhaps you'll think of eloping with him. I said I'd do my best to persuade you.'

Rosa laughed. 'I'm not in that much of a hurry,' she said.

Next morning, the photographer that everybody called The Basher was assigned to go with Rosa to take pictures of the runaway lovers. She waited for him in Cockburn Street. Looking sour, he grumbled as he hefted up his enormous camera case and opened her car passenger door.

'What sort of story is it this time? Another pair of

romantic halfwits? Bloody fools,' he said. There was not much romance in The Basher's soul.

He climbed into the car, muttering, 'Bloody Jimmy Goldsmith started something, didn't he? We waste our time chasing after these people. It's not real news . . .'

Staring ahead through the windscreen, and attempting to control her irritation because, no matter what story he was sent on, The Basher never seemed to be pleased, Rosa said, 'We can't always be chasing fire engines, now, can we?'

He stopped complaining and looked at her. 'OK, OK, so you think this is a good story. What's special about it?'

'I don't know, really. They're not the usual runaways. The girl's obviously very rich but the man isn't.'

'You can't blame him for wanting to better himself,' said The Basher, reaching into his pocket for a crumpled packet of cigarettes and lighting up.

When he saw Rosa eyeing him critically, he asked, 'Want one? I didn't think you smoked.'

'I do sometimes but I don't want one right now, thank you,' she said, in a deliberately prim voice to reprimand his bad manners. It was a pity that she sounded like Hilda though. To her irritation, he only laughed. He was infuriating.

She knew less about him than about any of her other colleagues. In fact, she did not even know his first name. His surname was McIvor but all she ever heard him called was The Basher. He was tall and gangly with straight brown hair and a nose that looked as if it might have been broken and badly reset.

As far as she knew, he was unmarried and appeared to have no regular girlfriend, though he was occasionally seen jitterbugging with great enthusiasm in the Palais with some of the blonde girls from the phone room. When the rest of the press gang met at the Cockburn, he rarely joined them. On the few occasions that he did, he only drank a couple of pints and then sloped off without apology or explanation.

Though she'd been out on lots of stories with him and found him extremely efficient and professional, she never succeeded in penetrating his reserve and suspected he agreed with Old Bob, the Chief Reporter, that a newsroom was not a suitable place for women.

Jake and Mary Lou were watching from the window of their Northumberland Street digs when the car stopped at their door. She waved from the pavement and they came running down, with Mary Lou leading, and Jake, less eager, following her.

Rosa and The Basher had to get out of the two-door car and tip up the seats so their passengers could ride in the back.

'Where are we going?' asked Jake when they settled down.

Rosa knew better than make any suggestions. No photographer took kindly to being directed by a reporter, and The Basher was the touchiest of them all. She looked at him with her eyebrows raised in enquiry, and he said, 'What about the castle?'

'Won't it be rather crowded there?' asked Jake Rosario.

'There'll be people about,' agreed The Basher. The tourist season was beginning and the projected visit of the Russian leaders Bulganin and Khruschev was also attracting a lot of sightseers to the castle and the Old Town.

'Perhaps it'll be better to take our pictures in a quieter place,' suggested Rosario.

Rosa felt The Basher bristle, and quailed, but, to her relief, he sounded fairly mild when he asked, 'Why's that?'

'Because Miss Makepeace suggested that you would take a long shot picture of us, sitting on a park bench or something. You can't take a long shot in a crowded place,' said Jake.

'Then we must follow Miss Makepeace's ideas,' replied The Basher icily.

She hastened to placate him. 'It was just an idea. Mr Rosario said he would prefer them not to be too recognizable because Mary Lou's uncle is against their marriage and might try to stop it if he knows where they are . . .'

She knew she sounded feeble for she'd only gone along

35

with Jake's suggestion because she wanted him to agree to being photographed.

'And can't the uncle read? You'll give their names in your story, won't you?' asked The Basher.

'I won't give their address, though,' said Rosa as she pulled the car away from the kerbside. They all sat silent and she was forced to ask, 'All right. Where will we go then?'

'Inverleith Park,' said The Basher with the air of a man who was coming up with his final suggestion. No one argued.

Inverleith Park was almost deserted except for a few people walking dogs. The last of the cherry blossom, swinging from tree branches like little candelabras in the spring sunshine, made a froth of fading pink, and a few greedy ducks, floating on the glassy surface of the pond, eyed the newcomers hopefully.

'If it's a bench you want there's one over there,' said The Basher, gesturing at a park bench on top of a slight rise overlooking the pond. Intimidated, Jake and Mary Lou walked towards it and sat down side by side like well-behaved children.

Rosa stood at the edge of the pond saying nothing. This, she knew, was going to take time. The Basher prowled around with his camera in his hand, staring occasionally through the big viewing aperture, sometimes crouching down, sometimes climbing to the top of the rise above the couple. Eventually, he found a place that suited him and knelt between a pair of birch trees to the left of the bench.

'Cuddle her,' he yelled.

'What?' asked Jake.

'Cuddle her for God's sake. Put your arm round her. Make it look as if you're madly in love,' yelled The Basher.

The couple obligingly leaned together and stared into each other's faces while The Basher stepped forward, took one shot and was shoving another plate into his camera when a Jack Russell dog came running over, barking wildly. When he waved it away, the dog caught hold of his trouser leg and worried it with awe-inspiring ferocity.

Pausing, he called to Rosa, 'Get rid of this bloody dog, can't you?'

She ran up, holding out a half-eaten bar of chocolate she had in her pocket. The dog snatched it and immediately went back to worrying The Basher.

'Don't feed it, kick the bastard,' he shouted.

'It's your own fault. You shouldn't have threatened it,' she snapped back.

'Threatened it? I'll kill the bloody thing if I get my hands on it,' he was saying as the dog's owner, a full-busted lady in a thick overcoat and a crocheted woolly hat came up jangling a dog lead.

'If you dare kick my dog, I will have you arrested, young man,' she cried. Bending down, she called, 'Come to Mummy, Cosmo.' Cosmo let go of The Basher's trousers and went meekly to her.

After again threatening The Basher with arrest, she stalked away, leaving Rosa staring after her with obvious respect. Cosmo's victim was furious and red-faced. For once he lost his cool and though Rosa badly wanted to laugh, she knew better than allow her amusement to show. 'Let's get this nonsense over,' The Basher called, and started firing off pictures as quickly as he could change the plates.

Regardless of the runaways' desire not to be recognizable, he took shots of them from many different angles, and then marched back to the car, leaving the others to trail in his wake.

Rosa attempted light conversation during the drive back to Northumberland Street, but The Basher stayed broodingly silent. After Jake and Mary Lou were delivered to their lodgings, he looked at Rosa and spoke at last. 'I don't like this, I don't like it at all,' he said.

'What do you mean?' she asked, wondering if he meant his encounter with Cosmo.

'There's something funny going on there.'

'With them, you mean? Rosario's a bit peculiar but the girl's all right,' she said.

'She's great looking, but she's as green as spinach,' said The Basher. He liked blondes, she remembered.

'I thought you said it was all right for him to better himself,' she reminded him.

'That was before I met him. I wouldn't trust him as far as I could throw him, but maybe you've hit on another good story.'

Mollified by the 'another' she said, 'It sounds as if you're interested in it after all.'

'Yeah, it's different. It's a watch-this-space story. If we follow it up though, I hope we don't meet any more mad dogs.'

Then Rosa allowed herself the laugh that had been building up inside her since they left the park. 'Cosmo was something else, wasn't he? But you'll be able to claim another pair of trousers on your expenses,' she said, and was relieved when The Basher laughed too.

Five

The Jake and Mary Lou story put Rosa's byline on the front page again, and, because she was basically optimistic, her natural ebullience came back. Jack's approval made her feel as if the world was filled with sunlight.

When Rutland, the new recruit, showed up in the office, Rosa and Hilda were the only reporters prepared to be unreservedly friendly towards him. The others walked warily round him like animals in the zoo, watching out of the corners of their eyes and wondering about his abilities.

Because journalism is such an egotistical business, their major concern was worry over whether he could outwrite or outsmart them. Mike was particularly concerned, and so was another reporter called Clive, who had recently come down from the branch office in Aberdeen determined to take the capital by storm, and did not much care how he did it.

When the time came for a tea break on Charles's first morning, Mike rose to his feet, and, towering over the new man, said, 'Coming to the canteen?'

Though Charles looked meek and mild, he was actually extremely sharp and as worried about the abilities of his new colleagues as they were about his. Putting on a friendly face, he said, 'Yes, I'd like a cup of tea.'

Mike grinned wolfishly and said, 'Tea or coffee's all that's on offer unfortunately. Come on, then. I'm Mike. What's your name again?'

'The Editor calls me Charlie but I prefer Charles,' said the newcomer as he followed Mike into a long dark corridor. They followed their noses like bloodhounds towards the smell of fried food, and once in the canteen, they sat opposite a girl who was sitting with her elbows on the table, dunking a doughnut into a cup of orange-coloured tea.

Charles thought she was quite pretty because she had a thick mane of dark hair curling round her face, and slightly slanted hazel eyes that were emphasized by thick, long lashes, but she was obviously not interested in fluttering them at him.

When Mike went off to buy the coffees, mentally noting to claim for them on his weekly expenses, she reached out a hand over the table and introduced herself to Charles. 'Hi, I'm Rosa Makepeace,' she said.

'I saw your story on the front page,' he replied and she beamed. When Mike came back bearing two thick china cups, he said to Charles, 'Rosa's Jack's favourite newshound. She was nearly murdered a while ago by a guy who killed her friend.'

Charles raised his eyebrows at this. 'That must have been terrifying, Miss Makepeace,' he said.

He's big on politeness, she thought in surprise. The male reporters she knew did not behave in a courtly way to women colleagues.

'Not too bad. It got her the front page and a byline,' said Mike, with a note of envy in his voice. Protective of his status as the paper's chief 'toe in the door' man, he resented anyone sharing the limelight, even for a short time.

'Only for a little while,' said Rosa. 'Nothing lasts long in this business. Today's big story is tomorrow's fish and chip wrapper. We all live in terror of running out of scoops.'

Charles regarded her with the soulful brown eyes of a dyspeptic spaniel. 'At least the Editor seems to be a very decent sort,' he said.

They laughed. 'Don't be deceived. Jack's all right so long as you're coming up with the stories, but he doesn't carry any dead wood. He can turn difficult just like that,' said Mike, snapping his fingers, and glancing at Rosa, whose expression told him that she too was thinking Charles Rutland would end up as kindling.

The pair of them secretly studied Charles, wondering

what it was about him that Jack saw and they didn't. He was pasty-faced and narrow-shouldered; his lank brown hair flopped down over his brow and his eyes were brown and pleading like the eyes of a hungry dog that was too well-trained to beg.

At least today he was not wearing his Fair Isle sweater – he'd heard Mike's comment on it – but was obviously very protective of his health, because he had on a woollen waistcoat and a brown muffler.

'Feel the cold, do you?' asked Mike, wondering what sort of underwear this stranger was wearing – probably woolly combinations.

'I've a delicate chest,' said Charles solemnly.

When Pat, another reporter in the newsroom, came in and sat down beside them, all three began to quiz the stranger, asking where he'd worked and what stories he'd done.

'What sort of stuff have you covered?' Mike enquired, anxious again for his own pre-eminence in the newsroom.

There was no way Charles was going to show them his carbon-copy story because he guessed they'd spot its falsity straightaway. Instead he said airily, 'The usual things. Your editor said he liked my style and when I showed him my stories, he seemed impressed, especially when I told him that I model my writing on Cassandra's.'

For a moment Rosa thought he meant Cassandra, the Greek prophetess of doom, but then the penny dropped and she realized he meant the *Mirror*'s William Connor and his sparse and jerky style. She preferred a smoother, more mellifluous style herself, but she'd heard Jack say that he was a Connor fan.

'As long as you don't share Cassandra's opinions,' she said lightly.

'Why?' asked Mike, eager for something to use against this threatening newcomer.

'Because he persecuted poor old P.G. Wodehouse in the *Mirror* and stopped him coming back to Britain after the war, didn't he?' she said.

'Did he?' asked Charles and it was obvious that, though he read Cassandra, he was more interested in the way his mentor wrote than what he actually said.

When the tea break was over, they watched him fish in his pocket to bring out a Rennie's stomach tablet in a little twist of white paper, which he unwrapped carefully and popped into his mouth. 'The tea was rather strong. It might upset my stomach,' he explained, and, with a smile, he followed them out of the canteen and went into the lavatory before returning to the newsroom.

As soon as he was out of earshot, Mike asked Rosa, 'What did you make of *that* then?'

She shook her head. 'He's either red hot or rotten, but Jack hired him and he's no fool. There must be some reason he took him on,' she said.

Mike fished in his pocket and brought out a ten-shilling note. 'Let's have a wager on it. Here's my ten bob to say he doesn't make it past the first month.'

Rosa could never resist a bet. She found another ten-shilling note in her handbag and waved it at Mike. 'You're on,' she said. 'If he's still here in a month's time, you owe me a pound. Will we give the money to Lawrie to hold for us?'

'Don't be daft. He'll lose it on a horse before a week's out. Remember when he took our bets for the Grand National and didn't back the horses? He still owes me a tenner from that. Let's give it to Hilda. She's the only person in the office who can be trusted with other people's money.'

'She has to have some purpose, I suppose,' said Rosa caustically.

It was not the tannin in the canteen tea that upset Charles's stomach – it was his easily awakened anxiety. What Mike and Rosa told him about Jack's intolerance for non-achievers made the palms of his hands prickle and a mild sweat break out on his forehead. He *had* to succeed; he *had* to make his name. There was no way he could slink back to Salford as a failure.

But so far neither the Editor, the Deputy Editor or the Chief Reporter had even acknowledged his existence. When the other reporters went out on their assignments, he was left sitting in the office trying to look busy.

When he'd secured this job on the *Dispatch*, he'd been elated by the thought that he would be writing stirring words under his own byline and had spent hours choosing a byline name for himself. Connor was Cassandra, could he become Spartacus, Socrates or Publicus? One thing was certain, he would never be Cedric.

Ever since he told Jack his name was Charles, he worried in case he inadvertently revealed his real name. I am Charles, he told himself over and over again, like a spy being brainwashed. If anyone asked his name, he must never be caught unawares. I'm CHARLES, CHARLES, CHARLES Rutland, he silently recited.

It sounded good. Giving up the idea of finding a classical byline, he decided that his future work would be signed *Charles L. Rutland*, which, to him, sounded dignified and authoritative.

As the newsroom emptied, he sat on alone, doodling his name on a bit of scrap paper. It looked good with a big *C* and an even bigger *R*, the tail of which curled under the *utland*.

He signed it over and over again till he perfected his signature into a work of art. Of course, in print, it wouldn't look like that, but when he was rich it would look good on his cheques. He counted the letters; fifteen of them – a good figure, not too many to look pretentious, not so few that his byline would be overlooked.

Charles L. Rutland would blaze on a front page one day, but if he was going to make a big name, he'd better start soon, because, as well as being hungry for fame, he was a pessimistic hypochondriac, convinced that he was doomed to die young. What if the talent that burned inside him never found an outlet before fate snatched him away?

Closing his eyes, he imagined his deathbed scene with a weeping mother and grim-faced father. Jack might give an address at the funeral about his unfulfilled talent. *He died too soon.*

He was slumped in his chair, weighed down by the misery of his imaginings when Mike came hurrying back, eager to write up his account of a car accident in Lothian Road.

Charles watched while the other man's stubby fingers flew nimbly over the typewriter keys. When he'd finished, Mike called across to him, 'Hey Charlie – I mean Charles – put this copy on to Jack's desk, will you?'

It was like being a copy boy again, but Charles lifted the sheets of paper and carried them across the room, reading as he went. Mike was fond of clichés, he noticed. None of the people he'd interviewed simply 'said' anything – they 'sobbed', 'gasped' or 'exclaimed in horror'. An ambulance had 'screamed up' to the scene and 'conveyed the injured to the Royal Infirmary'.

'It sounds like a bad accident,' he said when he went back to Mike's desk.

'It wasn't too bad. There was nobody really hurt. They've all been discharged from the hospital,' was Mike's reply, said in a tone that implied the victims had not really tried hard enough.

Charles laughed, and Mike laughed too, leaning back in his chair, both perhaps recognizing in each other a mutual desire for an exciting story. If the ice between them was not exactly broken, it was beginning to thaw.

Six

For the next week Charles continued to be ignored and left to twiddle his thumbs in boredom. When he consulted Mike about how to impress the Editor sufficiently to be sent out on a story, Mike only shrugged and said, 'Jack likes self-starters. He leaves people alone sometimes to see if they can come up with something on their own. He has a theory that good journalists make stories happen.'

Very aware that he was making nothing happen, and because he was feeling powerless, Charles's dyspepsia grew worse. He endured night after night of fitful sleep and was always wakened about one a.m. by a niggling pain beneath his ribs on the left-hand side of his body. The pain disappeared by the morning, only to start up again in mid-afternoon. Rennie's tablets softened it for a while, but his periods of remission were growing shorter and shorter.

On his tenth day at work, when he clocked in, he found the newsroom crowded with people lined up along the long windows that stared across at Princes Street.

Mike was banging his fists on the grey-haired Chief Reporter's desk and shouting, 'Bugger the calls. I'm off to Princes Street. Look out of the window. That's the best blaze we've had for years.'

When Charles joined the crowd at a window he saw an immense plume of black smoke rising towards the sky a short distance along Princes Street to the left of Waverley Station.

Rosa came running in, crying, 'There's a great fire in Princes Street! I'm going down there.'

Old Bob, standing up behind his desk, held up a hand and

told her, 'Mike can go, but not you. I've put you down for the annual general meeting of the Women's Rural Institute.'

She folded her arms in an attitude of defiance and said, 'I won't go. Send Hilda to the W.R.I. It's her kind of thing. I'm a *news* reporter, not a *woman journalist*.'

'I'll report you to the Editor,' shouted Old Bob, but Rosa paid no heed as she ran out after the departing Mike.

Jack arrived, shouting as he came through the door, 'Who's gone to that fire?'

Old Bob, suddenly subservient, said, 'I've sent Mike and Miss Makepeace.'

'That's good. They'll know what to do,' said the Editor, as he wrestled out of his overcoat and joined the group at the window watching the towering column of smoke. It enthralled them for at least fifteen minutes, and no other work was done until The Basher came loping in with a sheaf of photographs in his hands.

He slapped them down on Jack's work table and said in a casual tone, 'There you are – your first edition pictures.'

'Great, great,' crowed Jack, as he looked at them, 'How did you get these so soon? They're not bad at all.' That was as close as he ever came to fulsome praise.

'My next-door neighbour is a fireman. He gave me a shout when he was called out this morning at half past four,' said The Basher, who, Charles was surprised to see, was wearing a Fair Isle sweater. Why didn't they sneer at him?

'Look at this!' cried Jack, brandishing one of the prints towards Gil. It was a dramatic shot of a fireman on the top of a ladder silhouetted against a blazing inferno and a black sky.

'Well done, Basher, you'll make a name for yourself one day,' said Gil solemnly.

Everyone was jumping around with glee because of the fire and it didn't occur to any of them that there might be casualties or loss of life. If there was, that would make the story better in their eyes.

It was established that the blaze was in a big clothing store called C&A's and when Mike and Rosa returned half

46

an hour later, elbowing each other in their haste to get in the door first, Mike said that the fire had been spotted by a patrol policeman at four o'clock in the morning. After a tremendous struggle it was almost contained, but there were suspicions of arson, a development that cheered Jack immensely because it meant the story would run for days.

Rosa's contribution consisted of quotes from the members of C&A's staff who turned up to find their place of work an inferno of flame. She also had reports of opportunist looters and laughed as she told Jack, 'Do you know the fat doorman at the North British Hotel – the one that wears rouge and lipstick? I saw him coming out of the store carrying a bundle of evening dresses with big skirts and petticoats. He wasn't a bit abashed when he saw me. I wonder what he'll look like in them?'

'Put it in the story but don't identify him. We don't want to get the poor bugger into trouble,' said Jack.

Clive, to his chagrin, turned up too late to be sent to the fire. He asked hopefully, 'Any casualties?'

When Rosa shook her head, he said, 'Not even a fireman suffering from smoke inhalation?'

Another shake of Rosa's head.

'Couldn't you make one up?' asked Clive.

'No! I don't tell lies,' said Rosa sharply.

Everybody except Charles had work to do. As he sat disconsolate at his empty desk, the pain in his stomach grew worse. It felt as if all the devils in hell were scraping away at his innards with red-hot toasting forks.

Pain and nausea engulfed him but nobody noticed because they were all busy with stories about the fire. Mike and Rosa were particularly energetic, hammering away at their typewriters. Even Hilda was busy, telephoning C&A's head office in Holland to ask if they were planning to hold a fire sale of damaged stock.

Charles's stomach ached as if an ember was burning a hole in it. When he could bear the pain no longer, he grabbed his notebook, and sidled out of the office to take refuge in the library, which he had only just discovered. It was a dusty, quiet cavern, walled in by books, and presided over by a moth-eaten-looking old man called George who welcomed Charles's visit. Few people ever spent much time in the place, and George liked to talk.

As a haven, the library was only spoiled for Charles by the fug made by George's constant smoking. Pipe in mouth, he sat at one of the long tables reading a vast leather-covered tome about the buildings of Old Edinburgh.

'What can I do for you this morning?' he asked the new man with a smile.

'Have you any medical text books?' was the frantic reply.

George nodded. 'Third stack, second shelf from the top, right-hand end. Beaumont's *Medicine*, red cover. I don't usually encourage people to read books like that. They can end up very worried.'

'I'm doing some research,' said Charles and went in search of the book. When he laid it on a table, his nerves jangled with anticipation and a stab of pain shot through his gut. He was well aware that letting a hypochondriac like himself loose on a medical textbook was a recipe for disaster. God knows what he'd find out.

Running his eye down the list of contents, he was appalled by the variety of ailments on offer – *pyorrhoea alveolaris*, *visceroptosis*, *acute cholecystitis*, *laryngeal paralysis*, *granulomata* . . . Though he didn't know what they were, the names of these diseases brought him out in a cold sweat.

Against his better judgement, he started reading the section on the stomach. The words, 'Death is inevitable with phlegmonous gastritis . . .' immediately jumped out at him. Forcing himself to read on, he found that the death sentence only applied to cases of poisoning. His breath escaped in a hiss of relief.

The next section concerned *Chronic Gastritis*, and he thought that must apply to his case. 'The patient is usually an adult who complains of "indigestion". The chief symptoms are a poor appetite, an unpleasant taste in the mouth, regurgitation of food, heartburn or excessive thirst.'

48

That's my symptoms exactly, he thought, and read on till he came to words that froze him in his chair. 'Chronic gastritis predisposes to the development of gastric carcinoma.'

So his worst fears were confirmed! *What's the point of worrying about scoops? I wonder how long I've got?*

Beaumont had the answer to that question. On the next page was written, 'Carcinoma of the stomach cannot be excluded on the grounds of age alone . . . Death usually occurs within 6 or 12 months from the date of diagnosis. Prognosis – this is usually hopeless unless early operation has been performed.'

Charles laid his head down on the table and groaned, rousing George out of his abstraction.

'Is something the matter?' he asked in a sympathetic voice. The wan-looking lad was so unlike the usual reporter. Today he looked even worse. He was not nearly brash enough for this job.

Charles looked up with tragedy in his eyes, but couldn't bring himself to share his terrible secret with George.

'I don't think I'm settling in,' he sighed, straightening up. 'And I'm worried because I've been here a week and not been sent out on a single story yet.'

George was kind. 'Maybe you're trying to write the wrong sort of thing. You look more like a feature writer than a newsman to me. People should write about what they know. What sort of thing interests you?' he asked with sympathy.

I don't know much about anything really, thought Charles, as he looked past the concerned man to another window that took in a long sweep of Princes Street with its centre point of a still smoking building.

'Edinburgh interests me. It's so romantic and historical. Though I've only been here for a few days I already love the place and all the old buildings,' he admitted. The stark battlements of the castle, the awe-inspiring and dignified Holyrood House, the sideways-leaning tenements and dark closes of the Old Town, delighted him. He could wander happily around them for days if only he didn't have to go to work.

'Me too,' agreed the librarian enthusiastically. 'Look at this book I'm reading. It lists all the ancient buildings in the city and it's fascinating. There are places that most people – even Edinburgh people like me – know nothing about. I'll let you borrow it for a couple of days. Maybe it'll give you some ideas.'

When Charles went back to the newsroom carrying the book, Jack spotted him coming through the door. 'Hey, you! Have you nothing to do? Get yourself down into Princes Street and do a vox populi at least. Find out what people are saying about the fire,' he ordered.

Charles doubted if he could make a readable story out of buttonholing pavement gawkers on Princes Street, and, as he feared, when he reached Princes Street, the passers-by were generally unmoved by the fate of the chain store.

'I couldnae care less if it burnt doon, I've mair to dae than worry aboot that,' said a hassled-looking woman with a cotton scarf tied round a head that bristled with metal curlers.

A plump woman in a fur coat who was walking a Pekingese dog on a lead past the Scott Monument, looked at him with scorn when he asked for her reaction to the catastrophic fire. Though the smoking ruins of the store were almost directly across the road from her, she pretended not to notice and said indifferently, 'Has it burned down? But it was a very cheap place. Not my sort of shop. I buy at Jenners. Sorry to disappoint you, young man.'

A workman in a cloth cap replied to his request for a statement with, 'Is this a' you hae to dae? Away and get a proper job.'

Rather than go back to the office with such paltry comments, he desperately kept on walking towards the West End of Princes Street, not knowing where he was going but following his nose down Queensferry Street till he came to the Dean Bridge. Leaning his elbows on its parapet, embellished with fiercely curving metal spikes, he stared down into a valley full of trees. Then he crossed the road and overlooked the red tiled roofs of the Dean Village far below. It was a tranquil place, a village preserved from the past.

The walk soothed him, and, when he turned to retrace his steps, he noticed a strange house at the end of the bridge. Built like a miniature mediaeval castle, it was a place from a fairy tale with battlements and an ancient sundial sticking out of its end wall.

It rose up for three stories above the bridge, but there were several more levels beneath that, dropping down, and down again, almost to the level of the village at the bottom of the valley. 'Rapunzel, Rapunzel, let down your hair,' Charles whispered in fascination, leaning over the parapet.

Two wooden front doors, with Latin inscriptions carved over both, opened on to the pavement. One said *PAX INTRANTIBUS*, while the second was inscribed *NISI DOMINUS FRUSTRA*.

He had never seen such an unusual house and lingered outside in admiration for quite a while, wondering if he had the nerve to peer into the front windows. While he was loitering, to his amazement the first front door suddenly opened and a pretty young woman looked out to say, 'I saw you waiting on the pavement. Have you come to see the house?'

'I'd like to,' said Charles, wondering if she was psychic.

'Come in then. There's someone else coming at two o'clock but you'll be finished by then. Did the lawyer send you?' said the woman, standing back and opening the door wider.

Charles shook his head, and she frowned. 'How did you hear about it then? We haven't advertised it yet.'

'Is it for sale?' he asked.

'Yes. Aren't you viewing?'

'No, I'm a journalist, but I admire your house very much. I thought I might write about it.' The last remark slipped out, as his best ideas always did.

She seemed to be on the verge of telling him to go away, but he gave her his most forlorn, lost dog smile and she relented. 'My husband's downstairs. Come in and

I'll ask him what he thinks about that idea,' she suggested.

They went down a narrow staircase to another panelled room where a young man, with a baby in a playpen beside him, was wrapping pieces of china in newspaper and putting them into a tea chest.

He looked up at Charles and smiled. 'Come to view? It's a great house. We're only selling because my company is sending me to London.'

'He's not a buyer, he's a journalist who wants to write about the house,' explained the young woman.

The couple looked at each other, nonplussed for a moment, till Charles said, 'If I write an article, it could encourage buyers.'

'That's true,' said the husband. 'Come on, you look all right. I'll show you round. I hope you don't mind going up and down stairs. You need good legs to live here.'

The house was a delight and he genuinely wished he could afford to buy it himself. When he said so, he was invited to stay for a cup of coffee. The woman fetched her baby out of the playpen and it crawled around the floor while they chatted. Fortunately it was a very good-natured baby, and Charles, who knew nothing about such little creatures, watched its antics with fascination. He so enjoyed this interlude in his day that he completely forgot about his stomach ache.

An hour later, he emerged on the street determined to write a story that would make buyers flock to the young couple's house. Ideas coursed through his brain and the story was half written in his head by the time he reached the office again.

But first he had to write Jack's vox populi. 'Where the hell have you been? Get on with it! I need your piece for the next edition,' yelled the Editor as soon as he saw him.

Still wearing his overcoat, Charles sat down at his typewriter and started banging away, typing out a collection of fallacious quotes from fire-bystanders: 'A terrible tragedy. I bought all my children's clothes there'; 'An Edinburgh landmark has been eliminated overnight'; 'I've lost the best job I ever had! I'm ruined. What'll I do now?'

As he read these comments, Jack asked, 'What's the names of the people who said all this?'

'Did you want their names?' Charles asked, apparently lightly, whipping over the pages of his empty notebook in a charade of looking for them. In fact he had not been able to persuade any of his interviewees to tell him who they were.

'Of course I want their names. Put them in your story,' said Jack handing back the copy.

His future depended on it. There was nothing he could do but make up some names, so he used his ingenuity and named his interviewees Stanley Emerson, Ariadne Harold and Lizzie McIntosh.

Jack looked suspicious. 'Fact or fiction?' he asked when he got to Ariadne, but Charles's owlish blandness reassured him.

'Did you get their addresses?' he asked next.

'Addresses?' said Charles blankly.

'Where do these people live?' the Editor snapped.

'I don't know. I didn't ask them.'

Jack leaned his fists on his table and said, with a menacing air, 'I don't know what kind of rag you worked on in Salford, but on this paper you get people's addresses – and ages – as well as their middle bloody names. Don't forget that. There's a map of the city on that wall over there, look at it and make up addresses. Pick long streets with lots of houses and nobody'll complain. People like to see their street mentioned in the paper, as long as it's not them that's being quoted. It gives them something to talk about.'

When that task was finally completed, Charles made a resolve. He was going to forget the few remaining scruples he had about sticking to the truth, because he much preferred the world of imagination, and, as far as he could see, a brash liar would usually get away with it.

At last he opened the book George had lent him in the hope it mentioned the house on the Dean Bridge. To his tdelight, it did. 'The Dean Bridge,' Charles read, 'was built in 1829 by Thomas Telford. At its south end was a very old house, pre-dating the bridge, which was at one time occupied by a hirer of hansom cabs whose stables were in the Dean Village underneath the bridge. The first room off the bridge had been his office . . .'

Charles fished his notebook out of his pocket and read the Latin inscriptions, which he'd noted down when he visited the house. He knew no Latin, so was determined to find someone who could translate them for him. *George*! he thought. Rushing along to the library again, he asked the old man, 'Do you know what these mean?'

George furrowed his brow, nodded a few times and then said, '*Nisi Dominus Frustra* means without God on your side, you won't succeed, and *Pax Intrantibus* is a blessing – peace on those who enter here, sort of thing.' He was pleased to be able to demonstrate his erudition.

Charles thanked him for his help, and ran back to the office where he started typing frantically again. The others were preparing to clock off for the day and only Mike seemed interested in what Charles was doing.

'Big story?' he asked curiously.

'I think so,' said Charles happily.

'We're all off to have a drink. Would you like to come?' asked Mike.

Charles did not drink and his first instinct was to refuse the invitation, but he knew that if he did that, the invitation would not be repeated, so he said, 'I have to finish this first, I'm afraid. If I stop halfway through it might die on me.'

The word 'die' slipped out and sobered him a bit because it reminded him of his mortality. Judging by his stomach pains, he had no time to lose. To make an impact, his story should be as dramatic as he could make it.

Mike raised his eyebrows at Charles's eagerness to work overtime, but said, 'If you finish in the next hour, come and join us at the Cockburn. We won't be there after eight, though, because we either go dancing or to the pictures on Wednesdays.'

'I think it's going to take me a while, but perhaps I can join you tomorrow,' said Charles and went back to work. As if he had turned on a mental tap and accessed a hidden part of his brain, words and ideas poured out of him, amazing him by his own ingenuity. When he read the finished piece, he almost burst with pride.

The copy was lying on the Editor's work table next morning and Charles sat at his desk, watching eagerly, his upper teeth biting into his lower lip as Jack lifted his story, riffled through the sheets – four of them – but, alas, shoved it aside unread. It was not until half past eleven, when the first edition had been put to bed, that Charles's story was lifted up again.

His chest was hurting with the pain of holding his breath, and his stomach was clenching while Jack, with a frown on his face, read the copy. For the first time since he wrote it, Charles felt unsure of its quality and was on the verge of giving in to black depression again when the Editor looked across at him.

'Hey, this is *good*, but is it true?' he said.

Every tensed up muscle in Charles's body relaxed and he managed a smile. 'It's absolutely true,' he swore. He really thought it was.

'OK. Great,' said Jack, 'Take one of the photographers along to the house to get pictures of these people, especially the baby, and we'll use your piece tomorrow.'

The story, with the first use of his Charles L. Rutland byline, and three photographs taken by one of the paper's photographers, McGillivray, filled the middle section of the paper next day.

Did I write this? How clever of me, he thought when he read it. He felt no repentance about the unfortunate fact that the whole thing was a fabrication.

Most of his colleagues expressed their admiration of the piece but neither Mike nor Clive congratulated him. When they encountered each other in the men's lavatory, Mike said, 'What do you think of the cissy boy's story?'

'I think he dreamed it up,' said Clive.

'But the people who own the house were in the photos. If he made it up, how did he get them to go along with him?'

'They're selling the place, remember. Publicity is always good,' said Clive.

'Even that publicity? All that supernatural stuff? Wouldn't it put people off?' asked Mike disbelievingly.

'Some people are funny,' said Clive sagely.

In the office, Charles was surrounded by an admiring crowd of colleagues. 'How did you find that story? I've passed the house a hundred times and never suspected it was so unusual,' asked Tony.

'All the historical stuff about the cab office and the bridge building is in a book in the library,' said Charles modestly.

'But the rest? Where did you hear about that?' Tony said, gesturing at the article.

'I felt there was something special about the house, so I knocked on the door and asked,' said Charles.

'My parents knew people who lived there once and they never said anything about a ghost,' said Hilda.

'Perhaps it's not the sort of thing they wanted to talk about, or perhaps they weren't psychically sensitive,' suggested Charles.

'You haven't got the second sight or anything, have you?' Pat asked.

'No, I don't think so, but the house seemed to call me in a way,' said Charles.

Gil, listening to them, laughed. 'If I were you, then, lad, I'd keep my ears open all the time,' he said.

Going home in the bus, Charles re-read his story over and over again, folding the paper so that the middle section was visible to other passengers. It struck him as brilliant and he was particularly pleased that the subs had not changed a word of his copy. The great Cassandra would be proud to put his byline on it.

Not all ghosts are frightening. The other day I was in

56

a house where there is a friendly ghost. The people who live in the house have a two-year-old baby. The resident ghost loves babies. When the baby's parents put their daughter into her cot at night, they know she has a very unusual babysitter. If she wakes she doesn't cry. Instead she laughs because the ghost is tickling her . . .

The story went on for a couple of hundred words, describing the house on the end of the bridge and the family who lived in it, and told about a ghost that haunted the house and delighted in playing with the baby who responded with giggles and cries of delight.

The last words of the story were: 'Should you fancy living in a house with a ghost, the baby's parents are selling. Not because they have to, but because they are moving to London. The ghost does not want to go with them.'

Two days later a gift-wrapped bottle of champagne was delivered to Charles in the office, and the young couple that owned the house telephoned to say they were delighted by his story, and even more pleased that an eager buyer who read his article had snapped up their house for a thousand pounds more than the expected price.

Clive was not pleased by this outcome. 'Maybe you should give up journalism and become an estate agent,' he snapped when he met Charles in the canteen.

In the evening, however, Mike invited Charles to join him and the other reporters in the Cockburn where they always went for a drink on Saturday nights. Charles was pleased to accept. He felt he was coming into his own at last.

Seven

'I've burned my bridges,' thought Patricia as the train juddered out of King's Cross station.

She sat in a corner seat of a third class carriage, back to the engine, staring out of a misted up window at the passing panorama of London houses and brightly painted corner pubs.

It was not a disappointment to be leaving the capital because during her five months here she had been miserable. Work on the magazine was undemanding, her colleagues were hostile and she had made no friends. The evenings and weekends were passed in solitude, walking in parks or lying in bed reading.

She missed Edinburgh, she missed her large and noisy family who lived in claustrophobic closeness in a Musselburgh council house, but most of all she missed Hugh. When she left him and decided to go to work in London, she had no idea how much she would ache for him. The object of her move was to make him ache for *her*, but she was the one who could not bear the separation. If she had stayed in London much longer she would have had a nervous breakdown – or so she thought.

When the city suburbs were replaced by fields and farms, she frowned as she accepted the fact that she was giving up a career opportunity, and a large wage, so that she could go home. Somewhere she had read that it was a mistake to retrace your steps in life, but surely there were exceptions to that rule?

She knew that she would not be able to step back into her old job because she was determined to marry Hugh, and the

Dispatch did not employ married women. The company's wedding present to any female employee who walked up the aisle was their P45. It was suspected that Harriet, the *Dispatch*'s Women's Page Editor, had been married for years, but no one had ever been able to prove it, and grim-faced Harriet hung on to her job.

Patricia wanted to be Mrs Maling; she wanted to be introduced as Hugh's wife; she longed to go out on his arm and tell people, 'This is my husband'. What was the point of marrying someone, if you had to deny the link?

She closed her eyes and leaned back in the seat. Hugh, oh Hugh! She'd run him down at last. During their last phone call, he'd said that he would marry her, though he warned again that he would not make good husband material. That warning gave her no concern. All she wanted was him. He was a fixation with her and if she didn't get him, she might as well die.

Five and a half hours later the train pulled into Waverley. She was standing in the corridor when it came to a halt and the smoky, throat-choking station smell engulfed her. It was as welcome as a gulp of champagne.

Her luggage consisted of two large suitcases which she hauled out on to the platform and along to the left luggage office. It was half past seven in the evening. She had not warned Hugh about her arrival because she did not want to be disappointed if he failed to turn up and welcome her home.

'I'll go to the Cockburn and find Rosa. She's almost certain to be there tonight,' she thought. Her friend might be persuaded to give Patricia and her cases a lift to Musselburgh in her little car.

Her instinct was right. As usual, Rosa was in the Cockburn. So too were Mike, Lawrie, MacGillivray, Pat, Tony, Clive and, for the first time, Charles and Hilda.

Though he was pleased at being invited to join the gathering in the pub, Charles lingered in the office after the others left because he did not want to appear too eager.

When he did make for the door, in the corridor he almost bumped into Hilda who was standing looking forlorn in front of a big notice board where details of interdepartmental golf matches were displayed.

As he passed, she turned and asked, 'Didn't you go to the bar with the others?'

'I don't drink,' he said. For some reason he did not want to tell her that he was bound for the Cockburn too.

'Neither do I and they think that I'm not being friendly. It's not that, though. It's just that alcohol doesn't agree with me.'

'I know what you mean. I have a bit of a stomach problem too, in fact,' said Charles eagerly. He enjoyed medical discussions.

Hilda had something other than dyspepsia on her mind however. 'They never ask me to go with them because they don't like me,' she said piteously. Two spots of bright colour burned in her cheeks and there were tears in her eyes.

'I'm sure they like you,' he said feebly.

She shook her head. 'They don't. I'm an outsider because of Daddy being on the board. They avoid me. They don't want anything to do with me.'

'But you don't want to go to the bar, do you?' said Charles, confused by this illogicality.

'That's not the point. The point is they don't invite me. They go off in a crowd, all so friendly, and they never say "Hilda, are you coming too?" I feel left out.'

Sympathy woke in Charles's heart. She looked so miserable that he felt he ought to do something to cheer her up. Should he invite her to supper? But after the Cockburn he planned to eat at a cheap little cafe near his digs and it wasn't the sort of place where one would take a girl. He was also reluctant to spend the money on anywhere grander, for his stomach could not cope with fancy food.

'Why don't we both join them in the pub? The Cockburn's only next door,' he said.

Hilda stared at him. Her swimming eyes behind the

spectacles looked blue and trusting. 'Could we? I've never been in a pub,' she said.

Charles had accompanied his father to their local sometimes during the toughening-up phase of his youth, so he said airily, 'I have, and I think the Cockburn is quite respectable. I'll escort you.'

They walked up Fleshmarket Close, where Hilda cooed over kittens in the pet shop window, and covered the short distance down Cockburn Street to the shabby hotel. Inside its front door, in a little hallway, the words *Cocktail Saloon* were inscribed on a brown notice board with a painted hand pointing up a steep flight of stairs covered with fraying red carpet.

Charles led the way like a soldier going over the top in the trenches. Hilda brought up the rear, wrinkling her nose at the bar odour of stale beer and Jeyes fluid that floated down the stairs.

Looking like lost children in search of a familiar face, they paused in the cocktail bar doorway. Rosa spotted Charles first and waved a hand as she called out, 'Hi, come and join us.' Then she saw that Hilda was standing behind him. 'You too Hilda,' she managed to add, hiding her surprise.

Mike looked up to see who was arriving and moved his chair along to make room for them. He had wondered if Rutland would turn up in the pub, and now he was here, with Hilda in tow. Rosa, filled with guilty goodwill about her failure to be nice to Hilda, said, 'Let me buy you both a drink. What will you have?'

Charles knew he should not openly ask for two lemonades in this company so he replied, 'No thanks. I invited Hilda along so I'll buy our drinks. I'll go over and get them now.'

Rosa found a seat for Hilda and said to Charles, 'Then let me introduce you to Etta the barmaid. She likes to meet the new reporters.' She steered him towards a long, brown-painted bar that was presided over by a diminutive red-haired woman with a fierce scowl on her face.

Etta's features didn't soften at the arrival of customers,

though she liked Rosa well enough. Pointing her finger at Charles, she asked 'Whae's this then?'

'It's our new reporter, Charles Rutland. Charles meet Etta. She knows everybody in the Edinburgh press and it pays to keep on her good side,' Rosa said with a laugh.

Charles, feeling awkward, said hello to Etta who barely grunted in reply, but her shrewd eyes were taking him in.

'What do you drink?' she asked and he waited till Rosa went back to her seat before he replied, 'Lemonade – two, please.' He really wanted to ask for milk, but Etta looked terrifying, staring at him with her back to the mirrored glass wall that was covered by a range of shelves and multicoloured bottles.

'Two lemonades? Any chaser?' she repeated in scornful disbelief.

What was she asking him? he wondered. When he shook his head, she looked pitying and said, 'Hunh! You're not going to be good for business. Most of my customers take a beer and chaser of whisky with it. Not many teetotallers come in here.'

He felt duty bound to explain his abstention, if not Hilda's. 'I'm afraid I have a bit of a problem,' he said.

She raised black-pencilled eyebrows that did not match her hair and said, gesturing at the press group, 'Aw yes? Then join the club. All that gang have problems of one sort or the other. What's yours?'

'I'm threatened with stomach cancer,' said Charles softly.

'Aw my God! Dinna say that word,' gasped Etta, taking a step back as if he'd uttered an obscenity. As a gesture of pity, she pushed a glass bowl of peanuts towards him with her elbow when she passed over the lemonades.

He took the glasses to the press table, and went back to bring over the peanuts, which the assembled company fell on like starving animals. The nuts disappeared in seconds.

'I'm ravenous. Buying peanuts was a good idea,' said Rosa through a mouthful.

Charles felt constrained to admit, 'I didn't buy them. Etta gave them to me.'

Rosa gasped, 'Did she? She never gives them to anybody else. She must really like you.'

He smiled, feeling good because he'd played knight errant to Hilda, and also because the fearsome barmaid liked him. His first visit to the Cockburn was turning out to be quite satisfactory after all.

Then, something happened that he never expected – he fell head over heels, drastically, painfully, overwhelmingly in love.

'Hi-yeee!' cried a voice from the cocktail bar door, and everyone turned to stare at a girl who was standing there, waving a gloved hand.

She was delighted to find her quarry Rosa and so many more of her old colleagues hunched around their usual table. They looked exactly the same, as if only days had passed since she last saw them. Most were wearing the same clothes.

'Hello all,' she called again, advancing into the room, and remembering to place one foot in front of the other in the best model girl way. Although she was so much in love with Hugh, she was a coquette and could not resist making a good impression on other men.

The faces that turned towards her first registered curiosity – for they did not immediately recognize her – followed by astonishment when they did. Mike almost fell off his chair, she was pleased to see.

And no wonder, for Patricia looked amazing. Not only had she lost weight during her time in London, but she'd also acquired a sort of high gloss that made her look like the *Vogue* fashion model Barbara Goalen. They had the same long thin legs and slender bodies, and, like Goalen, Patricia gave off a remote, glacial aura that was totally at odds with her real personality.

Her passion for home dressmaking had been abandoned and she was wearing a smart, blue grosgrain suit with a sexy peplum and nipped-in waist over a long, full skirt. Her dark hair was combed back in a prim-looking French pleat, softened by a perky little blue cocktail hat with a half veil.

On one lapel of her jacket was pinned an enormous brooch made of rhinestones that caught the light and glittered like diamonds, as they were meant to do.

Rosa, still wearing her old blue reefer jacket, jumped up and cried out, 'Patricia! It's great to see you. Come and sit down. Let me get you a drink.'

Mike pulled out a chair between him and a solemn-looking stranger, who he introduced as 'Rutland, our new chap'.

She sparkled at Charles as she sat down and his heart turned over in his chest. It was as if he was having a revelation, like someone seeing a vision. This, he knew, was his ideal woman, the woman of his dreams, the woman who had lurked so long on the fringes of his unconsciousness, a woman from some romance read long ago and never forgotten.

Her polished sophistication, her sparkling hazel eyes, gleaming hair, and the fetching, sexy gap between her front teeth, all enchanted him.

He seemed to be breathing at an unnaturally fast rate, but for once that did not worry him. He wanted to lean across, take her hand and say, 'Don't look at anyone else, don't speak to anyone else. We are meant for each other. Marry me.'

What he actually said was 'Hello.'

Normally sharp-eyed Rosa, standing at the bar, was amused to see how Mike and the rest of her male friends perked up at Patricia's arrival, but she failed to notice Charles's stricken state.

The vision of metropolitan sophistication that was now Patricia caused her a quiver of disquiet and, it had to be admitted, jealousy, which she immediately rejected as being unworthy, for this girl, newly back from London, was not the one who left Edinburgh five months ago. Clever people learn quickly.

Etta, the Cockburn barmaid, was staring at Patricia too. 'That's your old pal, isn't it?' she asked.

Rosa nodded and said, 'Yes, she's come back to get married.'

'Humph,' said Etta. 'First wedding of many by the look of her.'

Rosa asked, 'What do you mean?'

'Let's put it this way. If she was marrying my son, I wouldn't waste money on buying her a washing machine with a ten-year guarantee,' said Etta, and Rosa realized for the first time that the barmaid didn't like Patricia.

When she went back to the table carrying two Babychams, which was the drink she and Patricia had always preferred, she was greeted with a tinkling laugh.

'Babycham! How sweet. Do you really still drink them?' asked Patricia.

'I got them for old times' sake. Actually, I prefer beer these days,' apologized Rosa.

Patricia replied, wrinkling her nose, 'A dry Martini's my preferred tipple now.'

But she took the drink and swallowed it down, flashing her eyes at Charles over the rim of the glass. When he reddened, she laughed.

Then she put a hand on Rosa's sleeve as she said, 'Sweetheart, will you do me a favour. I left my cases at Waverley because I couldn't face dragging them on the tram all the way to Musselburgh. Will you give me a lift home?'

Rosa laughed. 'You're in luck. I brought the car to the office today. Of course I'll take you home. Do you want to go now?'

Suddenly Patricia felt deathly tired and she nodded as she admitted, 'Yes, I do. Can you tear yourself away?'

'Of course,' said Rosa, getting up. 'Come on.'

After the girls left, the rest of the party sat in silence for a bit till Charles gathered himself together and asked, 'Who's that girl?'

Mike said, 'Patricia Aitken. She used to be on our paper but she went off to work in London and now she's back because she's getting married.'

'Who to?' asked Charles. Only Hilda noticed how his voice quavered.

'To Hugh Maling, a complete bastard,' said Mike.

Tony shook his head and said in his tolerant way, 'Don't be too hard on him. Maybe it's just us who don't like him. But Patricia's changed, hasn't she? I hardly recognized her.'

Mike snorted, 'If she's marrying Maling she's still the same girl underneath – a mental masochist.'

The departure of Rosa and Patricia broke up the party, and people began to drift away. Charles escorted Hilda to her bus stop in the High Street and walked home to Mayfield Road, with his mind in turmoil. That wonderful girl who had erupted into his life could not be allowed to throw herself away on a man who Mike said was a complete bastard.

He almost bumped into lampposts as he walked along, dreaming up ways for Patricia to realize that their destinies were entwined. Perhaps he could save her from some life-threatening accident? Or, like Cyrano de Bergerac, could he besiege her with love letters in someone else's name? He'd wait for her for years if necessary. He was a man with a mission.

When Rosa and Patricia ran out of the Cockburn, they headed for Rosa's car which was parked near the bottom of the steep street. They were laughing in the same way they used to when they got into it.

After they collected the suitcases, Rosa headed the car towards the east side of the city and looked at her friend, leaning back in the front seat. Under her glossy veneer, Patricia looked tired and anxious.

'Are you pleased to be back?' Rosa asked.

'Of course,' was the reply.

'Won't you miss the big time?'

'I'll get another job. I wrote to the *Express* before I left London and I have an interview next week,' said Patricia.

Rosa nodded. Patricia was a first-class writer, and her reputation had been high before she left for London. Someone else would be glad to take her on.

'But the money won't be so good,' she said.

Patricia turned to stare at her. 'There are things more important than money, you know.'

'Like what?'

'Like love. I really meant it when I said I was coming back to marry Hugh. He's said he'll marry me and I'm going to make him keep his promise,' said Patricia.

'He should be begging you, not having to be coaxed into it,' protested Rosa.

Patricia made a face. 'You have some very unworldly ideas, darling. That's why you let your car salesman slip through your fingers. You think it's the man who has to do the courting. In fact, it's nearly always the woman who forces the pace.'

Rosa winced, but she said, 'I think it would be nice to be wooed, to feel safe enough to fall head over heels in love, not to have to worry that he doesn't love you back . . .'

Patricia's voice was colder now. 'Do you think Hugh doesn't love me?'

In fact Rosa did think that. She thought he was a very reluctant lover, but she said, 'Of course not. I've no idea how things really are between you but—'

'But you think I'm the one that's doing all the running. Well maybe I am, but he's the man I want and I'm prepared to make every effort to get him. I'm not going to end up on my own or with somebody else wishing I'd tried harder. I'm marrying him as soon as possible. You said you'd be my bridesmaid, remember? I hope your romantic ideas won't stop you doing that.'

Rosa was stricken. 'Oh Patricia, don't let's fight. I only want you to be happy. And of course I'll be your bridesmaid.'

'Good. And Rosa, please realize that I'm well aware of the trouble I could have with Hugh. There's always one half of a couple who does the loving and one who is loved. In our case, I'm the lover, and believe me when I tell you that even if I knew that this marriage would only

67

last for three weeks, I'd still go through with it. He's the only man in the world I want – and I'm *determined* to have him.'

Eight

It was half past eight by the time the girls reached Patricia's home, a council house in a street of identical houses, in a small community of streets with almost identical names – Inveresk Street. Terrace. Place. Crescent. Avenue. Circle.

Rosa wondered how confused old people, or those who had too much to drink, ever found their way home. It was like a maze from *Alice in Wonderland*.

As they turned off the main road and into the first street, Patricia seemed to stiffen and sat forward in her seat, clutching her hands together.

'I can walk the rest of the way. Just let me out here,' she said on the corner.

Rosa replied, 'Don't be silly. I'll take you to your door. Those cases are too heavy to carry. Point out the house for me.'

'Turn left at the top of the road. It's the third down on the right,' said Patricia, her face tense.

When the car stopped, she almost fell out of the door, she was in such a hurry to get away. 'Sorry I can't invite you in,' she said to Rosa, 'but my mother gets very bothered about visitors. They might even have gone to bed . . .'

Rosa smiled as she opened the car door. 'That's all right. But let me give you a hand with your bags and then I'll be on my way.'

Hurriedly Patricia pushed her back in her seat. 'No, stay there. I can manage. Goodbye. I'll see you tomorrow or the next day. I'm coming into the office to speak to Jack. I want him to give me a good reference for the *Express*.'

'I'm sure he'll give you a good one. You were always

69

his favourite,' said Rosa, wrenching at the car's long gear stick and trying not to feel offended by Patricia's obvious keenness to be rid of her.

As she pulled away from the pavement, she looked into the mirror and watched her friend's elegant figure walking up the concrete garden path. Coming down the street towards her were two young women in flimsy coats and headscarves, walking arm-in-arm and laughing. They turned into the gate of the house next door to Patricia's, and called out something to her. She called back and waved a gloved hand. Compared to them, she looked like a bird of paradise among starlings.

Poor Patricia, thought Rosa, *she's ashamed to invite me into her house.* The realization was deeply disappointing, for she'd always thought that Patricia and herself were above such considerations. For the first time, however, she realized that their friendship was based on life in the office or socializing after work and she knew little about Patricia's family or home life.

Rosa, however, always talked a lot about the cottage in the country where she'd grown up with her widowed father, but she had never taken Patricia down there. There was no occasion ever to do so but there was no snobbery in her and she expected her friend to know that. For Patricia to treat her like a potential critic was a blow.

Patricia stood on the doorstep of her home and watched the gradual dwindling of the winking orange indicator that stuck, like a little arm, out of the side of Rosa's car. She felt terrible because some demon inside her had been driving her on to be nasty to her friend. In the Cockburn, she'd been catty about the Babycham, which she knew Rosa had only bought as a sort of private joke, and she'd deliberately looked pityingly at Rosa's old brass-buttoned jacket, making sure Rosa saw her doing so. Yet Rosa had been decent enough to bring her home without complaint, and then she'd sent her off without as much as a 'thank you' because she was terrified she would have to invite her in.

Throughout their friendship she'd listened with envy to Rosa's chatter about her home in the country, and her eccentric father, the failed inventor, who, in spite of never selling any of his ideas, still managed to provide his daughter with a pony, all the books she wanted, pet dogs and cats, and send her to Edinburgh University.

How could someone like Rosa understand what it was like to grow up in a house where the three brothers bedded down in the only spare bedroom every night, and Patricia and her sister slept on a bed-settee in the living room?

How would Rosa react to a family who ate their meals in relays at a kitchen table covered with oilcloth? Where money was always short; where there were no books except the ones she borrowed from the local library; where she knew it was impossible for her parents to pay for higher education because they needed the extra money she could earn the moment she was old enough to work.

Her English teacher almost wept when she told him she was leaving school at the age of fifteen. 'But you have such enormous potential. You could win a university scholarship. Let me talk to your parents,' he'd pleaded.

She'd turned mulish. 'No. I don't want to go to university or anything like that. I won't go. I want to get out into the world,' she'd snapped and nothing anyone said would change her mind.

In fact, she dreamed of going to university. There was nothing she wanted more, but as soon as she began working, she started educating herself and made a very good job of it. She knew she was more intelligent than anyone else in the office. She longed to better herself in every way, but she loved her parents and her brothers and sister. They were a close family who looked after each other, and as long as she lived, she would help any of them who ever needed money or support.

One of the reasons she was so besotted with Hugh was because he represented a world that was unknown to her except through books. He was a university graduate – with a Cambridge degree; his knowledge of literature and classical music was impressive; his background was even more different to hers than Rosa's, for his father was a Church of Scotland minister with a large parish outside Inverness.

He told her that the manse where he had grown up had fourteen rooms and his father, happily possessed of a private income as well as his stipend, owned an extensive private library with a large and valuable collection of books on the Roman Empire. His mother was a passionate gardener from a county family who had imbued her only child with a strong sense of his superiority in every way – social, mental and physical, for he was a handsome man.

To marry into a family like that would be a triumph for Patricia and she wondered how her parents would react when she told them about her plans, for, so far, she had kept Hugh a secret from them. How he would react to them was another problem that she would face when the time came. If everything went as she hoped, that time would be soon.

Rosa was feeling glum and rather stupid when she reached her lodgings in Northumberland Street. What an idiot she'd been to imagine that the old friendship with Patricia would pick up where it had left off the moment she came back. Patricia had changed. Perhaps Rosa had too. She'd have to try to find out if their old companionship could be re-established – and she'd have to get rid of her pea jacket for she'd seen the scathing way Patricia looked at it.

Mrs Ross, her landlady, was lurking in the hall when she turned her key in the lock. 'Your father telephoned tonight, my dear,' she said. 'He told me to ask if you could perhaps go down to see him this Sunday.'

Rosa's face paled. Her father never rang up if he could avoid it, for he had a long established distrust of telephones and put off even the most important calls till the very last minute. If she called him, she knew she would have to let it ring out for ages because he usually lost the receiver beneath piles of old newspaper, cushions and discarded clothing. He'd told her only to telephone if it was absolutely necessary. Otherwise they communicated by an exchange of jokey postcards. He was particularly fond of sending her ones showing black and white terriers posing with tartan bonnets on their heads. When she could find them, she sent him saucy McGill cards that showed fat ladies and puny little husbands at the seaside.

'Why did he phone? Is he all right?' she asked Mrs Ross.

'He sounded extremely well, and very cheerful. He just said to ask you to go down on a visit, and not to ring back because he was going out tonight. I'm sure there's nothing to worry about, my dear.' Mrs Ross treated Rosa like a daughter now, and showed a disturbing tendency to want to run her life, for she was sure Rosa was not going about that the right way. If Mrs Ross had her way, Rosa would be having fittings for a wedding dress and making arrangements to marry Roddy.

The reassurances that her father was well did not really soothe her however. Something had to be up for him to phone. 'If he rings back, tell him I'll be there on Sunday,' she said and went upstairs to have a bath.

As she sat in scented water, she pondered the problem. Mrs Ross said he was cheerful. Had he won the pools? But he didn't do them. He said they were a waste of money. Was it possible that he'd sold a patent? She doubted it.

Disquiet niggled away in her mind all day Saturday and when work was over, instead of going back to her digs or off with her friends for their usual drink-and-gossip session in the Cockburn, she got into her car and headed for the Ettrick Valley.

She had been home three times since her drive down there pursued by the murderous Sergent Boyle, and for the first couple of times she kept remembering her panic that night. On the third occasion she was less scared, but there had still been parts of the road where she remembered seeing his car tailing her and felt herself begin to shake.

Tonight, however, she was calmer – or perhaps more distracted with concern for her father – and also it was still daylight so she was not frightened by the sudden appearance

73

of headlights in her rear-view mirror. The road was much more leafy and the trees less skeletal than they had been when she'd sped down it in January, but the landmarks were still hauntingly familiar: the turn-off for Heriot, the long twisting road through Stow, the hairpin bend before the road that branched off to Clovenfords, Boleside gate-house, and Yarrow church. Though she could have taken her father's favourite short cut, she opted to drive the long way round as she did on that terrifying January night, to help exorcise her memories.

Feeling much less haunted, she drew up at last in the cobbled yard that fronted her father's cottage. She looked at her watch. It was half past eight. The black and white sheepdog, Jess, recognized the sound of Rosa's car and came bounding out of the shed, wagging her plume of a tail, but not barking. She never barked at people she knew.

I'm home! Rosa thought with delight as she opened the car door and stuck out her legs. At the same time she noticed with disappointment that another car was parked beside her father's ancient Volvo. It was a neat, dark-coloured little Hillman like the one Iain had driven.

Calling out 'Hi!' she pushed open the unlocked door and stepped into the cottage kitchen. Her father, looking perfectly normal, thank God, was sitting at the scrubbed wooden table and, standing before the Rayburn cooker, was a tall, white-haired woman wearing an apron. They both stared at the newcomer in surprise and Rosa's father said, 'But I said Sunday. I didn't expect you till tomorrow, darling.'

Tears filled her eyes. 'Shouldn't I have come?' she asked.

He jumped up and went over to hug her, 'Of course you should come! It's lovely to see you,' he cried. The stranger, a good-looking woman with a long bob of well cut hair that was prematurely white, untied her apron and said in an embarrassed voice, 'I'm going now, Sandy. I'll ring tomorrow.' Without looking back she hurried out of the house, got into the Hillman and drove away.

Rosa and her father looked at each other in silence. She was the first to speak. 'Who was that?' she asked stiffly.

'Her name's Jean Hedley. She's the new headmistress at the village school,' he said.

'*And?*' asked Rosa.

'And she's a widow and a very nice woman. She comes over to play chess with me sometimes . . .'

'*And?*' Rosa persisted. She knew there was more.

'And we're thinking of getting married.' It came out in a rush.

So that was it! That was the reason for the mystery summons home. She slammed her handbag down on the table top, making the china rattle. 'I knew something was up. You might have warned me. I've been so worried about you. I thought you'd gone and blown yourself up again or something.'

'But when I rang I told your landlady there was nothing to worry about,' he protested.

So this is the next wedding! They're coming at me thick and fast. Mary Lou and Jake, Patricia and Hugh, and now my father and this unknown woman, Rosa thought. Part of her wanted to laugh, but she was also angry at him for springing such an enormous surprise on her. And she was jealous too. Since her mother's death when she was twelve, nearly thirteen years ago, there had only been him and her, and she didn't want to share him with anybody.

He was rummaging in the wall cupboard for a bottle of sherry and two glasses, which he brought out saying, 'Sit down, have a drink and listen, my dear.'

She sat down, still staring at him and thinking she'd never seen him looking so authoritative.

He spoke quietly but with obvious sincerity. 'I want you and Jean to like each other because I love you both very much. Since your mother died I have been very lonely. I never thought I'd find someone else to take her place and meeting Jean has transformed my life. Please be happy for me. It takes nothing away from you. I love you as much as ever.'

Her heart softened and her eyes filled with tears. Too overcome to speak at first, she eventually whispered, 'I am happy for you, Dad, I really am.'

'There's more good news,' he went on, as he filled their glasses. 'One of my patents has been taken up by an American manufacturer. There'll be quite a lot of money involved. I'm telling you this first, even Jean doesn't know about it yet. The letter only came yesterday.'

For years he had been inventing things, most of which did not work, but she had always hoped that, one day, he would have success. So far her hopes had come to nothing.

'What have you invented?' she asked in a doubtful voice.

'A typewriter that works by electricity. I'll arrange for you to get one of the very first,' he said with a laugh, tossing back his sherry.

'Gosh, that's a good idea, but are you sure it's safe?' she asked, remembering that some of his other ideas had been very dangerous. Many times he'd been rescued from his wrecked or burning shed by their only neighbour, Eckie.

'The Americans are making sure it won't electrocute anybody and they're giving me quite a lot of money for the idea. When I get it, I might go to live in France. Jean'll like that because she loves the sun and speaks good French. And I'll give you a share of the money too,' he told her.

'Don't be silly, keep it. I'm earning a good wage now. I don't need money,' she said.

He shook his head. 'I'll give it to you anyway. It'll be a sort of dowry for you. Maybe one day you'll want to buy a house or something. Anyway, I think my luck's turned. I've several other good ideas in the pipeline. Finding Jean has changed my fortunes, I think.'

'Has she any children?' asked Rosa, wondering if she was about to gain a family as well as a stepmother.

He shook his head. 'No. Her husband, another teacher, died during an operation for appendicitis when he was thirty. They'd only been married for a year and had no children. She wishes she had some though and that's why I want you two to love each other.'

Rosa got up from her seat at the table and ran round to him. 'I am glad for you. I really am. If you love her, I'm sure I will too,' she sobbed, throwing her arms round his neck.

They were drinking another sherry, laughing and crying at the same time, when the cottage door opened and Eckie came in, whisking off his cloth cap the moment he stepped over the threshold.

His hair was snow white and he seemed older and more gaunt than the last time Rosa saw him. She couldn't bear the thought of the people she loved and had always known, changing and growing old.

'Eckie,' she cried, going over to hug him too and pull him towards the table where her father was already pouring out a whisky for the visitor. Eckie drank nothing else and would have considered the offer of sherry almost an insult.

'Hae ye telt her yet?' Eckie asked Rosa's father as he lifted his glass.

'Yes,' was the reply. *So Eckie knows all about the romance*, thought Rosa with some resentment. But of course he knew. He knew everything that went on in their part of the valley.

Eckie turned and talked to her as if she was still a child. 'Now Rosa, I want you tae ken that Mrs Hedley's a guid wumman. She's what this yin needs. He's been gey lonely since you went away.'

'I'm very happy for them,' she said solemnly and they clinked their glasses in a toast to hope and happiness.

Next morning Jean Hedley came back to be formally introduced, and to Rosa's relief, she liked her very much indeed. She was handsome and dignified but did not resemble Rosa's mother in the least so there was no question of her father falling for a lookalike substitute.

Rosa's mother had been small, chubby, blonde and giggly; Jean was thin and tall with a patrician face and long elegant hands that she used with exquisite grace. Rosa was pleased to see how unobtrusively solicitous she was towards her father, chaffing him fondly about the chaos of his home but not harrying him by trying to tidy it up too much, though she was obviously very much at home there. They were probably sleeping together, she realized with a certain amount of shock; Rosa was a puritan at heart.

As evening approached, she was preparing to set out for Edinburgh again when Jean said, 'Why not stay here another night and leave early tomorrow morning? You'd still be in your office in plenty of time. I've brought my accordion because we sometimes have a sing-song in the evening. Eckie comes over too and makes music with us.'

'You can play the accordion?' Rosa asked in surprise.

Jean laughed. 'I do. It's not very dignified or feminine, is it?'

'She's very good,' said Rosa's father proudly, and indeed she was. When Eckie appeared with his fiddle, they sat singing and playing old Border songs till darkness crept in over the hills and stars began spangling the sky.

Before Rosa went up to bed, she went out to stand in the overgrown garden and stare at the encroaching, comforting hills which she loved so much. Her father followed her out and put an arm over her shoulder, drawing her close in an affectionate hug.

'Do you like Jean?' he asked.

She looked up at him and said with absolute sincerity, 'Very much.'

'I'm glad,' he said. 'I wanted you to like each other. I never thought I'd find someone else after your mother died. It doesn't mean I'll ever forget her, but I'm finding out that I have an infinite capacity for loving. It doesn't mean you have to take anything away from one person in order to love another. It's as if our hearts have elastic sides. That sounds funny, doesn't it?'

She shook her head. 'No, I understand. I think you're very lucky.'

'I know that. Jean and I don't see any reason why we should wait months before we get married. We've known each other for three months now and we're very sure it's right. Would you mind if we get married very soon?' her father said.

'I think that would be a good idea,' she told him. 'How soon?'

'In three weeks. On a Saturday, we thought, so that all the neighbours and friends can come. We'd like to have a big party. Can you get that day off?'

The speed of everything that was happening made her feel slightly giddy, but she nodded and told him that she would make arrangements to have time off for his wedding day.

'And do you think you could bring Fanny with you?' he asked.

She laughed. Great-aunt Fanny was the last remaining relative of Rosa's mother, a grim retired schoolteacher who regarded her father with barely concealed disapproval. The way he lived in rural isolation, trying to invent things that never worked, made her despair of him.

'You coward! I bet you haven't told Fanny you're getting married again,' she said.

He laughed too as he said, 'Of course not. I was hoping you'd do that for me!'

'Gosh, she'll be very surprised,' Rosa said.

'Try to persuade her to come to the wedding though. She's a good old stick at heart,' he said.

When she eventually went to bed, Rosa stood at her little attic window staring out at diamond stars sparkling in a velvet black sky and thought, *Everything's happening so fast. If Father and Jean go to France, I won't be able to come back here any more. How I'll miss this place! But I'm glad that he's so happy. She'll be good for him. It's up to me to look after myself now.*

Nine

On Monday morning Charles looked ghastly when he appeared in the office. His stomach was playing up again because he had woken up to the terrible realization that he was about to start the last week of his trial period and so far Jack had said nothing about keeping him on.

His moment of glory with the haunted house story had been brief and was supplanted by Rosa's triumph with the tale of the American runaways. He was beginning to realize the truth of the journalistic saying, 'You're only a good as your last story'. His last story had been about the opening of a Princes Street shop that sold clan histories to American tourists and it was tucked away at the bottom of page five. He had to do something better than that to impress Jack, who was looking increasingly threatening every time his eye fell on Charles.

I have to stay, I have to stay! he told himself. Not only was he desperate to hold on to his hard won job, but he could not bear to think of leaving Edinburgh now that he had met the woman of his dreams. Patricia, with her glossy appeal, filled his thoughts, and every waking moment was taken up with fantasizing about ways of making her see that he was the man for her. His fertile imagination wove so many plots and scenarios that they even confused him.

He had never actually been in love before because his previous infatuations had all been conducted through the pages of novels, dreaming about fictional women. For the first time, this was the real thing and it hit him hard.

When he sat down at his desk, he wondered why his neighbour Mike held up a ten-shilling note to Rosa on the other side of the room and she grinned back. He groped in his pocket for a stomach tablet and sucked it in desperation. The effect it had was to stiffen his resolve, something the manufacturers did not stress in their advertising.

I'll make Jack keep me on. I'll make him recognize my abilities, he determined as he rolled a sheet of paper on to his typewriter carriage. Though he had nothing to put on to it, he began banging away at the typing exercise The Quick Brown Fox Jumps Over the Lazy Dog. Anything to look busy . . .

Old Bob was marking up the diary for the day, and everyone was watching him because he held their destiny in his hands. If he did not send you on good stories, you had no opportunity to shine.

As his eye ranged along the faces of his staff, he noticed how ashen-faced Charles was looking. Over the top of his half spectacles he stared at this new lad, and felt slight remorse at the way he'd been treating him since he'd arrived. He'd been sending him on the most unpromising jobs ever since that bit of flash with the haunted house story. It was Old Bob's way of taking him down a peg or two. He resented what he called 'flashy' writers because he'd worked his way up through the ranks by being uncontroversial and reliable. The pyrotechnics of words that Jack appreciated left him cold.

He pulled the leather-covered diary across the desk towards him and looked at the events noted for the day. The American singer Johnnie Ray was holding a press conference in the Caledonian Hotel at noon; and a French fashion designer called Christian Dior was giving interviews in the George Hotel from twelve thirty till three p.m.

His pencil hovered tantalizingly over the open page, well aware that his reporting staff, who had all already sneaked a look at what was on for the day, were on the edge of their seats, eager to see who'd get the best assignments.

He was about to write Charles's name against Johnnie Ray when he noticed that there was also a lunch in the Assembly Rooms held by a group of Edinburgh society ladies who called themselves the Soroptimists. From the look of Rutland, he could do with a good meal and the Soroptimists always put on a magnificent spread, though their speakers never said anything that demanded great attention. As an unusual act of philanthropy, Old Bob assigned Charles to the lunch, and went on to scrawl other reporters' names against the remaining events: Mike to Johnnie Ray; Tony on the calls; Pat to the Burgh Court and one of the older men to the Sheriff Court; Rosa Makepeace, another one who needed taking down a peg, was put down for the A.G.M. of a charitable society that provided funds for Distressed Gentlewomen; and Hilda got Dior, the interview that Rosa wanted most of all.

When the diary was laid out for viewing, the reporters rushed over to see what the day held for them, but some were not as grateful as their chief expected.

'Hell! I've got Johnnie Ray. That's the guy who blubs when he sings about a cloud that cries, isn't it?' moaned Mike.

Lawrie, who was poring over the back pages of the dailies in search of a horse to tip for the day, laughed and began singing in a sobbing way, 'Cri-i-i-i-y, though your heart is breaking!'

'And he does Hernando's Hideaway too. He's big,' said Tony who was a Ray fan and resented being put on the calls where he'd miss all the fun.

'Huh, he's a fruit,' snapped Mike who preferred snooping about after the C.I.D. than reporting the words of a pop singer with a tendency to burst into tears.

Hilda paid no attention to this conversation because she was reeling with horror at the idea she was to meet Christian Dior. She'd heard of him, of course, but he did not impress her any more than Johnnie Ray impressed Mike because she thought that the wasp-waisted and full-skirted clothes he designed were not very *proper*. She preferred plain, ladylike wear, the sort of sensible tailored garments that were worn by her mother – and her grandmother too, come to that.

But Dior was famous and Hilda would be expected to come back with something significant.

What should I ask him? What if he only speaks French! My French is terrible, she thought in a panic as she looked again at the diary in the false hope that she had misread Old Bob's writing.

With no more enthusiasm, Charles saw that he was to attend the Soroptimists' lunch at twelve thirty. *What's a Soroptimist?* he wondered but didn't want to ask and show his ignorance, so he went to the library, where he discovered that a Soroptimist was a member of a sisterhood of optimists.

At least they'll be cheerful, he thought bleakly, for he himself was in anything but a cheerful mood.

When he arrived at the Assembly Rooms, it seemed that there were a great many female optimists in Edinburgh, for an enormous room on the first floor of the George Street building was filled with chattering women. Under three magnificent crystal chandeliers, white-draped tables were loaded with bowls of flowers, trios of glittering glasses of different sizes and gleaming silverware.

Apart from the waiters and a red-coated toastmaster, Charles was the only male present, he noticed as he slipped into a press seat near the door. Sitting opposite him was a ferocious buck-toothed woman reporter from the *Evening News* who raised her eyebrows in surprise and a touch of scorn when she saw that a man was covering the story for the *Dispatch*.

'This is a women's lunch. There won't be much in it for you,' she said, leaning across the table towards him.

He wished he had the nerve to say he would manage perfectly well so long as the speaker didn't talk about gynaecological matters, but held his tongue.

A kindly-looking woman on his right turned to beam at him and said, 'Don't you worry. It's lovely to see a man at this affair, dear boy.'

The meal was lavish and delicious, though his enjoyment was slightly squashed by the disdainful expression of the woman from the *News* when he turned down the wines on offer.

'You're rather young to be a recovering alcoholic,' she said.

He looked surprised. 'What makes you think that? I'm not.'

'What other reason is there for turning away Châteauneuf du Pape?' she said, swilling down a third glass.

After the dessert plates were removed and coffee cups took their places, the company sat back to enjoy the speech given by a famous flower arranger whose large bust was adorned by a corsage of purple orchids. Her theme was how to plant a garden that would ensure a year round supply of plants and flowers for cutting.

Charles produced his spiral notebook and dutifully took notes; spelling the flower names phonetically in the hope that he could look them up when he wrote his report on the proceedings.

The *Evening News* woman was covering page after page of her shorthand notebook with intricate whorls, hooks and dots and he wondered what she found so interesting about such a boring speech.

Most of the Soroptimists were not finding it any more gripping than he did, because many of them were happily drifting into post-prandial sleep, their hatted heads nodding like wilting flowers. Inwardly panicking, he thought about Mike interviewing Johnnie Ray and Hilda meeting Christian Dior. At least they had something to work on. How could he impress Jack with stuff like this?

When the speech drew to a close, the friendly lady by his side woke up and engaged him in conversation again. 'Have you been writing long?' she asked in a motherly tone.

'Not very long,' he told her, truthful for once.

She clasped her large, ringed hands. 'So you're at the start of your career! With all your future before you! Let me look at your palm and I'll tell your fortune. I'm psychic, you see.'

Because he hated and feared the idea of anyone predicting

what lay in store for him, he shook his head, but she would not accept defeat. 'Don't be shy. Give me your hand,' she said, masterfully grabbing his right hand, and, used as he was to obeying his mother, he surrendered it with only a small protest.

She stared into his open palm for what seemed like an age before she said in a solemn voice, 'You're the oldest of a large family. I think your mother died when you were very small but she's watching over you. You will marry and have six children. Your lifeline shows that you will enjoy a long life and have a very successful career. In fact, you are going to be famous. Isn't that good?'

He smiled back, saying nothing but thinking, *You're not much of a fortune teller because I have no brothers or sisters that I know of and my mother is still very much alive, but I hope you're right about being famous. Six children is overdoing it a bit though.*

He walked back to the office, worrying about how to write up the Soroptimists' lunch. The speech about flower arranging was certainly not good material, no matter how he tackled it.

How can a fellow become famous if this is the sort of stuff he has to cover? If only it had been Johnnie Ray or Christian Dior, he thought again.

Then one of his brilliant ideas struck him and once again his story was half written in his head by the time he was back in the newsroom.

When Jack read his copy an hour later, a grin split his face and he crowed, 'Where is this woman? Send a photographer out to get a picture of her.'

Charles shook his head. 'We can't get a picture because she went straight from the lunch on to a train to London.'

A look of suspicion crossed Jack's face and he looked at the clock. 'Which train?' he asked.

'The four o'clock,' lied Charles because the clock on the office wall told him it was now ten minutes past four.

'Phone the London office and tell them to send a photographer to page her at King's Cross. He can get her picture there and I'll run your story tomorrow,' said Jack.

Charles went into a phone booth and reluctantly lifted the receiver. The man in the London office was surly. 'Me, go to King's Cross? What's the story? What's the woman's name?' he scoffed.

'She's a fortune teller called Mrs Mary Brown,' said Charles. 'A large lady with white hair.'

'Bloody hell, half of the old wifies coming off that train will be large with white hair, and most of them'll be able to read the tea leaves as well,' said the London reporter.

'Jack says to page her.'

'So I'm to page Mrs Mary Brown in King's Cross? There'll be a dozen of them at least. You can tell bloody Jack to come down here and page her himself.' And the London end hung up.

Charles went back into the newsroom to lie to Jack. 'Someone will meet her at the station.'

When he went back to his desk, his fingers were crossed and he was praying that the London reporter would not go, but, if he did, that there would be no large, white-haired woman called Mary Brown on that particular train.

Next morning, though no photograph came through from London, Jack decided to run the story anyway and when it appeared in the first edition, in the middle of page three, it bore Charles's byline. Mike's piece on Johnnie Ray, and Hilda's paragraph about Christian Dior, were tucked away in less prominent slots.

'Good work, Charlie, but next time, get a picture!' Jack shouted across the room, and later, passing Charles in the corridor, he paused and said, 'You've got a job. I'll keep you on, but watch it, boy.' Charles felt giddy with relief, but he also knew he'd been given a warning to keep his imagination under control.

When the other reporters read his piece, Mike looked up and said sarcastically, 'So, this woman is predicting that

Christian Dior and Johnnie Ray will get married this year – to each other I presume?'

His sally set Lawrie off into loud guffaws, and he slapped Mike on the back in delight, crowing, 'Yeah, to each other! Good one.'

Hilda, who took everything very seriously and had no idea what Mike was getting at, smiled and said, 'It's a wonderful story and how clever of you, Charles, to think of getting the fortune teller to make a forecast about Mr Ray and Mr Dior. How did you think of it?'

He shrugged and said, 'It struck me that she might be able to comment on the people who are making the news in Edinburgh right now. She was pleased to do it.'

Hilda sighed. 'I wish I'd known about this when I met Mr Dior. I'm sure he'd be glad to know he's getting married soon.'

This set Mike and Lawrie off into fresh peals of laughter and even Charles felt his face splitting into a grin.

Ten

When Patricia came in to speak to Jack, Charles was sitting in one of the glass-walled phone boxes and enjoying a panoramic view of the office which allowed him to stare at her without being noticed.

He thought she was even more glamorous and exciting than the first time he'd seen her and his head swam as he worshipped from afar.

When she left, he emerged from the phone box and tagged on behind Mike who was making his way with Pat and Lawrie to the canteen. As he hoped, they began talking about Patricia as soon as they sat down.

Mike thought she was too thin to be a real stunner; Pat was impressed by her but said that the scathing looks she could hand out neutered him. Lawrie laughed. 'Neither of you would kick her out of bed though, would you?'

Charles felt the colour rising in his face and bent over his coffee cup to hide it as Lawrie began to elaborate on Patricia's bedworthiness. 'Those skinny women can go like snakes. I bet she's a terror between the sheets,' he said.

Before he could add any more specific details, Charles heard himself saying, 'Not that any of us are ever likely to find out.'

Mike laughed. 'Spot on. She wouldn't give us the time of day. It's poncers like Maling who ring her bells.'

Tony leaned towards him and said in a low voice, 'Watch out. He's behind you.'

Mike shrugged his padded shoulders. 'So what? He knows what I think about him. I've told him often enough.'

Charles turned his head to look at the queue of people

lined up beside the serving counter at their backs. 'Which one is Maling?' he asked.

'The Greek god,' snapped Mike.

That description suited only one man in the queue – medium height, blonde-haired with tousled curls falling loosely over his forehead in a way that made him look like an abstemious Dylan Thomas. It was a resemblance that he deliberately cultivated.

Charles studied him closely. He was wearing corduroy trousers, a polo-necked sweater and a brown sports jacket with leather pads on the elbows. The expression on his face was disdainful, and, if he'd heard Mike's comments, he gave no sign. It was as if he was enclosed in a bubble, apart from other people, as he stood in the queue

'She's a lovely girl. There must be some reason she goes for him,' Charles said.

'He treats her like dirt and there's a kind of woman who likes that. And because he's on the *Scotsman*'s literary section, he acts as if he's the only person around with any brains or education. He looks down on common reporters like us. He thinks we're hacks,' said Mike bitterly.

Lawrie did not like Maling either so he chipped in, 'Oh, we're not good enough for him. He mixes with the literati, goes drinking in the Abbotsford in Rose Street where the intellectuals hang out, and spends his weekends hiking or climbing in the Cairngorms. We drink in the Cockburn and spend the weekends sleeping off our hangovers.'

Everyone laughed and were still laughing when Rosa came in. When she sat down, Mike produced a ten-shilling note from his pocket and passed it to Rosa who pocketed it without a word. *What is this thing between them about ten-shilling notes*, Charles wondered?

Seeing him looking at her, Rosa said to him, 'I heard Jack saying to Old Bob that he's confirmed you on the staff. Congratulations.'

Charles flushed when the other reporters joined in and congratulated him too, some more sincerely than others. Then Mike said to her, 'Patricia's been in the office and

89

we're tearing Maling apart. Join in the character assassination session, Makepeace.'

She made a face. 'I can't really. Patricia's my friend. I was coming in just now and met her. She's ecstatic because the *Express* is taking her on and she's getting married to the man of her dreams. What more can a girl want?'

'When is that happy event taking place?' asked Lawrie sarcastically.

'Next Tuesday. That's my day off and I'm the bridesmaid,' said Rosa shortly.

Charles's heart sank.

'That's about five days. She's still got time to change her mind,' said Lawrie. Nobody said anything to that, and he went on: 'And if she doesn't, her secret admirers can drown their sorrows at my farewell party.'

The atmosphere changed immediately and they all sharpened up again. 'Your farewell party? Where are you going?' asked Pat.

Lawrie had been looking forward to this. 'I'm sorry to tell you that I'm tearing myself away from here. I've landed a job in London.'

Mike's face showed consternation and disbelief. 'Fleet Street?' he asked.

'In Fleet Street. On the *Sketch*,' said Lawrie.

'They can't have hired you as a racing tipster. Don't they know that you haven't tipped a winner for months?' Mike was furious that someone as inept and lazy as Lawrie should have conned his way into a Fleet Street job, when he'd been trying unsuccessfully for months to get an interview down there.

But Lawrie only laughed. 'They've hired me for my good connections,' he said grandly.

'What connections? The only people who think highly of you are the Edinburgh bookmakers. They'll miss you. They must make thousands off the poor misguided punters who take your advice every day,' said Mike rudely but he still couldn't rouse Lawrie's temper.

'Come on, Mike, bury the hatchet. I hope you'll come

to my party. It's on the last Saturday in the month at my flat – 14 Learmonth Terrace, top floor. Everybody's invited. Even Maling – but only because Patricia won't come without him. It'll be the thrash of the year, maybe of the century,' he said.

Two reporters left in gloomy moods. Charles, who was grieving over Patricia's determination to throw herself away on a man nobody liked, took himself down to Forsyth's high-class clothing store in Princes Street and bought a new outfit: corduroy trousers, polo-necked sweater and a tweed jacket with leather patches on the elbows. It was a pointless gesture, he knew, but he wondered what it would feel like to go out dressed like Maling. Would it turn him into a different person? Would Patricia really notice him at last?

Rosa was equally low-spirited and overwhelmed by the weight of her social commitments. There was Patricia's wedding on Tuesday, Lawrie's party on Saturday, and her father's wedding two Saturdays after that. Why did everything happen at once – especially weddings? She was overwhelmed by them.

Thinking of weddings brought her mind back to Mary Lou and Jake Rosario. After she broke the first story about them, the dailies had swooped on Northumberland Street and besieged Mrs Neil's house. Jake, it turned out, was very agreeable to giving interviews to the bigger newspapers, so agreeable that Rosa was suspicious he had arranged lucrative money deals with the *Mail* or the *Express*, both of which practised cheque book journalism. When he was taken up by the big boys, he was unavailable to Rosa, though Mary Lou was still sweet and co-operative.

Why, she wondered, *was a man on the point of marrying a millionairess selling his story to newspapers*? Another odd thing was that, though the couple had been in Edinburgh for quite a while, they had still not posted the notice of their intention to marry. Why the delay? Were they waiting to see if Mary Lou's family would relent and agree to the wedding?

Rosa resolved to try to find out.

When she went back to her digs that night however, the problem was resolved for her. No sooner was she inside the front door, than Mrs Ross came out of her sitting room and exclaimed, 'I've some news for you. Mary Lou and Jake Rosario next door have posted their banns at last. They're getting married in fourteen days' time.'

Rosa groaned and exclaimed, 'Oh, no, another wedding!'

'Yes, and they've invited you and me to the wedding breakfast – in the George Hotel, no less.'

'At least they haven't asked me to be their bridesmaid,' snapped Rosa.

Mrs Ross smiled as if she was party to a wonderful secret. 'Actually, Mary Lou wants to do just that. How did you guess?'

'I refuse. I absolutely refuse. I'm up to my neck in weddings,' said Rosa.

Though she was tired, Rosa went next door to speak to Mary Lou and Jake. She found them ensconced as usual in Mrs Neil's first floor drawing room, and Mary Lou, at least, was pleased to see her.

'Did your landlady tell you that we've fixed a date?' she cried.

'Yes, she did. When is it exactly?'

'Two weeks today. That's a Thursday. It's in the Queen Street registrar's office.' Mary Lou pronounced the word 'registrar' with emphasis, to show Rosa she'd taken in the original correction.

'Well, you've been here long enough now to get married,' said Rosa.

Jake butted in, 'Mary Lou's uncle's been in touch. We thought he might give us his blessing and we could have gone back to the States for the marriage, but no such luck. He's as difficult as ever.'

Rosa looked him in the eye. 'That's hard luck,' she said. The Basher was right – much as she wanted not to agree with him – there was something very shifty about Jake.

Mary Lou came over and took Rosa's arm. 'Will you be my bridesmaid, Rosa? I think you've been good luck for us, because you were the first person of our own age we met when we arrived here.'

Rosa shook her head. 'Sorry, Mary Lou. I'll be a witness if necessary, but not a bridesmaid. You see, my best friend's getting married soon and so's my father. I have to be bridesmaid to both of them and there's an old saying: "Three times a bridesmaid, never a bride".'

Mary Lou looked shocked. 'Gee, we can't let that happen to you! I'll do without a bridesmaid, that's all.'

It was a dejected Rosa who went back to her digs at last. All those happy people, all that romantic billing and cooing that had been going on around her recently, was making her feel sick.

Once again, Mrs Ross was waiting for her. 'The doctor phoned and he's phoning back any minute,' she gasped.

Rosa sat down on the upholstered love seat in Mrs Ross's hall and looked round the big, empty space. She was happy enough in Northumberland Street but it was not her home. Was she doomed to spend her life in digs, living in someone else's house and using the phone on sufferance? Would she grow old and shrivelled like the sour old maids in the newspaper's clerical departments?

I can't bear much more of this, she thought, and at that moment the phone trilled.

She stared at the telephone receiver for what seemed like a long time before she picked it up. It was Roddy on the other end of the line, sounding as safe and as sane as he always did.

'I rang to let you know that I'm coming home on leave in four weeks' time and I hope you'll be able to get some time off,' he told her.

Before she had time to think about what she was saying, she blurted out, 'That should be all right, but I have to change one of my days off soon because my father's getting married again.'

His voice sounded careful when he replied, 'What do you feel about that?'

'Her name's Jean. I really like her. She's nice. I think

93

they'll be happy. She'll be good for him. And Patricia, my friend, is getting married soon too,' she said enthusiastically.

'Weddings seem to be in the fashion. Will you marry me?' asked Roddy solemnly.

She sat silent for a long time, listening to his breathing on the other end of the line.

At last she said, 'But I'm not in love. I don't think I'll ever be in love.'

'That doesn't matter to me because I'm in love with you,' he told her.

'Oh God, Roddy, how can you be? I'm a rotten person. Why do you want to marry me?'

'Because you're the most interesting rotten person I've ever met,' he said. 'Will you marry me, Rosa?'

'I might, I very well might,' she said. As soon as the words were out she wished she could pull them back like bits of elastic, but they were said and that was that.

Mrs Ross was hovering when she hung up. Of course she'd been listening with her ear pressed to the crack in the door and was unable to conceal her interest. 'How is the doctor today?' she asked.

'He's very well. He asked me to marry him and I said I might,' Rosa told her in a flat voice.

Mrs Ross clasped her hands in enthusiasm. 'I'm so glad. That is wonderful. He is such a decent man, and in a respectable profession too. Can I tell Mrs Neil?'

Rosa shook her head. 'I'd rather you didn't. I've not really decided yet. He's coming home on leave in four weeks' time and we'll see how it goes. Until then, please don't tell anyone.'

'When will the wedding take place?' asked Mrs Ross, her eyes shining as she decided to overlook Rosa's lack of enthusiasm.

Rosa shivered as she said, 'I can't think about that yet. Not for ages probably – if ever.' Her lack of enthusiasm depressed Mrs Ross, who would rather Rosa had jumped around waving her arms in the air and exulting at having caught such a good man.

Eleven

Saturdays were usually quiet days for general reporters because most of the work in the office consisted of sports reports. That Saturday of Lawrie's party, Rosa wrote up her story about Mary Lou and Jake fixing their wedding day – which, as she anticipated, also appeared in the *Express* that morning – and decided to slip away as soon as possible to buy something eye-catching to wear at Lawrie's party. Everyone was going to it – even Charles who had started tagging on to Mike like a schoolboy best friend, something that caused hard-boiled Mike a considerable amount of anxiety.

Rosa wanted new clothes because Patricia's critical expression when she looked at the old reefer jacket in the Cockburn had not escaped her. After her friend went to London, she stopped paying so much attention to her clothes for she cared little about fashion and, without Patricia giving her advice, happily wore the same outfit day after day. For Lawrie's party, however, she thought it was necessary to keep her end up with her fashionable friend.

In warm sunshine she walked to Jenner's, an imposing shop that always made her slightly giddy because it was a temple to fashion, built up in a series of balconies staring down into an elegant ground floor. Today its imposing ambience made her feel even more disorientated than usual.

In a floor-length mirror, she caught sight of herself, and stared in horror at the girl in the threadbare jacket, flat-heeled shoes, and a battered leather handbag slung over one shoulder. Her hair needed cutting too because it was long and curly.

I look like a down-and-out. I have to transform myself, she thought.

A determined shop assistant bore down and found it easy to talk her into buying a scarlet taffeta dress with a V-shaped neck and deep tucks round the hem of a full skirt fluffed out over several frilly petticoats. It cost Rosa three weeks' wages.

There was no point wasting the ship for a halfpenny's worth of tar, so she next went to Allen's, the exclusive shoe shop in George Street, where she invested what seemed an enormous sum of money in a pair of high-heeled Italian shoes made of leather so soft it felt like velvet. They added at least three inches to her height and made her feel like a queen, though she doubted she'd be able to dance in them without breaking an ankle.

Across the road from the shoe shop was a hairdressing salon, where a man with a moustache like Cesar Romero fluffed up her hair with a disdainful hand and said he'd do what he could with it. When she emerged, her hair was cut in a close cap of curls. She was not sure she liked the new style but since most of her hair was now lying on the hairdresser's floor, there was nothing she could do about that.

Spending money made her euphoric and she forgot about the office, preferring to float around town, filling carrier bags with more luxuries: two pairs of sheer nylons, a box of scented soap, a new lipstick and a bottle of really good wine. When the shops began to close, she went back to her digs, made herself a sandwich and lay down in bed to read *Love in a Cold Climate.*

The party was meant to begin at half past nine, but she knew there was no point in turning up then, for no one else would be there, not even the hosts. Nothing would happen till the pubs closed at ten thirty.

She dozed and read till half past nine when she ran a bath, and sat neck deep in hot water lathering herself with the scented soap. Normally she wore little make-up, but tonight she carefully painted her face in the way she'd often seen Patricia doing, combing her eyebrows, brushing mascara on to her lashes and putting lipstick on to her mouth with a little paintbrush.

Before she put on her scarlet dress, she decided that she needed perfume. Roddy had given her a bottle of Schiaparelli's Shocking in a bright pink box for Christmas, and she opened it, spraying under her arms and into her cleavage till the exotic scent hung around her like a veil.

In magazine beauty columns, she'd read that it was bad form to be able to smell your own perfume, but she went on spraying, thinking, *What the hell! I love it. Why shouldn't I enjoy it too?*

Finally she put the new shoes into her big handbag, along with the bottle of white wine, and walked to Learmonth Terrace in sensible brogues. It was best to leave her car at home if she was going to drink a fair amount, as she fully intended to do.

She arrived at Lawrie's door at the same time as a trio of jubilant fellows from the *Daily Mail*, one of whom sniffed the air around her and said, 'Hey Makepeace, you smell like a whorehouse.'

Since she was in high spirits, she did not mind his crack, so she said, 'Then it must be a very expensive whorehouse because I'm wearing Schiaparelli.'

'*Oh, pardonnez moi*,' he said and they all collapsed into laughter.

Lawrie's flat was on the top floor of the tall building and there were three flights of stairs to climb. She changed her shoes on the top landing, leaving her brogues tucked behind a plant pot, and followed the *Mail* contingent through the door that stood hospitably open.

In the hall, a pleasant *Dispatch* sub called Andrew was sitting beside a white enamelled bucket that looked as if it had been filched from a hospital maternity unit.

'Put your booze in there,' he said, pointing to the bucket, which was half full of sludge-coloured liquid.

The *Mail* men poured in their offerings: a half bottle of rum, a bottle of vodka and a screw-top bottle of beer – stingy, that one – and then it was Rosa's turn. She peered into the bucket and said, 'Ugh, there's everything in there. It'll turn them blind.'

Andrew laughed and said, 'That's the object of the exercise.'

She held out her bottle to him and said, 'Look, Drew, I bought a really good bottle of wine. It's a pity to mix it with that stuff.'

He read the label and nodded. 'Yes, it is good. Where did you get it?' He had a nice voice with a sort of gentle stutter.

'Justerini and Brooks,' she said sorrowfully. She did not want to waste such an expensive but impractical purchase.

'It's too g-g-good for this lot,' he said, producing a corkscrew from beneath his chair. 'I'll open it and keep it for you.'

'We can share it,' said Rosa generously.

Drew nodded in appreciation. 'Good! I love wine. When it's finished we can go on to the g-g-gut rot like everybody else.'

The flat was crowded and Tennessee Ernie Ford's voice was blaring out from the main room:

> *On Top of Old Smoky*
> *All Covered with Snow,*
> *I Lost my True Lover*
> *For Courting Too Slow.*

With a glass of wine in her hand, Rosa pushed her way through the crowd and was surprised to see The Basher, who normally avoided parties, in a black silk shirt smooching across the floor like Rudolph Valentino. His partner was a very pretty, virginal-looking blonde girl from the cuttings library. *The Basher and his blondes*, she thought.

Lawrie, looking as lecherous as Pan, was dancing with his curly dark head snuggled into the cleavage of a girl much taller than himself. Tony, Pat and Mike were all stepping out with various females, and Clive was trying to flirt with a timid looking girl from the *Glasgow Herald* and plying her with glasses of the lethal brew from the bucket.

The biggest surprise was Charles Rutland in a corner in earnest conversation with Hilda. In the rollicking crowd they looked totally out of place. Charles was dressed in a sports jacket with leather elbows and corduroy trousers. Hilda looked as if she was attending a meeting of the Women's Rural Institute for she was wearing a matronly skirt, a fawn twinset and a string of coloured beads.

McGillivray, the photographer, flushed and happy, dashed here and there with a camera taking pictures of the revellers. He was snapping Rosa when Mike came over and invited her to dance.

As she took his hand and stepped on to the floor, he said in surprise, 'You're looking great, Makepeace. What have you done to yourself?'

'I spent too much money on new clothes,' she told him.

'You should do it more often,' he said twirling her round.

While they were dancing, Patricia came into the room, clutching Hugh by the arm as if she were afraid he was about to run away. He looked disgruntled, not bothering to hide how much he despised the company and the occasion. However, Patricia positively glowed in a black, sophisticated dress that was swathed tight round the hips and into a fishtail at the back. As soon as she saw that dress, Rosa felt that her scarlet suddenly seemed flashy and her high spirits sank a little.

Mike too saw the newcomers. 'There she is, showing off and upstaging everybody,' he said.

'She doesn't mean to,' said Rosa loyally.

'Don't be stupid, of course she does. She'll make sure everybody sees her and then she'll leave,' he snapped back.

He's hurt because he's always been sweet on Patricia and now she's marrying somebody else, Rosa thought.

She kept the newly arrived couple in her sight and noticed how much Hugh resented any other man coming up to talk to his companion. As soon as a man approached – and many did – he positioned between them, cutting off Patricia. *He's jealous of her!* she thought, and was pleased at the thought because it meant he felt something for her friend.

When the music started again, Rosa took the floor with Lawrie, who twirled her round and said, 'You're a good dancer, Makepeace.'

'Thanks,' she said.

'You know what they say about good dancers, don't you?' he asked.

She was saved from thinking of a reply by a hand on her shoulder and Patricia's voice saying, 'What a lovely dress, darling! Jenner's, isn't it? I saw it there. But there's such a din and what a crowd in here! We're not staying because Hugh can't stand this sort of thing.'

'That's a pity because it's going to be a good party,' Rosa said, remembering the many times she and Patricia had revelled in parties like this.

'It's only for people who enjoy mindless entertainment,' interrupted Hugh, staring around loftily.

'Is it the sexual energy you don't like? Is that a challenge to you?' Rosa asked. Patricia looked sharply at her friend, who smiled back blandly as if she had no intention of being nasty to Hugh. He did not deign to answer.

'Talking of sexual energy,' Patricia said, lowering her voice, 'there's an old friend of yours in the room next door. Have you seen him yet?'

'Seen who?' asked Rosa. As far as she could make out most of her friends were on the dance floor.

'That car salesman you went about with last year. He's here with Anna from Accounts.'

Long-legged, pouting Anna was famously popular among the male employees of the *Scotsman* building because of the indiscriminate way she distributed her favours. It was almost a male rite of passage to have it away with Anna.

'Do you mean Iain? But he's married. What's he doing here with Anna?' said Rosa in surprise.

'What is any man ever doing with Anna, but why don't

you ask him? We're off, darling. I'll come to your digs tomorrow night to talk about the wedding. Don't forget.'

The party filled two big rooms, and both were crowded. For a long time Rosa resisted the temptation of going into the other room to check on what Patricia said, but at last, when she'd drunk another glass of wine and her watch told her it was half past twelve, she yielded and went through.

It was in semi-darkness for the benefit of canoodling couples on the sofas and in the corners. She struggled past entwined couples towards a window seat where she could perch and have a good view of what was happening.

Her lovely shoes were killing her so she slipped them off and put them up on the ledge beside her. It was not long before her eyes adjusted to the dim light and then she saw him. She could always pick him out in a crowd because he was so very handsome, tall and broad-shouldered with a male grace that still turned her heart over. Patricia was right. He was with Anna from Accounts, and they were entwined on a sofa beside the fireplace, kissing passionately while the rest of the party surged round them.

Damn, damn, damn, I wish I hadn't seen him, she thought. She was over him, she didn't want him back, but the sight of him revived the old hurt, opened the wound in her broken heart. Grabbing her shoes, she jumped down from the ledge, and, with scarlet skirts swishing, ran back to the dancing. As she passed the embracing couple, he looked up and saw her.

Andrew was by the record player, beating time to Guy Mitchell's 'Singing the Blues', and she ran up to him saying, 'Have we any wine left, Drew?'

'Sorry, I drank the last of it, but there's still a lot of stuff in the bucket. Help yourself. Some people who've just arrived poured in a bottle of gin and a bottle of whisky,' he told her.

What the hell! she thought and went to dip a cup into the poison brew, though she knew it would be her undoing.

She was whooping and dancing to 'Rock Around the Clock' with Tony when Iain came into the big room and stood watching from the door. Exhausted at last, she flopped into a chair, and when she looked up, he was bending over her.

'You're looking marvellous,' he said.

God, she thought, *you look marvellous too*. Her face was stony, though, as she brushed tendrils of damp hair back from her face and asked, 'What are you doing here?'

'I was invited,' he said.

'By Anna from Accounts?' she asked.

'We're old friends,' he said with a lascivious grin.

'Where's your wife?' she asked.

'At home with her swollen legs up. The baby's due next month,' he said.

'And where does she think you are?'

'Visiting my mother.'

'You really are a shit, aren't you?' Rosa snapped.

'But that's what you like about me, isn't it? Why don't you and I go someplace? Remember how we used to drive to Cramond and walk on the sands. You used to like that.'

'What have you done with Anna?' she asked stonily though her stomach was clenching with desire. She'd loved walking on the sands with him; she'd loved their passionate embraces.

'Anna won't miss me,' he said and held out a hand to her. Her head swam. That cup of stuff from the bucket was really strong.

What does it matter? she thought. She could go with him; she could let him make love to her. That would get him out of her system once and for all.

Swaying, she stood up and looked around for her shoes. Grinning in triumph, he put a hand on her shoulder, and then boldly slid it down past her waist to her right buttock, which he squeezed as if he owned it. All of a sudden her mood changed and she was filled with anger and revulsion.

He's a cheating, lying rat, she thought. She had no loyalty or friendly feelings towards his wife or Anna from Accounts, but she would despise herself if she played any part in his philanderings.

102

Turning on one spike heel like a striking cobra, she swung out a fist and caught him on the chin. It was a lucky hit. To her amazement, he gave a grunt, went down on his knees, then toppled sideways very slowly.

Feeling marvellous, and free at last, she stepped over him and was making for the door when Anna came in. Rosa pointed at Iain's unconscious body and said, 'You'd better ring for a taxi and send him home to his wife.'

It was time to go. She grabbed her overcoat and found her sensible shoes behind the flower pot, before she bolted down the steep stairs. The street door was heavy and when she pulled it open, chilly night air flooded in.

She blinked, jumped down three steps on to the pavement, and swayed as the witches' brew from the bucket caught up with her.

Giddy, she clutched at the metal railings that ran along the basement areas beneath the tall houses of the terrace, and thought, *My God, I can't stand up.*

She leaned her forehead against one of the cold iron stanchions and nausea rose in her. Her legs felt peculiar, as if they were made of cotton wool.

I'm going to fall down, I'm going to pass out, she was thinking in anguish when a hand reached out to hold her up and a voice said, 'How are you getting home?'

It was Mike. He stood on the pavement with The Basher, both of them looking somewhat the worse for wear but not nearly as bad as her.

'I . . . am . . . walking . . . home,' she said slowly, with as much solemnity as she could muster. Then, for no accountable reason, she felt better and began to giggle.

'All the way to Northumberland Street?' asked Mike.

'It's not far. I'm quite capable,' she slurred.

'That I believe. You pack a good punch anyway. You knocked that guy out cold,' said The Basher and laughed.

As usual he brought out the worst in her and she became belligerent. 'If you don't watch out I'll knock you out too,' she said.

Both of them roared with laughter and took hold of her

elbows. 'Come on, we'll take you home. What number do you live at? You might as well tell us because you'll never make it on your own,' said Mike.

They were standing in a circle of light thrown down by a street lamp and, when she stared at them, she was surprised to see that they had turned into one of The Basher's photographic negatives – bits that should have been dark were white, and the pale bits – faces and teeth for instance – were dark. Something had gone wrong with her eyes. She started laughing again. She felt liberated and free.

'I live in number seventeen but I'll get there on my own, thank you,' she told them.

The Basher propped her upright against the railings and said, 'Don't be daft. You'll never make it in one piece.'

She stared at him and slowly realized he was right. Could she trust this pair? She decided to do just that because her legs didn't seem to work and she wouldn't be able to run away from them.

'What was in that bucket?' she groaned, as she linked arms with them.

'Have you been drinking that gut rot? You should have taken your own bottle and kept it in your pocket. Some people can't be let out on their own,' said The Basher dismissively.

'We're not all as smart as you,' Rosa managed to say and slumped into semi-consciousness, only surfacing now and again to recognize landmarks like Mrs Ross's front door.

It was a tremendous relief to wake in her own bed next morning. She was lying fully dressed beneath the satin-covered quilt. Her new shoes lay on the pillow, one on each side of her head as if they had been deliberately put there.

For a while she stayed flat on her back with her eyes closed, trying to stop the room whirling round. When she eventually sat up, she remembered the events of the previous night and what was most vivid in her mind was the pleasure she got from hitting Iain.

Then she remembered meeting Mike and The Basher on

the pavement. They brought her home. Oh God, did they carry her upstairs? What did Mrs Ross think? She might give her tenant notice to leave because she had a rule that no lodger was allowed to take a man past the front hall.

She got up and looked in the wardrobe mirror. Her lovely scarlet dress was horribly crushed but not marked with any stains, she was glad to see. Groaning, she staggered around in search of aspirins and water. Her clock told her it was half past one.

Stripping off her party clothes, she went to bathe, trying to run the water slowly so that its flow might not be heard, but she was wasting her time. Mrs Ross was waiting on the landing when she emerged from the bathroom.

'How are you feeling?' the landlady asked.

'All right,' Rosa lied, though her head was throbbing in agony.

'Have you been sick? Do you want me to call a doctor?' asked Mrs Ross and it suddenly struck Rosa that her landlady was not angry. She was anxious.

'Oh no, I'll be all right if I lie down for a while,' she said reassuringly.

'Your gentlemen friends told me that you'd eaten fish that was off and it made you very ill. They were worried about you. I let them carry you upstairs because you really looked dreadful and they were very kind,' Mrs Ross said.

Rosa felt a fraud. Poor Mrs Ross did not for a moment imagine that her pet lodger had been hopelessly drunk.

I'll never do it again, she silently promised, as much for the sake of her stomach, which was churning hideously, as for her landlady's feelings.

She went back to bed and slept till six when she was wakened by Mrs Ross calling up the stairs, 'A lady to see you, Rosa.'

Because she was female, and did look like a lady in her blue suit and perky hat, Patricia was allowed upstairs. When she stepped into Rosa's room she wrinkled her nose and said, 'My God, what a smell of drink! You must really have gone for it last night.'

Rosa was not prepared to fill in the horrible details for her. 'I had a little too much, but I'm all right now,' she admitted.

There was more on Patricia's mind that Rosa's hangover, however. 'Are you all right for Tuesday?' she asked.

'Oh yes, I'll be better by then,' said Rosa.

'I don't mean that. I mean what are you going to wear for my wedding?'

'I haven't made up my mind. What are you going to wear?' Rosa asked.

'A cream silk dress and coat. My hat's cream too, and my flowers will be white camellias,' said Patricia.

Rosa was surprised. 'I didn't realize you'd be dressing up so much for a civil wedding.'

'Because we're marrying in an office, it doesn't mean I want to look dowdy. So what are you going to wear?' asked Patricia sharply.

Rosa looked around, feeling hunted. 'I've nothing very smart. I haven't even got a hat.' Neither did she have any money to buy one because she'd emptied her bank account during her Saturday spending spree.

'You don't need one. Let me see what you have in your wardrobe,' said Patricia and it struck Rosa that her friend was relieved there was no danger of being upstaged on her big day.

She watched feebly as Patricia rummaged through her wardrobe and eventually hauled out her best suit, which was grey with a tight skirt. 'Wear this. You won't need a hat,' Patricia ordered.

'Is it going to be a big wedding?' Rosa asked.

'Not really. Only my family will be there. Hugh's people can't come,' said Patricia, and it struck Rosa that Hugh's family had probably not been told that he was getting married. Her friend seemed very brittle and defensive, certainly not a blissful bride.

Why is she going through with this? It's doomed to disaster. I must say something, Rosa thought.

'Are you *sure* you're doing the right thing?' she asked.

For a moment it seemed as if Patricia's composure would crack and the vulnerable girl that had been Rosa's friend would show through again.

They stared at each other for a moment, then Patricia tightened her lips and said sharply, 'Don't ask silly questions. I know you don't like Hugh. You've been making no attempt to hide it.'

'I'm sorry. I'm not jealous or anything and I don't want to hurt you, but Hugh's simply not right for you,' said Rosa.

Patricia put the grey suit back on its hanger and said in a cold voice, 'Please don't upset yourself. I'm the one that's marrying him and, if he isn't right for me, there's always divorce.'

Rosa remembered Lawrie's cynical comment and said, 'But that's awful. You shouldn't be thinking about divorce before you're even married. You don't have to go through with it, you know.'

Patricia turned back with one hand held up to warn that the subject was taboo and said, 'I've told you already. I'm obsessed with him. He's what I want more than anything or anyone else in the world.'

Twelve

On the Monday morning after Lawrie's party, Charles was first in the office. He had spent the weekend thinking about Patricia, going over and over the glimpses he'd caught of her and Maling at the party. He'd noticed they seemed at odds with each other and that made his spirits rise.

Perhaps his colleagues were right when they predicted that the marriage, if it took place, would not last. He would be ready and waiting for her when it broke down. He knew that he was not as handsome as Maling, but was confident he was just as clever. What he had to do to enhance his chances was to build himself a reputation, become a leading light in the world of Edinburgh journalism, so that she would notice and appreciate him. Charles was not overmodest. Life-long devotion and admiration from his mother provided him with a great amount of self-esteem.

He looked up in surprise when Rosa arrived early, because she usually came in late, trying to avoid Old Bob's accusing eye. Today she seemed extremely downcast and puffy-eyed. Early rising obviously disagreed with her.

'Did you enjoy the party on Saturday?' he asked as she settled at her desk.

'Yes, I saw you and Hilda there. Did you go together?' she asked.

He shook his head and said, 'We met on the doorstep. We were the first people there actually, but we didn't stay long. We left about half past ten. Hilda felt that she ought to turn up to say goodbye to Lawrie, and it was the same with me.'

'It was nice of you to go,' Rosa said, relieved to hear Charles had not been there to see her knocking out Iain. The ribbing she was going to get from the rest of her colleagues, especially Mike and The Basher, would be hard enough to bear.

Charles was chatting on: 'There was a lot of drinking going on at that party, wasn't there? It amazes me how people can drink so much. They must feel terrible next morning. My stomach wouldn't stand that sort of abuse.'

Rosa gave a heartfelt groan. 'You don't think of the consequences at the time. To be perfectly frank, I still feel rotten. I hope I'm fit enough to cope with Patricia's wedding tomorrow,' she told him with feeling. Her head was still aching even though she had breakfasted on Alka Seltzer.

'Is it tomorrow?' he asked, in a painfully achieved light tone.

She nodded. 'Yes, it's in the registrar's office at Abbeyhill. I've to be there, bright eyed and bushy tailed, at twelve o'clock.'

He laughed, but his heart was pounding.

When Jack came in, he rustled about among the papers on his work table, dashed to and fro from it to his office, shouted at one or two unfortunates who had crossed him, and then pointed at Rosa.

'Take yourself along to the photographers' department and get a mug shot taken,' he ordered.

She stood up and asked, 'Why?'

'Because I'm going to let you have a shot at writing personality profiles and I'll give you a byline with a picture. You're doing well with that runaway couple story, let's see what you can do with a series of profiles of Edinburgh MPs.'

She groaned. 'They are such sticks!'

Jack laughed. 'That's all the more reason to see if you can make them interesting. Make appointments to interview two, and if I like the results you can do all six.'

A surge of resentment rose in Charles when he heard this.

I should be the one doing the profiles. I'd do them very well, he thought and, before he had time to hide his feelings, he glared at Rosa with undisguised dislike. She caught this glance and realized that, no matter how friendly and affable he seemed to be, he did not like rivals.

When he saw how she'd caught him on an off-guard moment, he became friendly and whispered to her, 'That's a great opportunity for you. You'll do it well, I'm sure.' His words put her on guard against him. She much preferred the outright competitiveness of Mike.

Walking along to the photographers' department, she hoped that The Basher would not be on duty because she wanted to give him as long as possible to forget what had happened at Lawrie's party. With any luck, weeks could pass before she saw him again.

A red warning light was burning above the darkroom door and when she knocked, it was his voice that answered. 'Wait!' he shouted.

For a moment she wondered if she should run away but she was more frightened of Jack than of The Basher, so she sat on a chair beside the door and waited for him to finish whatever he was doing.

When he finally opened the door, he looked at her as if he had never seen her before. 'Yeah?' he asked.

'Jack wants you to take a head and shoulders shot of me for a byline,' she said, thankful that he was not making any clever cracks.

'OK, hang on a minute till I finish with these negatives,' he said and shut the door again.

Minutes ticked by and she wished she'd brought a news-paper with her. When she was on the verge of falling asleep, he opened the door again and, as if he was seeing her for the first time that day, again said, 'Yeah?'

She glared at him in fury. 'Let me remind you that I am only here because Jack wants a head and shoulders picture taken of me. Can you do it please and let me get back to work?'

He laughed. 'All right, all right. Keep your hair on.

Come in and sit down over there. I'll take it in a minute.'

Once he began taking her picture, however, he was very quick, positioning her against a blank wall and shooting off three exposures in as many seconds. 'Tell Jack I'll send it along in half an hour,' he said as she turned to go.

I bet he's deliberately made me look awful, she thought, pushing open the dark-room door. She was almost through it and safely away when he called out, 'Hold on a minute!'

When she turned irritably around, he said with a broad grin, 'You make a very cheerful drunk, Makepeace.'

'Bugger you!' she said furiously.

Half an hour later, she was pounding away at her typewriter when The Basher brought in his prints and threw them down on Jack's desk without a word. She watched the Editor's expression as he spread them out and looked at them.

After a few moments, he called Gil over and together they bent their heads over the pictures of her, comparing them and picking the one they liked best. She wished she could give her opinion too but was not invited to look.

Jack got out his ruler and cropped the selected picture, saying something to Gil as he worked. They both laughed and raised their heads to look across at Rosa who felt herself colour beneath their gaze.

'What were you saying to The Basher when he took your picture?' Gil asked.

She felt her face redden. 'I was telling him to bugger off,' she snapped. They both laughed.

I'm so hung over it wouldn't be hard for him to make me look a hundred years old, she thought miserably. Rather than sit and be stared at, she dashed out of the office and went to look at her reflection in the ladies' lavatory mirror.

The face that stared back at her did nothing to raise her spirits, for it was chalky white with haunting bags beneath the eyes. She hated the idea that the *Dispatch*'s readers would think she looked like that all the time.

Charles, hiding his resentment, followed her out of the

office a few moments later, but headed for the outside world. Because it was a fine day, Edinburgh was thronged with visitors. On Princes Street he thrust his way through lines of people walking three or four abreast and blocking the pavements till he turned up Hanover Street to George Street. He had no real idea where he was going till he reached one of his favourite sanctuaries, the Edinburgh Bookshop, and mounted the stairs to its first-floor tea room.

There were a few places tourists did not know about in the city, and the bookshop cafe was one. Today, as usual, its patrons were gossiping women and bankers, lawyers or accountants from the offices of George Street or Charlotte Square. In spite of the pleasant weather, they were all clad in business suits and the hat rack at the top of the stairs to the cafe was loaded down with their bowler hats.

These men were traditionalists for whom it would be unthinkable to go to the office casually clad. They never relaxed their standards, even if it meant running the risk of collapsing from heat stroke.

Charles surveyed them with pity. 'It's very warm,' he said to a conventionally dressed man sitting next to him on one of the long leather-covered benches.

'It is, but it won't last,' was the guarded reply.

Charles shrugged off his jacket and sat in his shirt-sleeves. When he saw his neighbour looking disapproving, he explained, 'I feel the heat, I'm afraid. I'm glad I don't have to wear a business suit.'

The man rustled his paper as a sign that their conversation should come to an end. 'At least you know a man's respectable when he's properly dressed,' he said stiffly.

Charles laughed. He wished he could say, 'A business suit and a bowler hat would be a good disguise for a villain then.'

Instead he sat back silently and sipped his tea. Like a divine flash, another idea was born in his fertile mind. It was brilliant. Leaving the cup of tea unfinished, he got up, grabbed his jacket and ran all the way to the office.

When he was going back in, he met Rosa leaving. She

was on her way to interview her first MP and to combine that with a trip to Jenner's where she intended to buy a wedding present for Patricia.

After enduring an hour of self-important cant from the politician, she went with relief to the Princes Street store, where, in the basement floor, she looked at tooled leather desk sets and fine glass paperweights, but nothing she saw seemed right for her friend. Then her eye fell on a silver-plated cocktail shaker. It was exactly right because it looked as if it should dress the set of a 1930s black and white Hollywood movie.

It was purchased and carefully gift-wrapped up in paper printed with silver wedding bells which Rosa knew Hugh Maling would regard with scorn. She didn't care. The present was not for him. It was for Patricia.

Before she went back to work, she realized that there was another, even more important wedding on her agenda. She must buy something for her father and Jean. Because they were planning to go to France, she settled for two elegant suitcases – a his and hers set.

Packing one inside the other, and with the gift-wrapped cocktail shaker inside them all, she dragged her booty back to the office and put it in the ladies loo to be collected later.

When she sat down to read her shorthand notes about the pontificating MP – how could she make him sound even remotely interesting, she wondered with despair? – she noticed that Charles was banging away enthusiastically on his typewriter as if the words in his brain were coming out too fast for him to get them all down. Another Rutland exclusive was being born.

Thirteen

On Patricia's wedding day, the sultry weather broke, rain drifted down Arthur's Seat and a shroud of grey mist hung over the jagged roofline of Edinburgh's Old Town.

When Rosa woke, she sat up in bed and stared out of the window at the bleak rain-streaked houses on the other side of the street. *What a pity the sun was not going to shine for her friend's big day*, she thought. It was like a bad omen. 'Happy the bride the sun shines on', went the old saying. What did it go on to say about brides who ran to the altar through rain? She did not know.

As she was dressing, she remembered that Patricia's wedding present, and the suitcases for her father and Jean, were still in the *Scotsman*'s ladies' loo. She'd forgotten to bring them home. The ceremony was booked for noon, so she had enough time to call in at the office and collect them. Lugging her burden towards the staff entrance, she met Charles in the corridor.

He grinned at the sight of her in her best grey suit with a large silk rose pinned on the lapel.

'Gosh, you're all dressed up. Where are you going?' he asked.

She told him, 'Patricia's getting married today. I'm going to her wedding.'

Charles looked at the big suitcase in her hand and said gallantly, 'That looks heavy. Let me carry it for you. Where are you taking it?'

'To my car. It's parked at the top of the steps,' she said, glad to hand over her burden.

When they got to the car, she unlocked the boot and, as

114

he was putting the cases in, he said, 'I think it's a pity that an ambitious girl like your friend is marrying a man like Maling.'

Rosa shrugged. 'She loves him and he's her choice. He's maybe got hidden depths.' She looked at her watch, and gave a little cry. 'Gosh, it's a quarter to twelve, I have to rush.'

He looked around as if reluctant to be overheard and said, 'The marriage is in Abbeyhill, isn't it? I was going to Meadowbank and that's nearby. Do you think you could give me a lift?'

She frowned. 'I can't go as far as Meadowbank or I'll be late.'

He nodded. 'Abbeyhill will do. I can walk the rest.'

For some reason she was not keen, but there was no reason to refuse, especially since he'd helped her with the cases, so she opened the car door and said, 'OK, get in.'

The registrar's office was in the middle of a line of low, grey stone buildings on the left-hand side of the road and a forlorn little group of people were already waiting there beneath a trio of large black umbrellas, when she stopped the car beside them.

Charles climbed out of the passenger side, thanked her for the lift and ran across the road to a newsagent's where he disappeared through the door. She stared after him and noticed that there was a big placard on the pavement beside the shop door. Scrawled on it in huge black letters were the words:

BEWARE BOWLER-HATTED BEGGARS!

What on earth is that about? she wondered, but had no time to find out. Her watch told her it was five minutes to twelve.

'Have the bride and groom arrived yet?' she asked a young man on the pavement who she recognized as Patricia's brother because he looked so like her.

He scowled as he replied, 'She's on her way but I widnae care if he never came.'

So Hugh isn't any more popular with his new in-laws than he is with me, she thought.

At that moment a hired car drew up at the kerbside and Patricia, looking magnificent in cream satin with a hat made of silk roses, stepped out with her red-faced father who seemed as unhappy as her siblings.

Grouping round her like a guard of honour, the members of the wedding party escorted her into the office. It was three minutes to eleven and there was still no sign of Hugh.

With a quiver of hope, Rosa considered the possibility that the groom would not turn up, but at one minute to the hour, he came running down the street accompanied by his best man, a supercilious journalist called Maitland Crewe who worked for the BBC and did radio broadcasts about bird watching in the Highlands.

There was no time for introductions, no hands were shaken, and in unseemly haste the party was ushered into the office by a harried-looking registrar, who said he had another wedding scheduled for twenty past twelve.

The rain falling outside made everything look bleak and unwelcoming, and even if the sun had been shining, it would still have been a depressing place. The only floral decoration was a vase of plastic gladioli on a side table, and the registrar, who looked like the statue of John Knox in St Giles cathedral, was sniffling with a severe head cold that was obviously not improving his temper.

At breakneck speed, he read through the ceremony, and barely waited for the couple to make their responses before rushing on to the next part. Rosa stood with her head bent, hardly hearing the words because she was thinking how sad it was that someone who looked as wonderful as Patricia was throwing herself away on graceless Hugh.

Though passably handsome, he had taken no care with his turnout. His jacket was baggy at the elbows and his shoes, though good, were unpolished. There was no flower in his buttonhole but as the ceremony proceeded, one of Patricia's brothers pulled a white carnation out of his own lapel and passed it to the groom who accepted it with bad grace.

In what seemed like seconds, it was over. They were pronounced man and wife and asked to sign the register. When everyone was out in the rain again, Patricia, with happiness beaming out of her, hugged her parents and cried, 'Darlings, I've booked a table upstairs in the Cafe Royal. Let's go there now.'

A taxi was hailed; Patricia, Hugh and her parents got into the hired car; Maitland Crewe, mumbling about work, disappeared at a trot in the direction of Regent Road; and the rest of the guests piled into Rosa's Morris Minor.

As she was indicating to pull away from the pavement with her carload of guests, Rosa was surprised to see Charles Rutland still standing inside the doorway of the newsagent's, intently watching the goings on at the registrar's office on the other side of the road. In his hand he was carrying a copy of the first edition of the *Dispatch*.

In the Cafe Royal eight bottles of champagne were standing in silver buckets of ice but it soon transpired that it was a mistake for Patricia to be so lavish with the drink. Eight bottles were far too many for her small party, and she looked anxious when her brothers began drinking with enthusiasm.

By the time the meal was served, they were ganged up in a sullen trio, muttering dangerous words like, 'Thinks he's too guid for the likes of us, does he? Where's his folks? Stuck up bastard . . . Let's fill him in.'

Rosa heard them and whispered to one of the brothers who had travelled with her, 'Please don't start anything. It's your sister's wedding day after all.'

He stared at her with opaque eyes. 'OK, I'll no' upset my mither. She's on the verge of greetin' onywey. I'll wait till she goes hame before I hammer him.'

But Patricia was well aware of the growing danger. After the dessert was served, her parents got up to leave, and she rose too, saying, 'Hugh and I are going as well. We're taking the train to Inverness tonight. Everybody else stay and finish the champagne. It's all paid for.'

Rosa did not feel up to accepting that invitation. Forcing

herself to look pleasant, she shook Hugh's hand and congratulated him on marrying a wonderful girl. Then she kissed Patricia, passed over the gift-wrapped cocktail shaker and said, 'I hope you'll be very, very happy. You'll keep in touch, won't you?'

'Of course I will. We're only going away for two days to stay with Hugh's parents. You'll see a lot of me because I'm starting with the *Express* next week. They're paying me very well and I'll be able to buy a flat,' said Patricia.

Looking over her friend's shoulder, Rosa saw Hugh's face darken.

I'll be able to buy a flat, Patricia had said. The cracks in the marriage were showing already.

Outside, the light rain had become a deluge and was falling heavily when Rosa emerged on the street. She was grateful she had opted to wear flat shoes instead of her lovely Italian stilettos. Her curly hair was plastered to her skull and her jacket shoulder pads soaking when she slipped into the driving seat and leaned back with a feeling of utmost relief. She loved her car and always felt safe in it, as if it was a kind of burrow.

On her way home, she remembered about the 'Bowler-Hatted Beggar' poster, and drew up beside the old woman who sold newspapers from a stand at the top of the Waverley Steps to buy a third edition copy of the *Dispatch* which she threw, closed, on the seat beside her.

At Mrs Ross's front door, because she was curious, she reached over for the paper and opened it. In the middle of the front page was a big piece. When she read it, Rosa gasped.

'Beggars in Bowlers Besiege Our City,' it proclaimed and went on to tell how the reporter, Charles L. Rutland, was shocked to be approached by a well-spoken, well-dressed man in a business suit and a bowler hat who asked him for a handout.

'I was astonished and asked him how much he wanted. He said half a crown would do very well,' wrote Charles, and

118

went on to tell how, in return for his coin, the gentlemanly beggar told him that there was an organized gang of bowler-hatted mendicants patrolling the city streets, preying on residents and visitors alike. Their favourite begging site was in Charlotte Square or outside Edinburgh's exclusive New Club in Princes Street.

He ended his report with: 'This is a warning. The well-to-do fellow in the bowler hat walking beside you today might not be a businessman. He's probably a beggar.'

Not unexpectedly, by the time Rosa read the piece, Charles's story had already started a storm of protest. Telephone calls flooded in from outraged city councillors, and business gentlemen wearing bowlers in central Edinburgh were astonished and deeply offended to be sneered at – or worse, offered money by passers-by, especially soft-hearted American tourists.

For three days furious letters of protest from the business community filled the Letters Page of the *Dispatch* and important citizens petitioned their local councillors to have something done about the importunate beggars. Some people even called on the city police to find the culprits – or else.

The staff of the rival newspapers were divided in their opinions of Charles L. Rutland. Half of them were furious because he had scooped them and editors berated their reporters for not finding stories like his. The other half were sceptical about the truth of his report.

Leo Fairley, star reporter of the *Daily Mail*, sat in his favourite watering-hole, the Doric, and said to his friends, 'Doesn't anyone think it odd that Rutland finds stories no one else does? Doesn't anyone wonder why there's no photograph with this piece of his? Why can't any of us follow it up? As far as I can see, it's because it's all airy-fairy nonsense and I don't think he'd sue me if I said to his face that he's a liar.'

A jubilant Mike carried Fairley's comments back to Charles, who only looked disdainful and said, 'Jealousy is what's wrong with Leo Fairley.'

119

He was delighted with his success. Everyone was talking about him and that was what he wanted. The manic strain in his personality made him determined to continue with his fabrications. He wanted to see how far he could go.

Fourteen

On a brilliant summer morning, the new bride Patricia, elegant in a cream linen suit, walked round an empty flat in a tall building called Blackie House, off the Lawnmarket in the Old Town. It was a long, narrow apartment of five big rooms with six windows like watching eyes looking out from its north side towards the shores of Fife glimmering on the other side of the azure river Forth.

For four hundred years, the flat had endured a mixed history. The panelled walls and painted ceiling beams on some of the floors showed that it originally housed important people, but for the past century and a half it had been sub-divided into tiny apartments where working class families were born, lived, and died, often sleeping four to a bed.

Now, after generations of being slums, the tenements of the Old Town of Edinburgh were on the verge of gentrification. Smart, astute people like Patricia had begun looking around the ancient buildings for flats where they could live in the style of the grandees who occupied them long ago.

Yes, this will do very well. I'll be able to make an impressive home here. We'll invite interesting people in to drink wine and hold stimulating conversations. I'll have a salon, she thought. She would be a perfect hostess and, with work, the flat could be made very elegant. Hugh would appreciate that. It might give her status in his eyes.

And she needed status badly. After their marriage, they had gone to Inverness where Hugh's father picked them up at the station in a rattly old car and drove them to his manse, an imposing building set alongside a grassy glebe where sheep grazed. The rooms of Hugh's family home were packed full of beautiful old furniture that he said airily were family pieces. Though most of the rooms were never occupied, his parents showed no sign of giving any of these valuable pieces away. The newly married couple received no wedding present.

Hugh's parents were condescending, and spoke to Patricia in the same, slow, well-enunciated tones that some British people used to foreigners on the Continent. She was obviously 'not the right sort'.

Goaded into opting for honesty, she told them her father drove a brewery lorry and they chuckled gently as if she'd made a joke. When they were leaving to return to Edinburgh, Hugh's mother hugged her son and wept as if he was going off to war. She did not hug her new daughter-in-law.

After the visit, Hugh's treatment of his wife had grown even more dismissive. 'Was it absolutely necessary to tell my people what your father does for a living?' he asked her as soon as they got into the train for Edinburgh.

'Why not?' she snapped.

'If you don't know why, there's no point me spelling it out for you,' he replied.

They had been married for ten days, and every day saw a deterioration in their relationship. Perhaps this flat would patch things up between them for she knew she could turn it into a home of which he would be very proud.

The rickety, cage-like lift, that cranked its way up a narrow tower at the back of the building, was not working when she tried to leave the empty flat, so she was forced to negotiate the twisting stairs – down, down, down for five stories. Swaying on her high heels, she made her way out of Lady Stair's Close to Market Street and the *Daily Express* office, deliberately walking in the shade because the brightness of the sun after the shadows of the ancient courtyard made her giddy.

Already she enjoyed special status as a star feature writer at the *Express*, where she was contracted to write her own column, so she had no qualms about using the office telephone for personal calls. First she contacted the lawyer who was letting the flat for its owner, and told him that she was prepared to pay the high rent demanded for a long lease. Her cheque would be with him tomorrow morning, she said. He sounded impressed.

Though Hugh was still in bed when she'd left for work in the morning, he did not answer the telephone in the tiny bachelor flat in Rose Street, which they had shared since their marriage. He'd lived there as a bachelor and it was extremely small and shabby, but when she complained about it, he always said, 'Of course, you're used to much better places, aren't you? A council house in Musselburgh with all your family – two bedrooms for six of you, am I right? I don't call that gracious living.'

In public or in private, he treated her with disdain, but after she told him how well the *Express* was paying her, he became even more scathing and it struck her that he was jealous.

His most cherished ambition was to write a literary novel, but his talent was mediocre. Night after night he sat up late, writing and re-writing the first chapter of his epic, but was never satisfied and most of his attempts ended up in a trash basket full of crumpled sheets of paper. It was agony for him when his contemporaries – people he knew and despised – succeeded in getting published, while he was employed to write criticisms of their books. He got rid of some of his spleen by the cruelty of his printed comments. The rest of his bitterness he vented at his wife.

Not a day had passed since their wedding without him reducing her to tears. Sex between them was now perfunctory and unfulfilling and she was left with a feeling of emptiness, wondering what there was about the sexual act that made people like Lawrie and Anna in Accounts so voracious.

In the evenings, Hugh often came back from work with his friend Maitland Crewe, the supercilious broadcaster and Hugh's best man. Crewe had a wife called Sonya, but he never seemed to go home to her and Patricia had never met her.

He and Hugh sat talking till the small hours about highbrow books and ignoring Patricia. If she complained or tried to join in the conversation, Hugh told her to go to bed because she did not understand what they were talking about. He jibed, 'After all you weren't university material, were you?'

In desperation she began reading the books he and Maitland discussed and found she enjoyed, and could very well understand, the works of Albert Camus, or Christopher Isherwood, one of whose books was in her handbag when she looked round the new flat.

Even she was mystified by the way she put up with Hugh. If she were to see another woman going through the cruelty being inflicted on her, she would not hesitate to say, 'Get out, get out now!' But it seemed she enjoyed being tormented, though she did not understand why.

She did not lack confidence and knew she was an attractive woman. Men made approaches to her and she knew she could find another lover within weeks, if not days, but it was Hugh she wanted – because he did not want her. In her eyes, their marriage was like an emotional wrestling match. Either she would make him hit the mat, or she'd be the one to end up bloody and beaten.

After taking on the lease of the flat, she left the office again in search of her husband at their old flat where she found him in his dressing gown drinking tea and surrounded by more crumpled paper.

'I've found us a lovely place to live, darling,' she said brightly.

'A council house in Sighthill?' he asked sarcastically.

'Of course not. It's a beautiful big flat in the High Street with a view down the Mound and across to Fife,' she said sweetly, ignoring his jibe.

'You're moving in your family? All those High Street flats were multi-occupied by working class families,' he said. She kept her temper and pretended to laugh but felt her back teeth clenching.

'Of course not! I've told the lawyer that we'll take it.

You'll love it. We can look at it now if you like. I've still got the key,' she told him.

'Isn't that nice? So you've taken it. Haven't I any say in where we live?' he snarled.

'But it's a wonderful flat. I know you'll like it. The whole building's been done up by the owner. There's only one flat on each floor.' She had to have that flat, no matter what he said.

'Spacious living,' he sneered, but she could tell he was interested. Being married to him was very hard work and today she was even more irritated than usual by their constant bickering.

'Let's go to see it now,' she pleaded, and, amazingly, he agreed.

Outside again, the sunlight bouncing off the grey walls and pavements dazzling her eyes, she thought she preferred Edinburgh when it was in its normal gloomy guise. In hot weather, the stifling heat radiating from the solid, close packed buildings made her head swim. As they walked up the Mound, a car horn hooted behind them and she turned to see Rosa at the wheel of her little car.

Leaning out of the open window, her friend called, 'Hi, Patricia! Where are you going? Do you want a lift?'

Patricia bent down and said, 'It's not far. Only to the High Street. I've found a lovely flat and we're going to view it. Do you want to have a look too?' She thought Hugh's venom might be diverted a little if there was a third person around while they looked round the place.

Rosa was flattered to be asked. She had not seen Patricia since the wedding party at the Cafe Royal and was pleased by this sign of a renewal of their friendship.

'I'd love to. It's such a lovely day, I was going up to the Observatory for a walk.' she said. They both ignored Hugh who stood on the pavement staring at the Old Town skyline.

Patricia opened the passenger door, and climbed into the back of Rosa's car. To her relief, Hugh got into the front without complaint. 'The flat's in Blackie House,' she told Rosa.

They parked at the entrance to Lady Stair's Close, walked across the courtyard, and toiled panting up the steep stairs of the building because the lift was still out of order. When Patricia turned the key in the lock and threw open the door to the flat, Rosa exclaimed, 'Gosh, it's lovely. What a find!'

They walked into the main room and stood at the windows, staring out at the magnificent panorama spreading before them. 'You have a bird's eye view of Edinburgh, you lucky things,' Rosa said.

Hugh said nothing but wandered around with his hands in his trouser pockets, kicking at the wainscoting. 'What's the rent?' he asked at last.

'Three hundred a year,' Patricia said, and he whirled round. 'What! That's robbery!'

'We can afford it. I'm earning two thousand a year,' she said stiffly, knowing that his salary was seven hundred and fifty.

In embarrassment Rosa began examining the painted ceiling beams. 'Look at these. They're beautiful,' she said in an ineffectual attempt to divert them.

The couple, who were eyeing each other like prize fighters, did not answer her and she felt very out of place standing between them.

'I love the flat, but I must rush and leave you to look round on your own,' she said in an embarrassed voice, and bolted for the door.

As soon as she disappeared, Hugh turned on his wife and snarled, 'So, you earn two thousand a year, do you? Did you think it was putting me down to tell me that in front of your sidekick? Don't ever do that again!'

She said nothing, but she was thinking, *He's trying to break me. It's war between us. And I must win.*

That afternoon she signed the tenancy agreement for the flat.

Next morning Rosa received a phone call at the office from Patricia. 'Darling,' she gushed in her new, over-the-top way, 'why don't we meet at the Chinese today?'

126

There was a moment's pause, then Rosa said, 'Great, what a good idea. One o'clock?'

It was nine months since she and Patricia last lunched in their favourite restaurant and she wondered why a rendez-vous had been arranged now.

The Chinese restaurant was hardly changed though the red and gold tinsel lanterns looked a little more tarnished than they used to do. Yellowing scrolls covered with inscrutable lettering still fluttered on the white painted walls, and the owner was as impassive as ever. At the cash desk, his blank-eyed wife in her faded black cheong-sam, still seemed lost in her alternative world. Rosa and Patricia had always enjoyed going there, for they were often the only patrons, but the food was delicious and, as far as they knew, authentically Chinese.

Rosa turned up on time but Patricia, as usual, was ten minutes late. Eventually she came running up the stairs, apologizing before she sat down. Today she was wearing a full-skirted navy seersucker dress with a polka dotted collar, cuffs and belt. On her dark hair perched the tiny blue hat that looked like a patting hand.

'Darling, I've literally rushed away from Danny Kaye's press conference to meet you. That's friendship, isn't it?' she exclaimed, falling into her chair.

'Was he interesting?' asked Rosa.

'Massively egocentric, I'm afraid, but my piece'll be all right. Most of it can come out of the cuttings. These people say the same thing every time anyway,' replied Patricia.

Leaning forward on the table, she asked, 'Let's have all our old favourites: sweet and sour prawns for you, chicken spring rolls for me, egg fried rice and green tea. OK? It's on me, by the way.'

When they ordered glasses of lager and toasted each other, Rosa began to relax, feeling that their old ease was coming back. 'It was a pleasant surprise to be invited to meet you here again,' she said.

'Well, I thought you were looking a bit glum when you

were in the flat yesterday. It is a lovely flat, isn't it? I've signed the lease, you know.' Patricia kept her eyes on Rosa's face all the time she was speaking.

'That's excellent. It's a beautiful flat.' Rosa told her what she wanted to hear.

'I've been planning what I'm going to do with it – white walls, stripped floors, bright curtains, lots of plants and not too much furniture. The cocktail shaker's perfect by the way. You are clever to think of giving us that,' said Patricia.

Rosa grinned. 'I thought it suited you,' she said.

'Now, let me know what's happening in your life,' said Patricia, leaning forward.

'Not much. My father's getting married again, that's the most important thing at the moment,' Rosa told her.

Patricia knew how close Rosa and her father were so she asked, 'Do you like the woman?'

'Yes, I really do. The sad bit is that they are probably going to live in France,' said Rosa.

'But darling, think of the holidays you'll have! Far better than Portobello!' was Patricia's comment.

They both laughed, and then Rosa said in a more solemn voice, 'I'm at a bit of a crossroads in my life, as a matter of fact. I'm bored, I think. You've got married; my father's next. I'll be the only person left on the shelf soon.'

Patricia raised her eyebrows. 'Don't be silly. You'll find a wonderful man any day now. You're well shot of that Iain. And your work's going well. Jack's given you those profiles to do, hasn't he?'

Rosa grimaced. 'Spending my life making Edinburgh MPs sound interesting is not my be all and end all. I want a bit more than that. As for men, there's nobody I want to marry either. I don't think there ever will be.'

'Don't be silly. What happened to your doctor friend?' asked Patricia.

'I like him but I don't love him. But as a matter of fact I've told him I'll think about marrying him and ever since I said it I've spent my time wishing I hadn't.' Rosa sounded very low.

Patricia's face changed too. 'Maybe it's best to be the person who's loved rather than the one who does the loving. I'm far too eager to please Hugh. My advice is snap your doctor up. He sounds a good prospect and you'll have your own way for the rest of your life. Believe me, that's better than having to cater to someone else's whims all the time.' Her voice was bitter.

Rosa stopped eating her sweet and sour prawns and looked surprised. Patricia had never been so forthright about Hugh before.

'What's wrong? Are you and Hugh having trouble?' she asked, sorry that she'd been so involved with her own concerns, that she had not given much thought to Patricia's.

The question immediately changed the atmosphere between them. In a second Patricia stopped being approachable and became the sharp-tongued sophisticate again. 'What do you mean? Don't start lecturing me! Nothing's wrong with us. Why should anything be wrong? I'm married to the only man in the world that I want. He may not be the easiest, but I knew that before it started. Listen to what I'm telling you. My advice to you is to settle for marriage and safety. You don't want to end up living in a garret with only a cat for company, do you?'

She gathered her handbag off the floor, saying something about having to rush back to work. There was obviously no way the flickering flame of their old openness could be fanned into life again. She paid the bill and hurried away, waving her hand as if she was brushing Rosa off.

Rosa half rose in her seat and watched her go. For a moment she considered calling out, 'Stop. Come back and let's really talk' because she was sure that Patricia was running away to stop herself speaking more openly than she had done since she came back from London.

But Rosa, hurt, said nothing, an omission she came to deeply regret.

Fifteen

During the days preceding her father's wedding Rosa was kept busy. On Wednesday, the first of her MP profiles appeared as a middle page spread and she opened the paper with disquiet, remembering the hilarity her photograph had caused.

On one side of the page Jack had put a cuttings file photograph of the MP being profiled; on the other, beside her byline, was The Basher's snap of Rosa. She stared at it in disbelief.

Instead of looking haggard and hung-over, she seemed to gleam and glitter. It was the best picture of her that had ever been taken, so good in fact that she thought no one would recognize her. He had posed her slightly sideways on and she was looking over her shoulder like a screen vamp. Instead of being overcome with self-satisfaction at the way she appeared, she was slightly embarrassed, and the embarrassment was made worse by her original unfounded animus against The Basher when she was afraid that he would deliberately make her look awful.

Everyone in the office had their heads stuck inside the first edition as usual, and Rosa's article caused general amusement again. 'You should send that picture to Pinewood Studios. They might sign you up as a starlet,' joked Mike.

Just then one of the phones rang. Tony answered and shouted, 'It's Patricia for Rosa.'

When Rosa went on the line, Patricia said, 'I've just seen your middle page spread. It's good, and that picture of you is terrific. Who took it?'

'The Basher,' said Rosa shortly.

'He could make a fortune snapping girls. Ask him if he'll do one for me,' laughed Patricia.

When Rosa emerged from the phone box, she asked MacGillivray, who was handing over some pictures to Jack, 'Where's The Basher? I haven't seen him for days.' She didn't know whether she should apologize to him for her base suspicions, or tell him off for making her look so doe-eyed and submissive – which she was not and did not want to be.

McGillivray said, 'He's on holiday.'

Everyone was interested. They didn't associate The Basher with something as sybaritic as a holiday. 'Where's he gone?' asked Mike whose ideal destination would be either New York or Monte Carlo.

'To Spain. He was talking about some place where people used to go on pilgrimage,' said McGillivray.

Everyone stared at him in disbelief. 'Pilgrimage?' asked Tony, a minister's son. Pilgrimages did not cut much ice with the Church of Scotland. They were far too Romish.

'He wanted to take pictures of some cathedral,' explained McGillivray.

'I don't see Jack putting that on the front page,' said Mike with satisfaction.

In the canteen at break time, Rosa got down to the next item on her agenda. 'I want to swap some days off. Any offers?' she said.

'When?' asked ever-obliging Tony.

'This Friday and Saturday. I'm going to a wedding.'

Mike looked up and said, 'Another wedding? Who is it this time?'

'My father's getting married,' Rosa told him.

'Legitimizing you at last, is he?' he joked.

She took it in good part and corrected him, 'Married *again*. He's a widower.'

Mike shook his head. 'It should be you getting married, Makepeace. I'll marry you if you can't find anybody else.'

She laughed. 'What a rash offer. I might take you up on it one day. But, seriously, I need to be away Friday and

Saturday. The wedding's on Saturday but I'm taking my old aunt and she can't be hurried, so we'll go down the day before.'

Charles, who was always curious and could be relied on to ask questions about everything in the best journalistic tradition, asked, 'How old is your aunt?'

'She's well over eighty. She's my mother's aunt really, and she lives in Corstorphine, on the top of the hill behind the zoo. It's a terrible climb to her house but nice when you get up there. Sometimes she hears the animals roaring if the wind's in the right direction,' Rosa told him.

'Isn't she scared, living near these zoo animals?' asked Tony.

'She's lived there for forty years and, in a way, I think she relishes the possible danger because she's always going on about it. In fact, it's perfectly safe and the only animal that's ever escaped in all that time is a penguin. I tell her it would take a bold lion to confront Great-aunt Fanny, she's an ex-schoolteacher and quite terrifying,' Rosa said with a laugh.

After more discussion she swapped two of her Tuesdays for a Friday and a Saturday from Tony and Charles.

When Rosa turned up to collect her great-aunt on Friday morning, she was immediately and disquietingly struck by the frailness of the old lady. Fanny seemed to have shrunk even since the last time they met in January and she looked like a little, well-behaved child as she stood waiting for her niece at the gate into her tidy, rose-filled garden.

As they drove out of the city, with the sun through the windscreen lighting on her face, her deeply wrinkled skin seemed as fragile as tissue paper. The dark freckles on the backs of her hands and the way the skeletal knucklebones stood out, made Rosa's heart turn over with pity and fear. Fanny was growing old and it would be terrible to lose her, awkward as she could be at times.

As well as shrinking her, age had also softened her ferocity and she no longer made cutting remarks about Rosa's father or criticized her great-niece's dress sense.

When she said, 'You're looking very pretty today, my dear,' Rosa almost wished that the old Fanny would come back and ask why she was wearing cotton slacks; '*Not* the clothes for a real lady, I'm afraid,' she used to say with a sardonic twist of the mouth.

She was even pleasant about Rosa's father's re-marriage. 'I'm very happy for him. He's been on his own a long time and he did a very good job bringing you up,' she said.

Then she sighed and said, 'I had a bit of bad news yesterday. Do you remember my friend Miss Noble who lives in Clarendon Crescent?'

Rosa nodded. 'Of course I do. I like her very much.'

Miss Noble, a sharp-minded ex-schoolteacher colleague of Fanny's, helped Rosa when she was investigating the Boyle story.

Fanny sighed. 'I'm afraid she's becoming very absent-minded. She went out the other day and forgot where she lived so she couldn't get home again.'

Rosa was horrified. 'What happened?' she asked.

'The strange thing was, though she couldn't remember her own address, she remembered where I lived and asked a policeman to ring me up and ask about her. She obviously can't go on living alone, so she's selling her flat and going into a nursing home. It's the best thing, I think, but it wouldn't be what I'd want.'

Fanny turned her head to look full at Rosa as she added, 'I hope I die before I get like that.'

Rosa reached out and grasped the frail old hand. 'Don't worry. I'll look after you, I promise.'

She meant what she said. Even if it entailed living on top of that hill in Corstorphine, she'd not let Fanny wander the streets or languish away in one of those homes that smelt of urine and overcooked food.

Closeness and understanding grew between them during the two-hour journey to her father's house at Catslackburn, and, as they drove into the cobbled forecourt, Fanny recovered some of her old sharpness. 'Why is this place called by such a ridiculous name?' she asked.

'I don't know. It's marked as that on some very old maps,' Rose told her.

'I always thought it was selfish of your father to isolate you in such a lonely place while you were growing up,' said Fanny.

'But I loved it. I was very happy. And father was so broken-hearted about my mother dying that he wanted to be away from the world,' protested Rosa.

'At least he seems to have got over his heart-break,' said Fanny caustically, more like her old self, as Jean and Sandy came running out of the cottage door to greet them.

To Rosa's relief the two women got on very well, however. When Fanny discovered that Jean was a schoolteacher, she unbent and they discussed their mutual profession with enthusiasm.

Jean spared no effort to make her husband's aunt by marriage at ease and comfortable. Spotting that Fanny suffered from backache, she put cushions behind her in the armchair, plying her with cups of tea and glasses of sherry, bringing out photograph albums and watching without any sign of resentment as Fanny pointed out pictures of Rosa's mother, her niece.

Meanwhile, Rosa went for a walk across the moors with her father and he reassured her that marriage to Jean would not alter his feelings for his daughter.

'I know that,' she told him. 'I'm glad you're going to be happy again. Don't worry about me because I might be getting married myself soon.' She only said it to make him feel happier and it came out without premeditation, for she had not really intended to tell him about Roddy.

He stopped and threw out his arms in delight. 'Hallelujah! Who is he? Will we like each other?'

'I'm sure you'll like him. He's a young doctor I met when I was at university. But I'm not sure about getting married yet,' she said.

'Why haven't you brought him to my wedding so I can look him over?' he asked.

'Because he's in Cyprus doing his National Service, but

he's due home soon. He's asked me to marry him lots of times and the last time he did, I said I might.'

Her father looked sharply at her. 'Only might? What's his name?'

'Roddy. Dr Roderick Barton. He's twenty-eight, and comes from Edinburgh. His mother's a widow. She lives in Morningside. I think his father was a lawyer or something. Anyway, he left his widow well provided for,' Rosa told him.

'He sounds very suitable, but why have you taken so long to tell me about him?' asked her father cautiously.

She stared into his eyes. 'Because I don't know if I want to get married to anybody yet. If I do, we'd live in Edinburgh so's I can look after Fanny in her old age.'

He took her arm and said fondly, 'You make it sound very conventional but we're not that kind of family, are we? As soon as you can, bring Dr Barton to meet me and I'll decide if I want to give my consent or not. I know you're old enough to do as you please, but at least I can advise you.'

She laughed.'You'll like him, everybody does, even Mrs Ross. He has her eating out of his hand.'

After Fanny was taken to the Gordon Arms Hotel and installed in her bedroom, the rest of them held another impromptu concert and Rosa finally crept upstairs at one in the morning.

This is my father's wedding day. I wish I could cast a magic spell of perpetual happiness for him, she thought as she climbed into bed.

The morning dawned in glory, with birds chorusing joyously in the trees round the cottage. Rosa rolled over on the same lumpy mattress she'd slept on as a child and knelt to look out of the little window. The world shone brand new, untouched since time began. People living in the folds of those lonely hills had stared on to that same scene for centuries, ever since the first hunters tracked in after herds of animals that grazed the slopes when the glacial ice melted hundreds and hundreds of years ago.

The wedding was scheduled for eleven o'clock. Rosa put

on a dress of cream cotton patterned with fronds of green ferns, and her Italian shoes. At twenty to eleven, she, her father and Eckie, who was to be best man, began walking along the track to Yarrow church, which was tucked away behind trees and a stone wall in a bend of the main road. The collie dog Jess trailed behind them and slipped into the church at Eckie's back.

Inside, the church smelt of dust and roses, gathered from the neighbours' gardens, and massed in huge vases near the communion table. There were little nosegays tied on to the end of every pew as well.

Fanny, brought up by other guests who lived near the Gordon Arms Hotel, was sitting in a front pew so Rosa slipped in beside her and asked, 'Are you all right? Did you sleep well?'

The old lady was wearing a domed hat of cream straw that made her look like a little mushroom, and she turned with a smile as she said, 'I slept like a top, and they gave me a delicious breakfast. I like your dress. You'd better go out and wait for Jean arriving. She's very nice. Your father's a lucky man, but he deserves it for he's a good person.' Never before had Fanny been so pleasant.

Jean, in pale green silk that fortunately matched the bridesmaid's fern patterned dress, stepped out of the local taxi at the churchyard gate and hurried up the path towards Rosa whose throat unaccountably closed up with emotion when she saw her. The two women paused, looked at each other, then hugged with genuine affection.

'Good luck, good luck,' Rosa whispered as she followed the bride who walked down the aisle on the arm of one of her cousins.

The service was short but moving and Rosa had trouble not weeping while she listened to the couple taking their vows, especially when they looked into each other's eyes and whispered, 'Till death us do part.' Both of them had experienced sorrow and the loss of a loved one, so they knew what they were saying.

The atmosphere lightened when the organist – the minister's wife – burst out with a joyous voluntary and they walked back down the aisle as a married couple to the strains of Mendelssohn's 'Wedding March'. The whole church filled up with a feeling of love and as she watched the smiling couple, Rosa thought, *I hope it's like this if I ever get married.*

The reception was held in the church hall where long trestle tables were covered with food and wine, provided by the couple's friends and neighbours. People came and went, because the farmers were taking advantage of the fine weather and cutting their second crops of hay.

At intervals, speeches were made. Eckie's was very erudite and full of quotations from poets, especially his favourite Milton. The audience became silent and Fanny's face showed disapproval when he began to declaim:

> These two
> Imparadised in one another's arms
> The happier Eden, shall enjoy their fill
> Of bliss on bliss.

Rosa's father, however, brought things back to a more acceptable level when he rose to speak. He was funny and showed talent as a raconteur and while his audience laughed and raised their glasses in toasts, he turned towards his daughter and said, 'This might be the beginning of a spate of weddings at Catslackburn because our bridesmaid, my daughter Rosa, tells me that she's also thinking of getting married soon. Let's stand and make a toast to Rosa.'

Her cheeks flared red as all eyes turned towards her. They had known her since she was a child, and wished her well. *That's done it, I'll have to marry Roddy now or they'll think I've been jilted,* she thought in dismay for she didn't like the idea of doing something for the sake of appearances.

Late on Sunday evening she drove Fanny back to Edinburgh.

The old lady was tired and wan as they drove along, but she was intensely interested in the idea that Rosa might be the next bride. Question after question about Roddy flowed from her: What colour were his eyes? Did his mother own her house? Was he planning to work in Edinburgh? Did he smoke or drink?

Rosa answered as best as she could but when they got to the smoking and drinking question, she paused. Roddy took the occasional drink but he didn't indulge to the extent of her press colleagues – far from it. And, unlike them too, he didn't smoke.

Would she be able to live with such a paragon?

'He sounds very suitable. When will you bring him to see me?' asked Fanny.

'As soon as he comes home on leave. I promise I'll introduce you then,' said Rosa. She felt panicked, as if she was walking into a quicksand that threatened to swallow her up.

Sixteen

The Malings spent the weekend in marital disharmony. They found moving into their new flat an unsettling experience and turned on each other like snarling dogs, quarrelling about everything from where to position the furniture to the quality of their wedding presents.

Hugh's parents sent him a cheque for a hundred pounds, and Patricia's bought her a refrigerator which now stood in their kitchen with nothing in it except a bottle of gin, a jug of orange juice, some tomatoes and a plate of dried up and curling cold meat.

'I can't imagine why your people gave you a fridge. You never buy anything to put in it,' said Hugh.

'That's because you're never in to eat. How many meals have we had together at home since we got married? Probably two, and that includes breakfasts,' she snapped.

'Your friend Miss Makepeace had a good idea of the sort of present you'd prefer, even though she wrapped it up in vulgar paper,' he said.

'What do you mean?' she asked, from her perch up a ladder. She was hanging bedroom curtains printed all over with Sanderson's cabbage roses which he said looked like a typical middle-class matron's idea of heaven.

'The silver-plated cocktail shaker. She knew you'd put that to good use. I've been watching your alcohol intake and it's considerable. Keep it up and perhaps you'll drink yourself to death,' he told her.

'No wonder I drink. Anybody married to you would have to,' she said, coming down from the ladder and confronting him.

'So that's your excuse! I warned you I was not good husband material, but you didn't listen. I suppose you thought you'd mould me,' he sneered.

She wanted to hit him, and felt her hands clenching into fists, but knew better than to swing out because he would probably hit her back. A surge of misery overwhelmed her. They had not addressed a civil word to each other for days.

'At least my friend gave me a present. Your precious crony Maitland didn't give you anything,' she said, walking away.

He followed her through to the lovely, long drawing room where she stood staring out of the window that faced across the Firth of Forth towards the hills of Fife. It was a beautiful day and the river shimmered like a sheet of aquamarine.

The view did nothing to soften his mood, however, and he pressed on, wanting their row to escalate. 'What would you like him to give us? One of those plaster ornaments of a little boy with an Alsatian dog, perhaps? The kind that you see in the windows of council houses. That should make you feel at home.'

She whirled round. 'You bastard. Why did you marry me? Was it to torture me?'

He laughed because he saw he'd cut her to the quick. 'I married you because you plagued the life out of me. You hunted me down, and well you know it. You wouldn't take "no" for an answer.'

They stared at each other, Patricia wet-eyed and him stony-faced, both of them wondering the same thing: 'How did I get myself into this?'

She was thinking, *How can it have gone wrong so quickly? What can I do to make it right? I love him. I even love the terrible way he treats me . . . it's almost orgasmic being made to weep by him.*

He was thinking, *It's her awful acceptance that drives me on. Sometimes I wonder how mean and nasty I would have to be before she snapped.* He had been flattered when Patricia, the belle of the press world, the girl that all the men lusted after, made a set at him. She was beautiful and smart, sharp-tongued and apparently streetwise – but for some reason he could reduce her to jelly.

It flattered his ego that a girl like that just accepted his whims and caprices to go along with whatever he wanted. He liked playing cruel games. The first time she agreed to sleep with him, he lay in bed beside her all night and refused even to touch her.

'I don't want you,' he'd said, in case she was under the misapprehension that he was too chivalrous to take advantage of her innocence.

He enjoyed the way other men looked at her when they went out together; he enjoyed her style and the way she dressed and, in the beginning, he'd admired her talent for she was a star journalist. That was fine when she worked in London, but now that she was on the *Scottish Daily Express*, with her own weekly column, he was having second thoughts.

Everybody knew her. When they went out, she was fawned over. Head waiters showed them to the best tables, people wanted to talk to her at parties and receptions. Nobody was much interested in talking to him. In a few short weeks he had become Patricia Aitken's man, what's-his-name. Who does he work for again? That was the worst blow to his self-esteem, the one he found it hardest to forgive, and the one he was determined to avenge.

He turned away from her, and went back to arranging his books in a breakfront bookcase she'd bought at Lyon & Turnbull's auction house. She watched him for a moment and then went into the kitchen to pour herself a glass of gin from the new fridge.

She was swigging it back when there was a knock at the front door. She answered it, still holding her glass. Hugh's friend Maitland, with his frumpish wife Sonya, were standing on the doormat and she was carrying a parcel wrapped up in cream coloured paper printed all over with silver wedding bells.

Patricia's laugh pealed out very loud when the parcel

was held out towards her. 'A wedding present from us,' carolled Sonya.

'Hugh darling, Maitland and Sonya have come and look what they've brought us,' she called, running along to the drawing room.

He eyed the paper and forced himself to smile. 'That's very kind, Sonya,' he said.

Patricia was holding the gift up high. 'I can hardly bring myself to tear such lovely paper, but shall I open it?' she asked him.

'Oh, do,' he said, dusting his hands on his corduroy trousers.

'Perhaps it's a cocktail shaker,' she said and Sonya's face fell. 'How did you guess?' she said.

Patricia ran over and hugged her. 'That's just what we need,' she said, laughing almost hysterically.

Embarrassed and trying to break the tension, Maitland looked round. 'What a beautiful place. This must be one of the nicest flats in Edinburgh,' he said.

Patricia took his arm and said, 'Yes, isn't it? Let me show you round.'

She was rapidly transforming the place. The walls were painted pale cream, Indian rugs in brilliant reds, mauves and browns were thrown over wooden floors, and huge potted plants were placed where they could catch the light that streamed through the deeply embrasured windows.

'I'm keeping it uncluttered. I want as much light as possible to flood in,' she said to Sonya who blinked as she caught a strong whiff of gin from her hostess's breath.

'All this must be costing you a fortune,' she said, admiring an enormous palm tree in a pot.

'When I was in London I saved my money and now I'm spending it,' said Patricia, confirming their suspicions that little of the cost was being borne by Hugh.

'I'd offer you lunch but there isn't much available. I don't plan to spend my time sweating over a cooker. At least we can have a gin and orange out of your new shaker, can't we?' Patricia said when their tour reached the kitchen.

142

They accepted the offer and while the men began talking about a hill-walking expedition they had planned, the two mismatched women attempted to find some topic of mutual interest – but without much success.

When the visitors left, the door was hardly closed on them before Hugh flew at his wife, and sent her flying across the room. She crouched on the floor watching him as he raged but restrained himself from hitting her again. 'So you saved your money and paid for all this, did you? Are you making sure everybody knows you earn so much more than me? Don't think that makes them think highly of you. They know what you are – a nobody from nowhere, an overpaid hack.'

His jealous fury almost choked him, and she said nothing as he stormed out of the room and out of the house.

Patricia sat huddled in the sofa for a long time, wishing there was someone she could tell about her misery. Her parents would only be distressed and her brothers would probably want to beat Hugh up. At one time she could have told Rosa, and wished it was still possible to ring her up, but after their last meeting in the Chinese restaurant, when she had deliberately walked out rather than get into a meaningful exchange with her friend, she could not ask for help now.

As darkness crept in, and the shadows in the room closed round her, whispering that the room had seen many miseries and many joyful days as well, she stood up and went through to fetch another gin.

I've married him. I refuse to give up on him. I'll make him love me, even if it kills me, she resolved as the liquor bolstered her spirits.

Seventeen

In the hope of striking up an acquaintance with Hugh Maling, who he knew was a habitué of the Press Cub, Charles had started calling in there, and on a Sunday evening was rewarded by his quarry walking in and ordering a pint of beer.

There were not many people in the bar, and it was not difficult to start talking to Maling.

When Charles said he worked for the *Dispatch*, Hugh replied, 'So, you'll know my wife?'

Charles smiled. 'I got her job when she left. I don't know her but I've seen her.'

'Good looking, eh?' said Hugh.

'Oh yes,' agreed Charles in a neutral tone.

'But a bitch,' said Hugh.

Charles said nothing. From the days when he went to their local with his father, he remembered that the main topic of conversation for some men was the shortcomings of their wives.

After a little while, Hugh went off to phone Maitland, who soon turned up and joined the party. Though he guessed they would prefer to be left on their own, Charles stayed on, joining in their conversation.

Maitland, who was planning a radio programme about seabirds on the Isle of May, discussed his project at great length, giving imitations of bird calls and the howling of the wind.

'It sounds as if it will be very dramatic,' said Charles.

'Instructive, yes, dramatic, no,' said Maitland. He and Hugh, made loquacious by beer, went on to talk ponderously about the ethos of radio programming, which, according to them, was to educate the populace whether they wanted to be educated or not.

'Gravitas, that's what's needed,' exulted Maitland while his friend nodded in agreement.

'I'd like to try my hand at broadcasting,' Charles said.

Maitland looked at Charles critically before he answered, 'Some time I'm going to an interesting place, I might give you a ring and you can come along.'

Charles said he would be delighted. As he left he gave them his most hangdog, pleasant puppy smile, which hid his true feeling that they were a couple of pretentious asses.

Still, he thought, *it's best to get the measure of your enemy before you take him on.*

When he reached his digs in Mayfield Road he was surprised to find a note in his pigeonhole. No one had ever left him a hand-delivered note before. This one was from Ned Ingram, head of news at the *Express* and it said that if Charles should ever consider looking for a new position, he might like to call in and discuss the matter with Mr Ingram.

It was difficult to restrain himself from doing a war dance up and down the hall. They'd noticed him, they'd marked him down. A job on the *Express* meant he'd be working in the same office as the wonderful Patricia. He went to bed where he lay assessing his chances.

To be absolutely sure of Ingram hiring him, he needed one more big story, one more scoop. Where was he going to get it?

His adroit mind went into overdrive and by the time he fell asleep, he came up with several possibilities. The fact that none of them were true worried him not one bit. The stomach aches were momentarily forgotten and, because he had a glittering objective, he was a happy man, happier than he had been for ages. The fact that the woman of his dreams was married to someone else caused him only minimum concern. His ability to weave stories in his head convinced him that he would win her in the end.

On Monday morning, there was frenzied activity in the newsroom because Jack had deliberately started a scare story that was severely agitating the traditionalist residents of Edinburgh.

From a boring piece by one of the older reporters who covered the meetings of the City Council, he plucked out a comment by a left wing Councillor that a huge car park should be built over the site of Queen Street Gardens.

When he made it a front page lead for the last edition on Friday, he knew it would start a forest fire of protest, and he was not disappointed. On Monday, letter writers and phone callers deluged the office with their outraged comments.

Queen Street Gardens were hallowed ground; a long strip of trees, grass and bushes dividing Queen Street from Heriot Row, they were only open to the well-heeled – and very vocal – residents of the large houses of both streets. Robert Louis Stevenson had grown up in Heriot Row and it was said that he got the inspiration for *Treasure Island* from the little pond in Queen Street Gardens. To replace that with a car park was unthinkable.

Jack set his staff to transcribing the comments of the citizens and soon had a story that would fill many column inches.

Charles hated being given such boring work to do because it provided no scope for his creativity. With a phone clamped to his ear, he sat enduring the ravings of an angry councillor and stared through the window at blue sky. The day was fine, and he longed to be out, wandering around in search of his next exclusive story.

When he was eventually permitted to hang up, he went into the newsroom and told Old Bob that he was off to follow up a 'Save Queen Street Gardens Protest Group' that one caller had told him about. A lie, of course.

In Princes Street, he sniffed the air. It would be nice to be among trees, he thought. A bus came along with 'ZOO' written on its direction indicator and he jumped on board. Rosa's aunt lived near the zoo, he remembered. She heard wild animals roaring sometimes. In an instant his next story was born.

At the foot of Clermiston Hill, he got off the bus and looked around. A steep hill rose in front of him and, rather than toil to the top, he went up halfway and knocked at the door of a bungalow in a street near the bottom. By good luck, he chose the house of a curmudgeon who loved to complain about anything and everything.

'Good morning,' he said politely to the sour-faced old man who answered the door. 'I wonder if you're ever bothered by the danger of animals escaping from the zoo?'

The old man glared at him, taking in his look of puzzled innocence. 'Bothered, is it? I'm more than bothered. I'm always warning people to keep their back doors closed in the summer. My cat went missing last month. It could have been carried off by a predator from over there, couldn't it? I never found the body, so it was probably eaten!' He gestured with his thumb in the direction of the zoo on top of the hill behind him.

Charles made sympathetic noises, and the old man decided that he must be on some sort of information-seeking project from the Zoological Society. 'You can tell them from me that I've got my eye on them. Wild animals shouldn't be allowed to roam free. What's cages for?' he said.

Because Charles faithfully wrote all this down, he even agreed to telling him his name and age and finally closed his front door feeling that he'd made his point and would be listened to by somebody important.

In high spirits, Charles went from house to house, spreading alarm by telling the inhabitants that one of their neighbours was suspicious that a wild animal from the zoo had eaten his cat. They talked over garden fences, or ran to their telephones, warning each other to stay indoors because a wild animal was roaming the district. By noon, the police had been informed by an alarmed householder and vans of constables and veterinarians were cruising the streets with megaphones warning mothers not to leave their babies outside in their prams.

Children coming home from school were herded into posses and escorted to their homes by uniformed officers. One woman collapsed from nerves and had to be rushed to hospital, while concerned pet owners rushed around scooping up cats that only wanted to be left to sleep peacefully in the sun.

Unaware of the full extent of the chaos he'd caused, Charles found a telephone box, and rang the office to tell Jack he would have a good piece for the last edition. It might be an idea to send a photographer out as well, he suggested.

Tony answered his call, and rushed into the newsroom shouting excitedly, 'Rutland's on the phone. He says some animal's escaped from the zoo and he's out there now.'

Rosa looked up in surprise and asked, 'He's in Corstorphine? About an escaped animal? What sort of animal?' The short conversation they'd exchanged on the day she went to visit Aunt Fanny came rushing back into her mind.

He couldn't, surely he couldn't? she thought, but like many other people, she had strong doubts about the veracity of Charles's stories.

Tony said solemnly, 'I don't know what kind, but it's roaming gardens, eating cats.'

Rosa wondered what she ought to do. Should she say that Charles was causing chaos by making the whole thing up? On the other hand, she might be mistaken. Perhaps some animal really was running loose among the well manicured lawns of Corstorphine?

In the end she decided to play safe and rushed to the phones to ring up Fanny. Though she had deep suspicions about Charles's story she couldn't take any chances.

'Don't go out today,' she gabbled to her great-aunt. 'Stay in and keep your doors closed.'

'But, dear, it's such a nice day, I was hoping to sit in the garden.' Fanny sounded breathless and Rosa was sorry to worry her.

'Definitely do not go out! I've heard that some animal might have escaped from the zoo. It's not certain. It's probably only a rumour but I don't want you taking any chances,' said Rosa firmly.

'All right, dear, don't worry. I'll stay inside,' said Fanny soothingly.

'Have you enough food? I'll drive over with more for you tonight if you need anything,' said Rosa.

'The larder is full, and milk, eggs and bread are delivered every morning. Don't worry about me, and, if there's a wild animal roaming about, don't try coming out here either,' the old lady told her. She sounded weary as if she couldn't be bothered taking the rumour too seriously.

Meanwhile, as they spoke, Charles Rutland was working his way back along the suburban streets, selecting the houses to stop at by the quality of their gardens. It was Fanny's burgeoning standard roses that attracted him to her bungalow.

After she hung up the telephone, she sat down in her favourite armchair and was attempting to solve the *Scotsman* crossword when he knocked at her door. His earnest brown eyes and courteous manner reassured her that he wasn't a burglar.

The question he asked was carefully phrased. 'Good morning, madam, I'm trying to find out if anyone in this road has seen a strange animal that might have escaped from the zoo,' he said, gesturing with his hand in the direction of the wooded hilltop where the animals roamed or padded to and fro in their cages.

Fanny brightened. 'Yes, I've just heard about that. My niece rang and told me to stay indoors,' she said.

He could not believe his luck. 'You've seen the animal?' he asked eagerly.

She shook her head. 'No, but I often hear them if the wind's in this direction.'

She gave him her name and age without wondering why he wanted that information.

He had his story, so he hurried back to the office, started typing like a maniac, and in a short time handed his copy over to Jack who took it with a bemused expression.

Rosa watched and said nothing, but could not restrain herself from staring hard at Charles who smiled back with such a theatrical air of injured innocence that she was even more convinced he'd made the whole thing up. Her conviction became complete when she read his story in the paper later that afternoon.

It began: 'A killer is prowling the gardens of Corstorphine. People huddle in their houses, terrified to go out because of a mysterious animal that is thought to have escaped from the Zoo.'

He went on to quote people who said they had seen a mysterious black shape slinking through their privet hedges. Several weeping women testified that their pet cats had disappeared – 'eaten by the escaped animal,' opined Charles's article.

Halfway down the story Rosa came upon her great-aunt's testimony. 'My niece has just telephoned me to tell me not to go out because a wild animal is loose,' said Miss Frances Cooper, 82, of 17 Hillview Drive.'

Fury almost choked her. She walked across to Charles, who was reading his story with a satisfied look on his face, and whispered, 'That's all damned lies. You've made it up.'

He got up and walked to the newsroom door, saying, 'I'm going for a coffee', but she followed, hissing like a cobra.

In the canteen, he bought a coffee and sat at an empty table well away from other people. She sat down beside him and repeated, 'You made it up!'

He protested, 'But I didn't actually write that an animal *had* escaped from the zoo. I only said it *might* have . . .'

'And you've started a panic. The police are out carrying guns. Somebody could get shot by mistake! Tony and Pat are there now phoning in stories about children crying and people being too scared to step over their doorsteps. You'd better stop it before it gets any worse or I'll tell Jack you made it up – and how you got that quote from my poor aunt,' she threatened angrily.

'Which one was your aunt?' he asked with genuine interest.

'Miss Frances Cooper, 82, of 17 Hillview Drive,' she snapped.

'A nice old lady. She didn't seem to be too worried,' he said.

Rosa wanted to grab him by his tweed tie. She leaned closer towards him and said in a threatening voice, 'I don't know how you're going to stop this, but that's what you have to do. Perhaps you could lift the story of "Androcles and the Lion" and go to Corstorphine to take a thorn out of the *killer*'s foot or something. If Jack finds out you've started a city-wide panic, he'll fire you.'

Charles's use of the word 'killer' particularly annoyed her.

Her seriousness impressed him at last. 'All right, all right, I'll stop the story,' he told her in a placatory tone.

'How?' she asked.

'I'll think of something,' he replied.

When she returned to the newsroom, he did not join her, but turned in the other direction and left the office. He was not returning to Corstorphine however. Instead, he went down into Waverley Station and found an empty phone box that he could use without being overheard. When he was connected to the phone room, he dictated his last story of the day:

> The Corstorphine siege is over. The mysterious creature that has been stalking the suburb's gardens is back in its enclosure. Zoo keepers, doing their afternoon animal count, noticed that a female Siberian wolf, which probably escaped this morning, is back in its pen.
>
> As feed time approached, they think the wolf remembered its suckling cub and returned to feed it. It slipped back in through the same gap in the enclosure fence as it used to escape. The gap has now been mended. And a wolf has proved there is mother love among animals was well.

*   *   *

151

The story arrived in time for the last edition, and Jack made it his lead. While the *Evening News* still talked about terror in the suburbs, the *Evening Dispatch* put an end to the story.

Next day Jack wrote a thundering editorial accusing the Zoological Gardens of negligence and demanding enhanced security on behalf of terrified rate-payers living near the zoo. Instead of being fired, as he would have been if he was caught out in lying to such disastrous effect, Charles got a rise.

Rosa watched him smirking with self-importance and finally made up her mind what she thought about him. She did not like him at all.

Eighteen

The stout self-defence and protests of innocence put up by the Zoological Society caused Jack considerable concern. He called Charles into his office and, holding out the paper with the escaped animal story in it, he asked, 'Convince me. Is this kosher?'

Charles looked innocent. 'Kosher?' he asked as if he had no idea what the word meant.

'Come on, don't fuck about. Is it true?'

'Of course it is,' said Charles stoutly.

Jack looked at him with narrowed eyes and said, 'I'm not convinced and if I find out it isn't true and you've landed me in the shit, you're out. Just watch it.'

When, later that day, he was told that his star reporter Charles Rutland had been spotted calling on Ned Ingram at the *Express*, he shrugged and said to Gil, 'If he's on his way, I'm not going to stop him.'

Gil agreed. 'There's a whiff of unreliability about Mr Rutland, I'm afraid,' he said.

As a reminder to Charles not to get above himself, on a brilliantly hot day, when there was not a lot of news about because the warm weather acted as a deterrent to wrong-doers and the accident prone, Jack decided to send him on a story that would take him down a peg or two.

He detailed McGillivray and Charles to go down to Princes Street and fry an egg on the pavement. They looked at him in disbelief when he gave them the assignment.

'Fry an egg? On a primus stove or something?' asked Charles who hated losing his dignity by making an exhibition of himself.

'On the pavement, I said. Buy an egg, crack it and let it fall on to the ground. McGillivray will take your picture. When the egg gels, you have your story: "Edinburgh's pavements are so hot you can fry an egg on them",' said Jack.

'What if it doesn't fry? What if it stays runny?' asked Charles.

'It had better fry,' said Jack, who had a front page already set out in his mind.

Charles was furious. He took himself very seriously and felt demeaned by such a clownlike assignment. He didn't see the great Cassandra doing something like that, but Ned Ingram had not yet made him an offer, so he borrowed two eggs from the canteen and made his reluctant way to Princes Street with McGillivray.

They picked a site outside Jenner's and tried to clear a space of pedestrians, but seeing McGillivray with his camera at the ready, curious bystanders kept drifting over and standing on the pavement slab that Charles planned to use as his cooker. While the photographer kneeled in the blaze of the sun, Charles, egg in one hand, tried to hold back curious children and their parents with the other, but Jenner's uniformed doorman came rushing out and demanded that they move on.

'What do you think you're doing?' he asked.

'Frying an egg,' said Charles in a lordly tone.

Without a blink the doorman said, 'Go and fry it some-place else. This is Jenner's pavement. We're not a low-class cafe.'

Clutching an egg each, they moved along to Thornton's sports shop on the corner of Hanover Street, quickly cleared another space, and before anyone else could complain, Charles cracked his egg. Its yolk shivered but stayed in one piece. The white ran off in all directions. In desperation, he grabbed the other egg from McGillivray and cracked it too, but the same thing happened, though the extreme edges of the white went slightly solid, but it was not enough to show in a photograph.

They looked at each other. Without saying anything, they

both knew it would be a bad move to go back to Jack without taking a picture of a fried egg with them.

McGillivray saved the day. 'My sister works as a waitress in the Brown Derby. She'll ask the chef to fry an egg for us in their kitchen and we can carry it down to the pavement. Then I'll take its picture,' he said.

McGillivray's sister Nora, a pretty girl with a charming giggle, persuaded a white-coated chef to produce a perfectly fried egg on the cafe cooker and ran with it on a frying pan down the stairs of the Brown Derby restaurant to sun-baked St Andrew's Street. Using a fish slice, she carefully slid it on to the paving slab where it lay looking delicious, the wobbling yolk raised and brilliantly yellow, surrounded by a perfect white. She contemplated it with the satisfaction of an art lover in an exhibition while her brother took its picture.

This operation was watched by a bemused circle of passers-by, whose feet figured in the photograph that appeared in that night's last edition.

EDINBURGH BLISTERS IN HEAT WAVE
EGGS FRY ON PAVEMENTS!

Charles sulked for three days. He was a star feature writer, not a clown to be sent out to perform tricks in public, he said to Hilda, who listened to his grumbles and agreed with him. Jack had gone too far, he decided. He was not being treated with sufficient respect. It was certainly time to look for another position.

With a folder of cuttings, he went back to the *Express* and this time Ned Ingram gave in and hired Charles as a reporter. He'd wiggled his way in to work with Patricia. Step one in his campaign to win her heart had been achieved.

Gossip flew faster than light between the Edinburgh newspaper offices, and Jack heard about Charles's new job within twelve hours. Next morning he shouted across the office, 'If you're so keen to work for the *Express*, you'd better not hang about here any longer. Take your stuff and go.'

Charles made no protest. Ingram was pleased to start him early because there was a lot going on and he was short of staff. By afternoon, Charles was sitting at a new desk and beaming across at Patricia who looked magnificent in a cream linen suit. When she smiled back, he was transported to heaven.

Nineteen

The reason Ned Ingram was open to hiring more staff was because three of his men were taken up with following a new development in the Mary Lou and Jake elopement story.

Even Rosa had lost interest in the runaways because, when day followed day, and week followed week without them marrying, and the original wedding date was continually postponed, she grew more convinced that one or both of them was waiting for an inducement to return to America.

With only desultory interest she followed their story, until one night, when she was parking in front of her digs, Mrs Neil's front door was suddenly thrown open and Mary Lou came rushing out.

'I've been waiting for you,' she cried. 'Oh, I don't know what to do.'

Tears were running down her cheeks and she looked distraught.

'What's wrong?' Rosa asked. She was not in the mood for Mary Lou's dramatics.

'Jake's been arrested. The police came and took him away an hour ago. He's in prison and, if I can't stop it, he'll be deported.'

'Good heavens, why? What's he done?' Rosa asked, jolted into interest.

Mary Lou clung to her arm. 'Come in and I'll tell you. It's awful. It's my uncle, of course.

'But people can't be arrested for nothing. Even your uncle couldn't arrange that,' Rosa said, following the girl up the steps into the house.

Mary Lou burst into more tears. 'He can, he can! He has politicians in his pocket. He's saying awful things about Jake. He wants the Edinburgh police to send him back.'

Rosa sat down on a hall chair and sneezed, but she pulled herself together enough to cope with this story, which was rapidly taking an interesting turn.

'Well, you must have expected your uncle to do something or why didn't you get married long ago?' she asked.

'Because we thought he'd come round and agree to the marriage. We thought if we did something dramatic like running away to Scotland, he'd stop making trouble and give me full access to my trust fund,' sobbed Mary Lou.

Rosa nodded. Her suspicions were confirmed. 'What's your uncle done exactly?' she asked.

'He's accusing Jake of all sorts of things – stealing money and being married already. All lies, of course,' said Mary Lou.

A thrill of excitement swept through Rosa. The story is growing, she thought. Up till now it had only been a run-of-the-mill elopement, but now it was taking on another dimension. She wouldn't put anything past Jake.

She strove to hide her reaction as she said, 'But he won't get the Edinburgh police to arrest Jake unless there were very good grounds.'

Mary Lou brushed her corn-coloured hair away from her face and sobbed, 'Jake says none of it is true, but he's in jail!'

'That doesn't often happen on a trumped-up charge,' Rosa ventured.

'You don't know my uncle,' said Mary Lou vehemently. 'Jake's told me everything. He *was* married when he was nineteen but he got a divorce years ago. My uncle seems to have found out about that though. Poor Jake completely forgot it when he filled in the registrar's form here so they're getting him for making a false declaration. His marriage only lasted six months and he didn't think it was important.'

Uh huh, thought Rosa, smelling a very large rat. Surely

158

even a six-month marriage would not be forgotten so easily? She said, 'He must have documentation of his divorce.'

Mary Lou nodded. 'Sure he has, in the States. You don't carry things like that around like a passport or cheque book. He reckons his ex-wife is trying to shake him down. I've plenty of money. I can pay her off.'

Rosa got up and said, 'Fetch your coat. I'll drive you up to the High Street police station. You have to see someone there about this and you might be able to get Jake out on bail.'

Mary Lou stared at her with swollen bloodshot eyes. 'You are wonderful, Rosa. I knew you'd help.'

The square outside St Giles looked rainswept and desolate when they drove into it. Rosa parked her car beside the Mercat Cross and said, 'I won't come in with you. It might prejudice the police if they see you with a reporter and they know me. Go in and ask to see the inspector in charge of Jake's case. Tell him what you've told me about your uncle trying to stop you marrying and all that.'

An hour passed before Mary Lou returned. She was looking more cheerful when she climbed into the car. 'I spoke to a police officer and to Jake as well. They won't let him out tonight but I'm going to get a lawyer. I've been given the name of one in Walker Street – where's that? Thank you so much, Rosa. If he's allowed out we'll get married next week.'

'I'll drop you off at Walker Street,' said Rosa. From there she would go to the office and write up this story before the nationals got their hands on it.

That night a short bulletin about Jake's detention appeared in the stop press of the last edition. Rosa had scooped the nationals again.

Mrs Ross, bubbling with excitement, was waiting for her to return home. 'I heard about the couple next door,' she said.

'It's complicated but very interesting. Mary Lou's uncle says he's a thief and that he's been married before,' said Rosa.

159

'Isn't that awful, and he never said a word about being married!' exclaimed Mrs Ross.

'Mary Lou thinks he forgot,' said Rosa.

Mrs Ross scoffed, 'Does anyone forget getting married? I must admit he gave me a bad feeling from the beginning that one. I like the girl, but he's – he's *sleekit!*'

Rosa laughed. *Sleekit*, a Scots word meaning slimy and unreliable, summed up Jake perfectly.

Next morning, the daily press headlines declared:

RUNAWAY GROOM ALREADY MARRIED

and

'I'M NO LIAR' SAYS HEIRESS'S LOVER

Even the Walker Street lawyer could not free Jake. Mary Lou broke down in hysterics when she found out that her lover was to be deported in two days' time.

Twenty

It appealed to Charles's devious nature that he was playing a double game by socializing with Hugh and Maitland in the evening and charming Patricia during the day.

He fetched and carried for her, accompanied her to the Doric at lunch time, bought her drinks and sat nodding in sympathy when she told him that she was having trouble with her husband. Her words were precious to him, and he did not care that she was so frank only because gin and orange loosened her tongue. So far, in their conversations she was fairly cautious and only prepared to talk in generalities. Though she had many of them, she was never specific in her complaints about Hugh.

Because Charles was not an old friend, she could talk more freely to him than she could to Rosa who had too much knowledge of the past and might offer unwanted advice. Charles was uncritical and offered no advice. He only listened, but even so she did not want to tell him how miserable she was, how she knew that her marriage was a terrible mistake, how, in spite of terrible goading, her feelings for Hugh were still overpowering. She clung to the hope that sheer persistence on her part would triumph in the end and she would force him into loving her. They were in a duel to the death, she thought.

From his conversations with Hugh in the Press Club, Charles could have told her that a loving resolution of their problems was a forlorn hope. Her husband's first feelings for her, the original attraction that had drawn them together, were being poisoned by his jealousy. Daily her reputation grew because, no matter how inwardly miserable she was,

161

no matter how much she drank, her work was outstanding. Her flair for words never left her.

Hugh's completed précis and two sample chapters of his novel were sent off to a publisher, but they were returned with a curt rejection. 'Over-researched and not sufficiently original' was the comment. When he read the publisher's letter, Hugh crumpled up the paper and howled in frustration. If Patricia had been in the flat at the time, he would certainly have struck her. He couldn't bring himself to tell Maitland and Charles about his setback until he'd drunk three pints of beer. Maitland was positive: 'Everyone has their first novel rejected,' he declared. 'What you need is to get away from your problems, clear your brain. I'm planning a trip to Loch Skeen. There's a colony of peregrines there, why not come along?'

'I might,' said Hugh.

Charles, the perpetual questioner, asked, 'Where's Loch Skeen?'

Maitland's face took on an enthusiastic look. 'It's the most fantastic place, totally isolated, high in the hills above the Grey Mare's Tail, a waterfall in Dumfriesshire.

'Is it difficult to reach?' asked Charles.

'Well, a woman couldn't make it, of course, but it's not too much for a fit man. It's a seven-mile trek and the terrain isn't too bad – no rock climbing, but really hard walking. Even you could do it,' said Maitland.

Hugh looked mockingly at Charles as if he doubted that. 'I could try,' said Charles boldly. 'Can I come too?'

'Providing you don't hold us up,' said Maitland.

'I won't get tired,' said Charles, determined to hold his own against those two condescending fools.

'When will we go?' asked Hugh.

'Maybe this week,' said Maitland.

'As soon as possible as far as I'm concerned. Patricia's giving me trouble right now and I'm fed up listening to her,' Hugh said.

'I'm free to go any time,' said Charles, determining to go to the public library on George IV Bridge and read up on books on hill walking, and especially on Loch Skeen.

When Hugh returned home later that night, Patricia was sitting in their drawing room beneath the pool of light cast by a reading lamp. Her dark hair gleamed like silk, and her pale skin looked like carved ivory. At one time he would have paused in the doorway, struck by her beauty, but a surge of sheer dislike filled him when he looked at her and he knew that anything there had ever been between them was gone.

'No rolling pin?' he sneered as he stepped into the room.

She shook her head. Thank God she was not weeping. He could not stand her tears, because her nose always went scarlet and dripped. It revolted him.

'I was drinking in the Press Club,' he said.

She shrugged. 'I guessed that. We must talk,' she said.

'What about? Politics? The Suez Canal? Is Nasser mad? You choose the subject,' he said, walking across to the sofa and throwing himself into it.

'About us. We can't go on like this. It's killing me. I love you and I want to go on being married to you. Do you still love me?'

He could not resist toying with her. He might even make love to her tonight, but only so he could feel masterly over her. 'I've told you before. Love's a fantasy for cretins,' he said.

'I love you, I really do. You make my heart ache,' she said piteously.

'For Christ's sake, don't beg,' he snapped.

'Please, Hugh, let's talk to each other like we used to do before we got married,' she said.

'*Before*,' he said sarcastically. 'We've not exchanged a sensible word since.'

'That's because you won't. I try, but you turn me away.'

He glared at her. If only he could make her leave. If only she would be the one to pack up and get out. He would be able to stay on in the flat, which he vastly enjoyed though he would never admit as much to her. Even without her salary he could afford the rent because, unknown to her, he had a small private income from money left by his grandfather. It struck him that without her bothering him all the time, he would be able to stand back and look at his novel critically enough to rewrite it so that it could sell. Comparing himself to her all the time was holding him back.

Angrily he jumped to his feet and said, 'I'm going to bed. It's after midnight. I have to be up early in the morning, not like you. Are you coming?'

She stared at him. For several nights he'd been sleeping in the spare bed. Was this his way of extending an olive branch? When she too stood up he saw she was wearing a diaphanous, lace trimmed negligee through which he could see her shapely body, and the brown aureoles round the pink, erect nipples of her breasts.

'Come on,' he said.

In their big double bed, she turned to him and he slid his hands beneath the silken folds of her nightdress. As he felt the wetness between her legs, she put her face in his shoulder and sighed, 'Oh Hugh, I love you so much!'

Instantly he thrust her away. 'You're a tart. Get away from me. I don't want you.'

As she wept into her pillow, he got up and went into the spare bed.

When she woke next morning, it was ten o'clock and the flat was empty. An open packet of cornflakes sat on the kitchen table and there was a dirty cup in the sink. As she bent to put the cornflakes in a low cupboard she noticed a crumpled letter in the waste bin. The logo of a big publishing house was visible along the top of the page.

She fished it out and read it. It was dated three days ago. The rejection was very final. How disappointed he must have been when it arrived. No wonder he'd been so beastly to her last night. As usual, she was making excuses for him in her mind.

Daily newspapers like the *Express* did not impose early starting hours on their staff, so she need not be in the office till eleven. Hugh, with only a weekly column to produce, kept his own hours and hid himself away in his office like a sanctuary so he would probably be in the *Scotsman* by this time. She dressed, walked swiftly to her own office, and rang him up.

'Darling,' she said. 'I'm at work but I've been thinking about us. We have to talk'

He groaned. 'Not that again!'

'Yes, we must, because I can't go on like this. If things aren't going to get any better between us, we should separate. We can discuss that, but first I want us to be absolutely honest with each other. I don't want us to break up but we might have to.'

She could tell by the silence from his end that he was really listening to her. If she could only get him to sit down, while sober, and really talk to her, she was sure they could patch things up, but she was not going to say that in case it alienated him. His remark last night about her not begging came back into her mind. This time she was going to try a 'let's call the whole thing off' approach.

'Can we meet for lunch somewhere?' she suggested.

'This isn't the sort of thing we can talk about in public,' he said.

'All right, we'll meet in the flat. I'm in the office now and I've a story to do at five o'clock but I can take time off from about three. Let's meet at home then. Can you make that?'

He was intrigued. Perhaps she meant what she was saying. Perhaps they could cut their losses and split up. The marriage was less than two months old but he'd heard of that sort of thing happening before. Some people were just not meant to live together and when you got married you never knew if you were going to be among the losers. He was now sure that he wanted the marriage to end. She had to be made to accept that too.

'I'll see you there at three,' he said and hung up. Because she was out of the way, he could go back to the flat and re-read the manuscript of his novel without her knowing what he was doing.

The flat was empty, silent and tidy for Patricia had cleaned up the kitchen and made the bed before she went out. He opened the fridge and took out a bottle of milk, filling a glass. He drank the milk and ate a triangle of processed cheese. As he was throwing the silver foil covering of the cheese into the waste bucket, he saw his rejection letter, carefully folded, on top of the rubbish.

He remembered crumpling it up, and his heart leapt into his mouth. The bitch! She'd read it. She knew he'd been turned down. What a weapon that gave her against him.

I have to get in first. I have to spike her guns, he told himself. *How?*

His answer literally came calling at the door a little after two o'clock. When the door knocker rattled, he opened it to find Maitland on the mat.

'I rang your office and they told me you'd gone home. I thought you might like to hear my tape recording of the Bass Rock birds, so I brought my recorder along,' he said. He was lugging a large Uher tape recorder in a black leather case. It weighed him down on one side when he lifted it up.

'Hey, I'm glad to see you, come in,' said Hugh, opening the door. He did not tell his friend that his wife was due back in an hour's time and that she wanted to have a deep discussion about the breakdown of their marriage.

At half past two Patricia sat in the Doric Bar in Market Street, drinking brandy. She was deliberately hiding in a shadowy corner because she hoped no one she knew would come in and see her. Over and over again she rehearsed what she was going to say to Hugh. Would she sympathize with him about his novel? Better not, perhaps. She suspected he was jealous of her success, so perhaps she should offer to give up working – but that meant giving up the flat. She was even prepared to make such a terrible sacrifice.

Raising her hand she called over hobbling old Nellie who'd worked in the Doric as a waitress for forty years, and ordered another brandy. As she drank it, she reflected that the flat represented success to her.

166

Since childhood, she'd kicked against her circumstances and surroundings. For as long as she could remember, she yearned to better herself and move in a different class of society. Her intelligence, flair and good looks, all of which she knew were considerable, gave her a ticket to the world she read about in books, but love for her family, and her feeling of responsibility for them, tied her to the past, so she would never leave it entirely behind. That was how Hugh could hurt her so much, he knew her weakness.

She was on to her third brandy when Leo Fairley came in. Like most men he admired the lovely and hauntingly triste-looking Patricia, so he bought himself a beer and went to sit with her.

'Hi,' he said with a grin. 'Taking a tea break?'

She raised her glass, shook her head and flashed her eyes at him over the rim. *What would Hugh do*, she wondered, *if she took a lover*?

Jeer probably.

'I'm on my way home. Hugh and I have an appointment and I promised I'd be back in the flat by three,' she said.

The hands of the clock behind the bar stood at three minutes before the three o'clock closing time. They'd be thrown out of the pub any minute now.

'Let me buy you a drink before you go,' said Leo.

She did not refuse. 'I'll have a brandy if you can persuade Nellie to give you one,' she said.

Because Leo was a favourite at the Doric, licensing hours did not apply to him. As soon as Nellie brought the brandy over, Patricia swallowed it almost in one gulp and then ran for the door. Nellie and Leo watched her go.

'That was her fourth,' said Nellie with a shrug.

'Four brandies? At lunch time?' asked Leo in surprise.

'Oh aye. She can put them back, that lassie. She often comes in when it's quiet and drinks on her own. I aye say it's the solitary drinkers that are headin' for trouble,' said Nellie.

'Does she ever come in with her husband?' asked Leo, who knew and disliked Hugh Maling.

Nellie snorted, 'Him? God knows why she merrit that yin. She could hae found somebody better than that.'

The subject of their discussion ran up to the top of the Mound, and the calves of her legs ached because of the height of her heels. Out of breath, she stopped to stare across the road at Blackie House, which rose in front of her like a cliff face.

Her own windows, the windows of the flat she loved so much because it represented her ambition and success, glittered in the afternoon sunlight five storeys up. When her breathing calmed and her heartbeat slowed down, she crossed more slowly to the short flight of steps that led up to the courtyard of Lady Stair's Close.

Hugh hated tardiness and would be irritated if she was even five minutes late.

When she walked into the Lady Stair's courtyard, it was bleak and deserted. Tall tenements loomed round it like grim-faced sentinels. Tired after her run, it was an effort for her to push open the heavy outer door. The entrance hall, as usual, was dark, and when she pushed the bell on the rickety lift, nothing happened. Someone had left the door open on a higher floor.

In a sudden eruption of fury she rattled the metal mesh of the gates, shouting, 'Why don't you close the door? Close the damned door. Bloody hell, bloody hell!'

Total silence filled the building and nothing happened. She'd have to climb up five floors.

When he heard his wife rattling the lift, her husband was in their drawing room with his friend Maitland, who, listening intently to his beloved sea birds, had his head bent towards the Uher and did not hear Patricia's furious protests at the lift.

Hugh stood up, put a hand on Maitland's shoulder and said, 'Come on. Forget the birds. Let's go to bed. It's a long time since we did that.'

They had been lovers off and on for several years, and

enjoyed snatching sex at dangerous times. Neither of them was committed to the other. They enjoyed sleeping together because it was forbidden fun.

Crewe looked up in surprise from his machine. 'Now?' he queried.

'Yes, now. Why not? Patricia won't be back for ages and your Sonya wouldn't care if you slept with the Brigade of Guards, would she? Come *on*! It's better when it's snatched,' said Hugh pulling at his arm.

Maitland grinned and stood up. 'You are a wicked boy,' he said.

They were climbing into the double bed as Patricia, with a groan, began to climb the daunting stairs to her flat – fifty-eight steps altogether. It was hot and she was weary so she took her time, stopping frequently to lean against the wall. She'd been very tired recently and nauseous too. *Perhaps I'm pregnant. If I am, it's a miracle but it might save the marriage. I'll make a doctor's appointment tomorrow*, she thought.

She'd only had one period since she married and, though sex with Hugh was perfunctory, and for her unsatisfying, it had happened quite a lot in the first few weeks of their marriage.

The lift, gate open, was stopped on the fourth floor but she did not get into it for there were only twelve steps left to climb. She felt a surge of new energy at the thought of being pregnant, and almost ran up to the narrow landing outside her front door. He would not leave her if she was having a baby.

Hugh would be furious if she knocked and made him walk along to let her in, so she fumbled in her hand-bag for a key. As she slipped it into the keyhole, she admired the white eggshell gloss she'd painted on the door panels herself the previous week. The little brass doorknocker was cast in the shape of a cherub – *or a baby*, she thought. She was smiling as she opened the door.

Maitland heard her coming in, gave a gasp and tried to

struggle up in bed but Hugh, on top of him, pinned him to the mattress and hissed, 'Keep quiet. Lie still.'

'Darling, I'm home,' Patricia's voice rang out. The men heard her high heels tip-tapping along the wooden floor of the corridor towards the kitchen. After a moment's pause she called again in a questioning voice, 'Hugh?'

Maitland closed his eyes when he heard his lover call back, 'I'm here. In the bedroom.'

She hurried back along the passage and opened the bedroom door. At first she did not understand what she was seeing and asked, 'Are you ill? What's . . . ?'

Then her voice changed and the words were screamed, not spoken: 'Oh my God! Oh my God!'

Hugh sat up grinning, and pulled the stark naked Maitland up beside him.

'You might as well know. It took you a long time to tumble us,' he said, but he was speaking to his wife's retreating back.

Twenty-One

While Patricia was drinking alone in the Doric, Rosa was trying to cope with a hysterical Mary Lou who had rung her at the office.

'Oh Rosa, it's terrible! I don't know what to do. Please help. It's not Jake's fault!' sobbed the American girl. She was finding difficulty in speaking coherently.

Rosa could hear Mrs Ross's voice in the background so she said, 'Let me speak to Mrs Ross, please, Mary Lou.'

When her landlady came on the line, she asked, 'What's this all about?'

Mrs Ross sounded as if she was enjoying herself. 'Mr Rosario is about to be deported. I thought you would like to hear about that,' she said.

'When?' Rosa asked.

'The police have told Mary Lou he's to fly out today. At eleven o'clock tonight from Prestwick airport.'

Mary Lou's voice broke in, 'I want to go with him but they won't take me because my rotten uncle's made me a ward of court, whatever that means. Where's Prestwick? I'll hire a taxi. I must say goodbye to him, I must!'

'Don't be daft, you can't take a taxi. Prestwick's miles away. I'll take you,' said Rosa, making up her mind in an instant that no one else was going to hijack this story. If she didn't take charge of Mary Lou, another newspaper would.

'Oh I knew you'd help, thank you, thank you,' sobbed Mary Lou with obvious relief.

Rosa spoke to Mrs Ross again and told her not to let Mary Lou go back to Mrs Neil's but to keep her in Rosa's digs away from the rest of the press. 'Tell her I'll come to collect her. I'll pick her up at the mews behind your house. I'll ring you just before I leave the office and she can be waiting in your garage.'

Jack was enthusiastic when Rosa told him she planned to drive Mary Lou to Prestwick so that the lovers could say goodbye.

'Take an office car and keep out of the way of the rest of the press. The men from Glasgow will be out in force at Prestwick as soon as this story gets out so take The Basher with you. He's more up to the strong arm stuff than any of the others,' said Jack. The Basher possessed the streak of hidden madness that was necessary for a top flight press photographer.

When he was summoned from his darkroom, he didn't even raise an eyebrow when told where he was going and why. Rosa was furious that he still managed to look bored.

Jack was enthusiastic though. 'Make your story dramatic. Make it heart-rending,' he said, sending them off like warriors on to a battlefield.

Rosa did not want to attract attention from other pressmen as they left Edinburgh, so she and The Basher concocted a plan for him to take a taxi to the outskirts and her to pick him up as she drove out of the city. They decided the best place for the pick-up would be the Maybury roadhouse on the western side of Edinburgh where the road to Glasgow began.

After phoning Mrs Ross to warn her that Mary Lou should be waiting, trying to look casual, she sauntered down to Market Street and drove to the New Town. In Northumberland Street she saw a group of other journalists waiting on Mrs Neil's doorstep, so she turned off into the mews before she passed them. Fortunately the lane that led to the garages was semi-circular – she could go in at one end and out the other.

The door to Mrs Ross's garage was shabby and paint-blistered. It looked as if it had not been opened for years because tall weeds grew along the foot of it, but it could be accessed from the garden behind, and Rosa trusted that Mrs

Ross had managed to coerce Mary Lou into following her instructions.

Stopping at the garage door, she tooted the horn once. Thank God, the old door began to shake, but it was hard to open. It shuddered but did not shift, so, cursing, Rosa left the engine running and got out of the car to haul at it. With a supreme effort from both front and behind, it was eventually opened and Mary Lou ran out.

'Get in, lie down and hide yourself,' snapped Rosa, holding the car's back door open.

Saying, 'Thank you, oh thank you,' Mary Lou lay down on the floor with her arms over her head and they drove away. Every now and again, she tried to get up but Rosa was having none of it. 'Stay down,' she ordered. As far as she was concerned, Mary Lou should keep her part of the bargain. The lift to Prestwick was not an act of kindness. It was a journalistic project and must not be compromised.

At the Maybury, The Basher was sitting on a low concrete wall in front of the roadhouse. When Rosa's car slowed down beside him, he flung his camera on to the front seat and jumped in beside it. They were speeding out of the city by ten to five.

The trouble began when The Basher began criticizing Rosa's choice of route.

'You should have taken the road to Biggar,' he said, when he realized she was heading for Glasgow.

She felt her teeth grinding in annoyance. 'I prefer to go to Wishaw and then down the road to Strathaven,' she replied.

'It's longer,' he said.

'It's straighter,' she snapped back, and could not restrain herself from adding, 'anyway I'm doing the driving. You can't drive, so keep quiet.'

He shrugged. 'OK, keep your hair on. I'm just telling you . . .'

'We have a long drive ahead of us and I would be obliged if you could keep your advice to yourself,' she snapped.

They did not address a remark to each other for miles

but Mary Lou, ignoring the resentment between them, sat up perkily on the back seat and kept up a stream of conversation. She seemed to have forgotten much of her anguish about Jake and only occasionally remembered to squeeze out a tear and moan, 'Poor Jake, oh my poor Jake.'

She also seemed to have forgiven The Basher for trying to kick the dog Cosmo – something that had appalled her at the time – and became very coquettish towards him. Remembering his liking for blondes, Rosa was not surprised when he responded.

That's all I need. I do the driving while this pair flirt with each other, she thought.

When Mary Lou began questioning The Basher about his favourite music and what films he'd seen, Rosa snapped, 'Let's keep our minds on the job, can we? We have to decide how we're going to handle the situation at Prestwick because there will be lots of other reporters there.'

'Will that matter?' asked Mary Lou.

Rosa glared at her in the driving mirror. 'Of course it will. We want an exclusive about you saying goodbye to Jake. It mustn't be splashed all over the *Express* or the *Mail* tomorrow morning before our own first edition hits the street.' She was growing very tired of Mary Lou.

Her anger had a sobering effect on the others. Mary Lou said sadly, 'Gee, I wonder what'll happen to Jake when he gets to New York?'

'He'll be held in jail, then appear in court, I expect. He'll need a lawyer,' said Rosa.

Mary Lou's voice brightened. 'I'll organize that for him the minute I get back to Edinburgh. I'll phone somebody up. I'll get him the best lawyer I can find. I'm going to try to get home before he comes up in court . . .' Her voice trailed off as she mused silently, and then added, 'I sure hope I have time to call in at Saks in Fifth Avenue and buy something to wear. To make a good impression, you know. Saks have the loveliest clothes, Rosa. If you ever come to Manhattan to visit me, I'll take you there.'

Rosa wondered what impact Mary Lou in Saks clothes

would make on the visitors' room of an American penitentiary.

'What's Jake actually charged with?' asked The Basher.

'With being married already and not declaring it on his application to marry me – the police say his divorce was never finalized and my rotten uncle found his wife some place in New Jersey. I bet he paid her plenty. He's also charged with stealing some money from my uncle's office – only peanuts, a measly thousand dollars or something. He says he took the money so's he and I could run away together. Silly guy, I could have paid for us both. When I see that uncle of mine again I'm going to give him a rough time for causing us so much trouble. They won't shut Jake up in jail for a thousand dollars, will they? I'm kinda confused about things at the moment,' said Mary Lou soberly.

Jake's had it, thought Rosa and could see from the expression on The Basher's face that he thought so too, but she refrained from catching his eye because she was not prepared to show him any friendliness. Also, infuriatingly, he was being proven right about the route to take for Prestwick.

After a long time on the road, they finally reached Kilmarnock where Mary Lou said plaintively, 'I'm starving, and I need to go to the little girls' room. Can we stop?'

While The Basher bought fish and chips wrapped in newspaper from an Italian cafe, the girls found a public lavatory. Back in the car, he handed them their food but told them to eat it quickly. With a meaningful frown, he looked at his watch, saying, 'We've been too long on the road. It's twenty past nine. If we waste any more time, or take any more wrong roads, we'll miss him.'

For the last thirteen miles of their journey they formed a plan of campaign. Mary Lou was to get into the airport by a service door, contact Jake and his police escort and say goodbye.

'The police promised they'd allow me to see him if I got to Prestwick,' she said, grief-stricken again.

The Basher said he would go with her to take a picture of the touching farewell. 'And your job is to create a diversion so that other pressmen don't see what's going on,' he told Rosa.

'How do you suggest I do that?' she asked.

'By using your famous initiative,' said The Basher, sounding just like Jack.

Things were quiet when they arrived at Prestwick for there was only one plane still to go out. Cars were parked haphazardly here and there over immense empty stretches of black tarmac and, in the distance, lights glittered in the main airport building.

Facing its entrance, six press cars were drawn up close together. Rosa drove past them and headed for a dark corner as The Basher looked at his watch again and said, 'It's five past ten. Drive around till you see a police van and I'll have a look around.'

When they stopped beside a Black Maria, he unfolded himself from the front seat and strolled off into the darkness as if he had all the time in the world.

As the girls watched him go, Mary Lou asked, 'Is he married?'

'God no, I don't think so. Who would live with *him*?' said Rosa.

'I don't know. I didn't like him at first when he tried to kick that dog but now I think he's kinda cute,' said the American girl.

'He's the grumpiest man I've ever met and he's a bit mad. Our editor says photographers are all raving loonies,' Rosa said firmly, thinking that Mary Lou was a terrible judge of men. After all, she'd been taken in by Jake, hadn't she?

When he came back ten minutes later he still wasn't hurrying. Ignoring their eager expressions, he let himself into the car and settled down in the seat before he said, 'Yes, he's in there.'

Mary Lou immediately burst out, 'I must see him! They promised I could see him.'

'He's locked up in an office right now, but I told them you were here and they'll let you have five minutes with

176

him before they put him on the plane. Come on, let's go,' The Basher told her.

To Rosa he said, 'Leave the keys in the car and try to divert the boys in the main hall. They're all waiting for him to come through.'

'How?' she asked again. She was tired and her brain did not seem to be working too well.

'A striptease?' he suggested sardonically as he fished his camera off the floor of the car and ushered Mary Lou away.

A chilly wind coming in from the Irish Sea whipped round Rosa's legs as she walked towards the twinkling lights.

What will I do? What can I do? she wondered.

The Basher did not need much time to take his pictures because he was a swift operator, but she had to give him at least ten minutes. How?

Large glass doors opened inwards into the reception area. Through them she saw several journalists, including Leo Fairley and some others from Edinburgh, grouped round the central pillars or leaning on airline desks.

So that her arrival would not go unnoticed, she deliberately wrestled with the doors, pulling when she should have been pushing. Leo saw her and shouted, 'It's Makepeace. Where's the girl? Have you got her?' They knew that Rosa had a good association with Mary Lou.

It was easy to act like someone taken by surprise for she was genuinely terrified and her legs were trembling with fright. She took one step into the vast hall, stared at the crowd rushing towards her and took to her heels. Barging back through the doors again, she ran like a hare being hunted by a pack of hounds, across the car park towards a group of parked cars, in the opposite direction from where Mary Lou was saying goodbye to Jake.

It was years since she'd run any distance but she'd sprinted at school and could still summon up a fair turn of speed. On and on she went, dodging among the parked cars, and heading for a distant bus shelter where a single light shone. Her pursuers followed, calling out for her to stop. She wouldn't be running like that, they reckoned, unless she was guilty of something.

One of her sandals fell off as she pounded along and she kicked off the other, but still didn't stop. Her chest hurt, her breath was rasping in her lungs, she wanted to be sick but she kept on going.

Oh God, I'm dying, she thought. Reaching the bus shelter, she hid in the shadows behind its back wall. Her pursuers were closing in on her and she was ready to give herself up when a car drove up on to the grass verge by the shelter. Its door swung open, almost knocking her off her feet, and The Basher shouted, 'GET IN!'

His hand reached over and grabbed her by the upper arm, pulling her inside. She collapsed on the seat, retching and gasping as he accelerated away.

Mary Lou, hanging over the back seat, exclaimed, 'Gee, you sure can run!'

Rosa, in an undignified heap on the seat, examined her bare feet. The soles were torn and bleeding from running over the rough tarmac. 'Shit, I've lost my shoes. It's a good job they were old ones,' she said.

Then she glared at The Basher and said accusingly, 'I thought you said you couldn't drive a car.'

'It was *you* who said I couldn't drive, not me. Anyway it's amazing what people can do when they have to,' he said but it was obvious he could drive perfectly well. He probably preferred being driven to doing it himself.

Mary Lou put her arms round Rosa's neck from the back and said, 'Thank you so much. I saw Jake. I had time to tell him I love him and that I'll make sure he doesn't go to jail.'

Rosa glared at The Basher. 'I hope you got the pictures of all that.'

'Of course I did, and we got back to the car before the others caught her. I wanted another shot of her waving at his plane as it took off, but I couldn't risk hanging around any longer. Besides, I had to rescue you before they ran you into the ground.'

'I expect you'll be able to fake the second picture?' asked Rosa sarcastically.

The Basher nodded as he said, 'Yeah, I'll do that as soon as we're clear of this place.'

They had not gone far before she fell asleep and only woke when they stopped by a field outside Biggar where Mary Lou posed for another photograph, waving up at a crescent moon.

At half past three in the morning they reached Edinburgh. By that time Rosa was wide awake again, and Mary Lou was sleeping. They dropped her at Northumberland Street and Rosa said to The Basher, 'There's no buses running. I'll take you wherever you want to go. Where do you live?'

'I'm not going home. Take me to the office,' he said.

'Aren't you tired?' she asked.

He shrugged. 'I want to see those negs. I can't wait till tomorrow. I'll print them up and then go home for a sleep. You'll be in the office before me because you've the story to write. Tell Jack not to expect me till the afternoon.'

At they stopped at the top of the Fleshmarket Close steps leading down to the office door, Rosa yawned and said, 'I wonder what'll happen to Mary Lou now?'

'She'll be OK. She'll marry some rich guy – not Jake – and live in Manhattan. Maybe you can visit and go shopping with her in Saks like a couple of swells,' The Basher said as he jumped out of the car into a deserted Cockburn Street.

Then, to her amazement, he threw out his arms and began singing:

> We're a couple of swells
> We stop at the best hotels
> But we prefer the country
> Far away from the city smells.
> We're a couple of sports
> The pride of the tennis courts
> In June, July and August
> We look cute when we're dressed in shorts.

He went on singing but did not look back. Waving one hand he danced down the steep stone steps, past the locked up pet shop, still chanting, '*The Vanderbilts have asked us out to tea, But we don't know how to get there, no siree, no siree . . .*'

She watched in admiration as he danced away. Even so late, after such a strenuous day, he moved beautifully, a real dancer, jumping down three steps and then going back up two, bending and swaying without self-consciousness.

While she watched, a policeman appeared at the top of the steps, shining his flashlight down the dark gully. 'What's going on here? You'd better go home and keep out of trouble before I run you both in,' he shouted.

'*We're a couple of swells . . .*' The Basher's voice came floating up out of the darkness as he disappeared into the building and the door clanged behind him.

Twenty-Two

While Rosa was on her way to Prestwick, Charles was in the *Express* office enduring a dressing down from Ned Ingram. Though he dressed like a merchant banker and spoke like a BBC announcer, Ned was an astute journalist and a strict taskmaster to his reporters.

Charles had been sent to cover a song recital by Victoria Los Angeles who was one of the stars performing at the Edinburgh Festival, and had come back with an enthusiastic report of her performance.

To confine himself to eulogies about her singing would have been quite good enough to satisfy Ned, but he was unable to restrain himself from adding his own special touch to the story. In the audience, he wrote, there had been a man who claimed to be Miss Los Angeles' personal hypnotist. According to Charles, when she performed in Edinburgh, this man joined her entourage and sat in the audience mentally communing with her, encouraging her to do her best. He was also performing a similar function for his friend, the actor Donald Wolfit, who was appearing in a Festival play called 'The Strong are Lonely'.

Charles quoted the hypnotist as saying, 'As well as Miss Los Angeles, I'm very interested in Mr Wolfit. Without me sending my life force into him, he would not be able to speak a line on stage.'

When Ned read this, his face darkened. 'From what I know about Wolfit, it would take a drying-out course to make him word perfect. He's pissed most of the time and it's lucky he can walk on to a stage at all, far less act. How come this character talked to you?'

'We were sitting next to each other at the Victoria Los Angeles' performances and I noticed how he closed his eyes and concentrated on her. He was totally involved in the performance and when it finished, she looked as if she'd not sung a note but he was exhausted, totally wrung out, so I asked him why he was so tired and he told me.'

'I'm amazed he didn't knock you down,' said Ned. 'But if he's genuine, we need a photograph.'

Charles protested, 'He'll never agree to that. It would ruin what he does because then he'd be identifiable and all sorts of performers, untalented as well as talented, would be after him, wanting him to do the same thing for them. Imagine being approached by somebody like Max Bygraves? For him that's unthinkable.'

Ned spread the copy out on his desk and said, 'I find it almost unthinkable how you come across all these shrinking violets who won't have their pictures taken. I'm not going to run this story. I don't know why exactly but it just doesn't smell right. Watch it, lad. If you try to take me for a ride, I'll crucify you. There'll be no second chance.'

Chastened, Charles slunk away and was trying to pass the rest of the afternoon doing as little as possible, when one of the staff photographers came in and spoke to Ned who looked at the office clock and asked, 'Where's Patricia? I made an appointment for her to interview Sonya Dresdel at five o'clock but she's not turned up. Have any of you seen her?'

Charles looked at his watch. It was five past five. Ned was a stickler for punctuality.

'She told me she was taking a couple of hours off before she did the Dresdel job,' said another woman reporter.

Charles stood up. 'I know where she lives. It's not far away. I'll go up there now and remind her she's late,' he offered. He had made it his business to check out the building where Patricia and Hugh lived. Sometimes he even stood in the courtyard in the evening gazing up at their lighted windows and wondering what they were doing in the rooms high above the old streets of Edinburgh.

Ned nodded. 'All right. You might as well make yourself useful.'

Feeling cheerful, Charles strode up to the Mound thinking that this could be his opportunity to see inside the Maling home. They could hardly keep him standing on the doorstep if he turned up to escort Patricia back to work. She would probably need escorting too, because like other people in the office, he had noticed how her alcohol intake was increasing. He took that as a sign that she was growing disenchanted with her marriage.

Settling down with him would soon take her back to sobriety though. As he walked, his fertile mind was filled with mental pictures of their domestic felicity. He imagined Patricia fervently thanking him for saving her from the ravages of alcoholism – and from Hugh. He was a happy man.

He was smiling as he climbed the short flight of steps from the top of the Mound into Lady Stair's Close. The entrance to Blackie House was on his left and, as he turned, he saw that there was a small crowd of people clustered round the heavy wooden door of Patricia's building.

He hurried over, and one of the bystanders, a shocked-looking woman, said to him, 'You can't go in there. They're bringing her downstairs right now.'

'Who?' he asked.

'The ambulance men. There's been an accident,' she said.

So that's why Patricia is late, he thought. If she knew about the accident, and it was a dramatic one, she might have stayed behind to get the details for the newspaper.

'I'll wait,' he said and stood back while the heavy door, studded with immense nails, was swung open and a flustered-looking ambulance man in a dark uniform and askew cap backed into the paved entry, holding the struts of a stretcher. A second man held the other end and lying on the stretcher between them was a body totally covered with a white sheet.

The little crowd sighed and took respectful steps backwards like genuflexions.

The woman next to Charles whispered, 'Poor thing. She must be dead. They only cover them up like that when they're dead.'

Charles nodded. He knew he should whip out a notebook and start quizzing the policemen who stepped out of the hallway after the stretcher, but he was in a hurry to find Patricia. Someone else could cover this little drama.

The woman beside him wanted to talk. 'What a tragedy. I think it's that young woman who's not been living up there long. She and her husband moved into one of the high flats. Very smart she is – was – with lovely clothes. I used to see her from my kitchen window running across the courtyard. She was always in a hurry.'

Something awful clutched at his heart. He stared at her in horror and asked, 'What was her name?'

She shook her head. 'I don't know. I never spoke to her. Like I say she was new . . .'

He broke away and ran across to the policeman. '*Daily Express*,' he snapped. 'What's happened?'

The policeman looked at him and recognized his face. 'It didn't take you boys long to get here, did it?' he said.

'What's happened?' repeated Charles through tight lips. His heart was pounding and there was a mist in front of his eyes.

'A woman fell down the stairs and broke her neck,' said the policeman.

'Christ!' said Charles who never swore. Then he recovered enough to ask, 'What's her name?'

It can't be Patricia. It can't! he told himself.

'Her name's Maling,' said the policeman. 'Her husband's still up there but he's in an awful state.'

'I know them both,' said Charles and pushed his way into the building.

He did not even try to wait for the lift, which was clanking its slow way down to the ground with more policemen on board. Without thinking about the steepness of the climb, he ran up flight after flight of worn stone steps. At the foot of the final flight he collided with

Hugh who was standing talking to a man who looked like a doctor.

Without a preamble, Charles clutched at Maling's jersey sleeve and said, 'Is it really Patricia?'

Hugh stared at him with a bleak expression and nodded.

'Is she dead?' asked Charles. This was still difficult to believe.

Hugh nodded again. 'Yes, she's dead. For God's sake, go away, Rutland,' he said and turned back to the doctor, who glared at Charles and roughly told him to clear out.

Very, very slowly, as if he was carrying a heavy burden on his back, he walked back down the stairs. There were still some people in the courtyard, talking about the accident. Though they lived in the buildings adjacent to Blackie House, none of them had seen or heard anything unusual that afternoon.

'The police'll be speaking to the fowk in the other flats up there noo,' said one man, nodding up at the Maling's windows.

'They winna get much,' said an old woman. 'There's naebody on the top flair and the yins below her are oot at work a' day. They're no' like us, they're the fancy kind that moved in efter the place was a' done up.'

Charles walked back to the office as if his shoes were weighted down with lead. When Ned saw him, he raised his eyebrows and asked, 'No Patricia?'

He was surprised when the young man leaned both hands on a desk top, lowered his head and started to weep. 'She's dead,' he stammered through his sobs.

Twenty-Three

By a miracle of will, on the morning after the trip to Prestwick, Rosa woke at seven thirty, returned the office car in a sleep deprived trance, and forced herself into the office to concentrate on her story. By nine forty-five she'd finished the account of Mary Lou's tearful farewell to Jake and laid it on Jack's work table.

After that she folded her arms on the desk, put her head down on them and fell sound asleep. At ten, Gil put a hand on her shoulder and said, 'Go home. You're whacked. Take the rest of the day off. We're putting your story on the front page of the first edition.' He seemed to be treating her with extra consideration for some reason. Was her story that good?

She was struggling to her feet and yawning widely, when Mike came up behind her, slipped an arm over her shoulders and said, 'Have you seen the dailies yet?'

She shook her head. 'I haven't had a minute,' she told him. 'I've been writing up my Prestwick piece since I came in.'

He took her arm. 'Come along to the canteen, kid. I've something to tell you.'

'Oh, Mike, I'm whacked. I want to go home,' she protested.

He would take no refusal, only pulled at her arm. 'Come on, Rosa,' he said. She was surprised at that for he hardly ever called her by her first name – she was usually 'kid' or 'Makepeace'.

The canteen was empty because it was not yet official break time. Only one woman was manning the counter and Mike asked her for two coffees which he brought back to the table where Rosa was sitting, wondering what was going on. Before she had the chance to taste hers, he reached into his jacket pocket and produced a leather-covered hip flask. Unscrewing its cap, he poured a generous slug into both their cups.

'What's that?' she asked in surprise.

'Whisky,' he told her.

'But it's only ten o'clock. I don't want any whisky. Besides, I don't like whisky,' she protested.

'You will want this,' was his reply. Then he leaned forward and stared at her very hard. His face was stony and his eyes a cold shade of blue.

'Listen, Rosa. I'm sorry I have to tell you this but Patricia's had an accident and I know that you two were very close. I didn't want you to hear about it from anybody else so I asked the others not to say anything.'

She stared at him. 'Has she had an accident? Is she hurt?'

He nodded.

'Badly?'

Another nod.

'Oh Mike, she's not . . . ?'

He was glad she was quick on the uptake. 'Yes, she's dead, Rosa,' he said.

The eyes that looked back at him were enormous but dry. She obviously found it hard to believe what he was saying.

'Everybody's devastated, but I knew you'd be the worst,' he said.

'You're a very kind person, Mike,' she whispered. 'What happened? Maling didn't kill her, did he?'

He shook his head. 'I must admit I had the same thought when I first heard, but apparently not. She fell down the stairs in that block of flats where she lives.'

Rosa took a deep gulp at the coffee and the whisky in it burned its way down her throat, but seemed to clear her mind.

'Which flight? Those are awful stairs, like a precipice,' asked Rosa.

'The first flight down from her door on the fifth floor.

There's a small landing and then a twisting stair,' said Mike.

'He didn't push her, did he?' was Rosa's next question but Mike shook his head.

'No. They say she was drunk.'

'What time was it?'

'About three o'clock in the afternoon. She'd been drinking in the Doric with Leo Fairley.'

'But I saw him at Prestwick last night,' protested Rosa.

'He was in the Doric before he went to Prestwick. And I saw him up at Blackie House earlier this morning. He said Patricia was drinking brandy.'

Rosa shook her head. 'There was a reason for that. She was so unhappy! I knew from the way she kept avoiding the subject of her marriage with me. I'm sure Maling has something to do with this.'

'In all fairness, you can't say that. The only way he's involved is because they were married to each other,' said Mike sadly.

'Has anybody spoken to Maling?' asked Rosa.

'He's issued a statement but he's not speaking to the press,' Mike told her.

'I'm going up there now. I *have* to hear what happened,' she said and got to her feet.

Mike rose too. 'I don't think you should, but, all right. I'll come with you,' he said. She knew he was not going with her because he was afraid she'd scoop his story. This time, he was going as her supporter and friend.

They did not speak as they walked up the High Street to Lady Stair's Close. On their way, they passed a newspaper seller on the corner of Cockburn Street and printed in huge black letters on a placard beside him were the words:

UNTIMELY DEATH OF EDINBURGH WRITER

Rosa shivered. The word 'untimely' would not have been used about one of the establishment oldies like Compton

Mackenzie. It meant Patricia had died before she fulfilled her potential.

Eventually, they were standing under the arch that led to the courtyard, staring up at the windows of Blackie House. It was a lovely day and the sun was glinting off the glass.

'I hope he's in,' were Mike's first words since they'd left the office.

They climbed the stairs because Rosa distrusted the ramshackle lift. On the landing before the last flight, she stopped, terrified in case there was blood or some sign of the terrible thing that had happened there, but Mike put out a reassuring hand to pull her on. To her relief the steps were unmarked. There was absolutely nothing to show that a fatal accident had happened on those stone slabs. Rosa wondered if other people had fallen to their deaths there in the hundreds of years the house had been in existence.

As Mike rattled the cherub knocker, she stood two steps down staring up at his back, hoping against hope that it would be Patricia who opened the door. Maybe it had all been a mistake.

But Hugh Maling answered their knock. When he saw Mike, he grimaced and said, 'I've already said I'm giving no statements to vultures like you. Go away.'

In an adroit movement, Mike stuck his big foot between the door and the wooden jamb so that it could not be closed. 'We're here as her friends. Let us in, bugger lugs,' he hissed.

For a moment it seemed as if Hugh was going to defy him, but Mike pushed his broad shoulders into the half open doorway and stared him down. 'Try it, chum, just try it,' he said.

Because Hugh was half Mike's size, he opted for safety and stood back, but as Mike and Rosa stepped into the narrow little hall, he sneered, 'So, all the newshounds are out, are they?'

They were close together, facing each other. 'Tell me what happened to Patricia,' said Rosa.

'I've told everything to the police already,' said Hugh.

189

'Tell it again,' hissed Mike, and grabbed the other man by his collar.

He wriggled, red faced because of the strength of Mike's hold, and spat out the words. 'Can't you read? It was in the papers. She fell down the stairs. It was those high heels she wore. She tripped and fell.'

'Was she running away from you?' asked Rosa.

Mike slackened his hold and Maling recovered enough to become outraged. 'No, she was not. Maitland and I were in the sitting room. She went out on an errand. Because she'd been drinking she wanted to drink coffee to sober herself up, but there was no milk so she was going out to buy some. She told us where she was going. Then we heard her shout. I ran out and found her lying at the bottom of the first flight.'

So Maitland Crewe was in the flat at the time, Rosa registered that, but there was something else she needed to know.

'Was she killed instantly? Was she conscious when you found her? Did you try to revive her?' she asked in a shaking voice.

He stopped sneering and said in a flat tone, 'She was absolutely dead. Her neck was broken. The doctor said it was instantaneous.'

The words were stark. Rosa shuddered and leaned back against the wall. The thought that was haunting her was put into words without premeditation. 'Did you push her?' she asked.

Maling glared at her and said with menace, 'If you as much as whisper those words again anywhere outside I'll drag you through the courts. Maitland Crewe was here with me when it happened. He's a witness to the whole thing and he's given a statement. Your precious friend was drunk – drink and high-heeled shoes made her fall down the stairs.'

Rosa remembered what Leo had said about Patricia drinking brandy, but was that enough to make her fall downstairs? She wanted to ask more questions, but Maling walked away up the hall, shouting over his shoulder, 'Get out of my house the pair of you, or I'll call the police and tell them you're pestering me. GET OUT NOW!'

Mike took hold of her shoulder and pushed her back through the open door. 'Come on, Rosa, we're wasting our time here,' he said.

In the Lawnmarket, he hailed a taxi and put her into it. 'Do you want me to take you home?' he asked, but she shook her head.

'No. Thanks so much for your help. You've really been very kind.'

But before the taxi drove off, she leaned forward and said, 'Patricia always drank her coffee black. Why did she want to buy milk?'

Twenty-Four

Patricia's friends on the *Dispatch* held their wake for her in the Cockburn Hotel bar on the night before her inquest was due to open.

Though everyone was shocked by what had happened, work went on as usual – cars still bashed into each other, buildings still burst into flame, Festival stars still demanded publicity and unruly citizens still assaulted each other. Jack continued to rant and rave, and the voracious presses in the basement rumbled on, filling the building with the heady smell of printing ink.

After filling the front pages for one day, the death of Patricia became just another item from the past as far as the public was concerned. Only her family and the small world of journalism were deeply shocked and affected. Two members of that world were more stricken than the others.

Rosa Makepeace and Charles Rutland were in a state of grief, anger and confusion. Every morning when Rosa woke, her mind was filled with an unsettling feeling of foreboding and it took a few seconds before she remembered what had happened. Her talented, amusing friend was dead – at twenty-four.

What obsessed Rosa was the suspicion that the death, at best, could have been avoided, and at worst, had been engineered by Patricia's husband. She developed a corroding hatred for Hugh Maling.

That hatred was shared – and actually far outdone – by the feelings of Charles. Like Rosa, he blamed Maling for the death, though he did not know why. Perhaps it was only because he was Patricia's husband and guilty of living with her in that eyrie of a flat. He was also guilty of making her so unhappy that she drank too much and fell down the stairs. These accusations were undeniable, but what could not be proved was that Maling had any direct hand in his wife's death. Yet Charles, with his imagination and talent for invention, felt sure that he did. All he needed was something, no matter how small, to back up his suspicion.

When he heard about the meeting in the Cockburn, he decided to join his old colleagues and when he walked in, he was whey-faced, so ghastly looking that Mike suggested, 'You look as if you need something stronger than lemonade tonight.'

To everyone's surprise, Charles agreed. 'I think I'll have a brandy,' he said.

'Breakthrough at last,' said Mike, getting up. 'I'll buy it for you.' Then he turned to the rest of the party and said, 'In fact, I'll buy a drink for everybody. I've something to tell you.'

Etta dispensed the rounds, actually coming out from behind her bar with their orders on a large tin tray, something she never did usually, and Mike raised his glass to say, 'Brace yourselves. I'm leaving.'

Clive was the first to react. 'Where are you going?' he asked, for he was as jealous as Mike of colleagues' successes.

'To America, to Florida, in fact.'

Clive blinked in stunned envy. 'Not the *National Enquirer*!' That Florida-based scandal sheet was the acme for the toughest news reporters.

Mike nodded. 'Right first time. I've a mate over there and he's fixed it for me. I fly out next week.'

Usually this news would have created huge excitement and Mike would have been insufferably ebullient, but at this sad time, everybody's reaction was muted. His friends solemnly wished him every success and sipped the drinks he'd bought them with sombre expressions on their faces.

Rosa looked round and another wave of misery engulfed

193

her. With Patricia dead, and Mike moving on, everything was changing too fast for her liking.

It was Tony who brought up the subject of the inquest. 'Who's covering it?' he asked.

'I am. Old Bob told me tonight,' said Clive.

Rosa looked up. 'And I'm going as a spectator. Tomorrow's my day off.'

'If I'm on the calls, I'll slip away and look in on it too,' said Mike.

'I'm not covering it, but I'll be there. I think it was a tragedy and I want to know why it happened,' said Charles.

They all looked at him, wondering why he was so interested for he did not know Patricia as well as they did.

He looked back, aware of their curiosity, and said, 'We got to know each other quite well during the time I've been at the *Express*. She struck me as being very unhappy, especially on the day she died.'

That was true. Patricia was very tense that day. He remembered noticing her distraction at the time, but since then his mind had built up her behaviour into something more significant. During the few days since her death, he had not seen Hugh or Maitland Crewe but, when he did, he had a lot of questions to ask them.

'She was happy enough before she married that bastard Maling,' said Mike gruffly and Rosa suspected that his sudden decision to go to Florida had been prompted by Patricia's death. Like Rosa, he was aware of the need to move on and leave the past behind.

At the inquest, in the sombre Sheriff Court in the High Street, Patricia's family filled the front bench while her friends crowded in at the back. Clive was in the press seats, with his notebook open and pencil busy.

The first statements were from the ambulance crew, the police and a doctor who examined Patricia's body. A kindly-faced ambulance man described running up the stairs

194

of Blackie House and finding a woman's body crumpled at the foot of the stair between the fourth and fifth floors.

'I bent down beside her and it was obvious that she was dead. Her eyes were open and she looked shocked,' he said.

Charles, sitting next to Rosa, gave such a huge shudder at this point that she felt it through the sleeve of her jacket.

A policeman read out his statement in a solemn monotone. 'At three thirty-two a telephone call was received from Blackie House telling us that a woman had died following a fall down stairs. It is not the first time such a thing has happened. The stair of the tenements in the Old Town are notoriously dangerous . . .'

The doctor told the court that the deceased's neck was broken in the fall. Death would have been instantaneous. Mrs Maling was a healthy young woman, but when he was called to certify the death, he noticed that she smelled strongly of alcohol.

By this time the court room was stuffy and airless because the sun was blazing down outside. A terrible torpor seized the audience, but it was sharply broken when Hugh Maling stepped up to give his evidence.

Dressed in a dark grey suit and a black tie, he was solemn but very composed as he told the inquest that he and his friend Maitland Crewe had been listening to music – Beethoven – on the afternoon of his wife's death. He had not expected Patricia back till the evening but, about three o'clock, she let herself into the flat with her key. When she joined them in the sitting room, she seemed very cheerful.

'It did not strike me at the time that she might have been drunk,' he said sadly, looking down at his hands as if he was divulging a secret.

The coroner asked, 'Was your wife in the habit of drinking during the day?'

Hugh looked up and said, 'Sadly, yes, she was. I'd remonstrated with her about it, but I'm afraid that some journalists do drink more than is good for them. Before

195

she married me, she moved with a dissolute set. She was attempting to break her links with them though.'

At this, there was a sharp intake of breath from all the people in the back row. Even Clive seemed to bristle.

Hugh went on to tell that as the music played, Patricia went to make a cup of coffee. He heard her shouting that the milk had gone sour. The weather was hot and he had inadvertently left the bottle out of the fridge.

'She was quite angry when she popped her head round the sitting-room door to tell me she was going down to the corner shop to buy another pint.' he said.

'Then what happened?' asked the coroner.

'There was a cry from the front door, which she had left open,' Hugh closed his eyes as if the memory was agony to him.

'What sort of a cry?'

'A groan, quite loud,' said Hugh.

'What did you do?'

'I ran to the front door. It was still open. I stepped on to the landing – it's quite narrow – and saw my wife lying at the foot of the stairs.'

'There is a lift in your block, isn't there?'

'Yes, but when she came in she complained that someone had left the gate open on one of the floors and she'd had to climb up. It was still inoperative.'

'Was your wife in the habit of leaving the front door open when she went out?'

'It was a hot day. Besides, Mr Crewe and I were in the flat so there was no risk of a burglar or someone like that coming in. She hadn't far to go. It would only take a couple of minutes to fetch the milk because she'd close the lift doors on her way down . . .' Hugh sounded glib, as if he'd worked that answer out.

'What do you think happened? Why do you think she fell?' asked the coroner.

'I think she might have tripped on the door mat. Her shoes had very high heels,' said Hugh.

'What did you do when you saw her lying on the stair?'

'I ran down and tried to lift her up. Her head lolled. Her neck was broken. She was dead.' When he said this he looked thoroughly shaken, but Charles, watching him, was convinced he was not telling the truth – or at least not the whole truth. He seemed to be holding something back.

Rosa fidgeted in her seat beside him and whispered, 'Why did Patricia want milk? She drank her coffee black. Was Patricia carrying money or a handbag when she fell? If she had neither, how would she pay for the milk?'

He looked at her with respect. Both of these details had escaped him.

'Should I say something?' Rosa whispered again, but he shook his head.

'I don't think that's allowed,' he told her. He guarded Rosa's questions like treasure for they would go to building up his case against Hugh. Already he was planning retribution. The sight of Patricia's widower, so calm and controlled in the witness box, maddened him.

Hugh's testimony was followed by that of Maitland Crewe. Where Hugh was cool and collected, Crewe was ill at ease, stammering and unsure of himself, but his basic story did not contradict anything his friend had said.

They were listening to music – it was Beethoven, he remembered – when Patricia shouted. They ran to the door and saw her body at the foot of the stairs.

While Hugh tried to revive her, he telephoned for a doctor and an ambulance but knew she was dead because, during his Army service, he'd seen dead people.

No, she did not seem to be very drunk when he saw her, but that was only for a few moments when she stuck her head round the door to complain about the lift gates being left open and to tell them about the milk.

The coroner pounced on the comment about a shout. 'When she fell did she give a loud shout?' he asked.

Crewe looked confused. 'I don't really remember.'

'But it was loud enough for you to hear over the music of Beethoven?'

'It must have been.'

The coroner looked towards the policeman and asked, 'Did anyone else in the building hear a shout?'

The policeman shook his head. 'The top flat was empty and the couple in the fourth floor flat were at work. The lady on the third floor is old and slightly deaf. The gentleman on floor two was listening to his radio. The ground floor people were not at home.'

Evidence followed from Nellie and Leo Fairley, who both agreed that Patricia had been drinking brandy on the afternoon of her death.

Nellie said, 'Oh aye, I kent the lassie weel enough. She came in a lot – sometimes with the *Express* folk, but recently alone. On the last day, she sat in a corner as if she didnae want onybody tae see her and she put it back. Four brandies she had. She was a sad kinda sowl and booze cheered her up.'

Rosa bent her head as she thought over those words to herself. *'A sad kinda sowl' would not have been a fair description of her friend before she became involved with Hugh Maling. The old Patricia was sharp, funny and full of joie de vivre. What happened to her? Was it possible that she deliberately flung herself down the stairs? If she did, he drove her to it.*

When the coroner gave his verdict, it was accidental death. As the policeman said, many people met their ends by falling down the stairs of Old Town tenements.

Patricia's funeral was private, attended only by her immediate family and Hugh. Rosa was pleased that she could not go because she was afraid she would not be able to stand it without breaking down and making a scene. Her father and Jean drove up from the Borders to take her out on the day of the funeral. They drove to St Andrews and sat huddled on the dunes looking out over a dun grey sea, a prospect that did nothing to raise their spirits.

When they dropped her back at Northumberland Street, Jean told Rosa that they were returning to France soon.

'Why don't you come with us? Give up your job. You'll always manage to get another, but right now you need a break,' she said and her look of concern was obviously genuine.

Rosa gazed from her stepmother to her father and asked, 'What's going to happen to Catslackburn? Are you giving it up?'

Her father shook his head. 'No, of course not. Eckie's keeping his eye on it for us while we're away and we'll be back for Christmas.'

'I won't come to France, but if things get too much for me in Edinburgh, I might go down there,' said Rosa.

'That's better than nothing, but I wish you'd come to France. You need to change your life,' said Jean solemnly.

'Roddy's coming back soon. I might change it then,' said Rosa.

It was a time of upheaval both abroad and at home. The Hungarians rose in rebellion against their Russian overlords and Britain and France started hostilities in the Suez Canal Zone. With so much going on there was little space on the front pages for any local news and good stories were wasted or underreported. In the *Dispatch* office, the spice had gone out of life. Mike departed for Florida. Clive took over as chief crime reporter and made everyone's life misery by his boasting and bombast. Rosa sank into an angry depression as she mulled over the problem of Patricia's death. Something about that still bothered her. She was not alone in her suspicions. Charles was puzzling over it too – but unlike Rosa, he was doing something about it.

Twenty-Five

$\mathbf{M}$rs Ross was very proud of her lodger and kept a cuttings book of Rosa's bylined stories which she showed to her coffee morning friends. The last entries covered the Mary Lou story.

LAST EMBRACE FOR RUNAWAYS proclaimed one headline that carried Rosa's Prestwick story flanked on each side by photographs of Mary Lou, one of her hugging a handcuffed Jake, and the other of her weeping and staring up into a moonlit sky. The Basher's second shot really made it look as if she was waving off the plane.

Best of all, as far as Mrs Ross was concerned, were the words in huge letters: **by reporter ROSA MAKEPEACE and photographer ROBERT McIVOR**.

'You're the talk of the town,' she said to her lodger.

On the evening after Patricia's inquest, Rosa was lying on top of her bed, miserably mulling over all she had heard, when her landlady rapped at the door.

'Rosa,' she called. 'Mrs Neil has invited us next door to meet Mary Lou's uncle. He's come to take her back to America and she says he's charming.'

Rosa called back, 'That's all I need, for the wicked uncle to turn out to be the hero of the piece!' But she knew Mrs Ross wanted to go, so she reluctantly agreed to get up and meet the uncle.

They entered Mrs Neil's house by the back door and, calling out, 'Hello, hello,' made their way up the kitchen stairs to the first-floor drawing room where all the lamps were blazing and a handsome grey-haired man in his fifties stood in front of an open fire with a glass in his hand.

Mary Lou and Mrs Neil sat on the sofa staring at him in evident admiration. Mary Lou, no longer tearful and distraught, had recovered her old sheen and seemed to have put her worries behind her.

She jumped up and ran across to Rosa, putting an arm round her shoulders as she said, 'Uncle Joe, this is my friend Rosa Makepeace who took me to Prestwick – isn't Makepeace some name?'

Uncle Joe advanced on Rosa with his hand extended and bonhomie shining from him. 'I'm pleased to meet you, Miss Makepeace. You've been very kind to Mary Lou,' he said.

Rosa, impressed by his sophistication, stammered, 'I only did my job . . .'

'Not at all, not at all. You kept those press people away from her. You handled the whole thing magnificently.'

'But I'm press too and I wasn't the only one—' Rosa began, but she was not allowed to finish for Mary Lou interrupted, 'The photographer helped but he's the one who tried to kick a dog.'

So much for flirting in the car, thought Rosa. Mary Lou was definitely a fickle female. Not only had she jettisoned The Basher, but she seemed to have forgotten Jake as well.

The urbane uncle was busying himself at a drinks tray which, amazingly for the Neil household, held a bottle of gin, one of dry vermouth, a bowl of ice and a shining silver cocktail shaker, which had to be a relic from Mrs Neil's army days. Adroitly he poured generous measures of gin into the shaker, added ice, and looking over at the visitors asked, 'Martinis, ladies?'

Mrs Ross turned coy. She frequently told Rosa that alcohol never passed her lips, but now she seemed prepared to make an exception. 'A Martini would be very nice,' she simpered.

Uncle Joe uncorked the Vermouth, dropped a minute amount into the gin and ice and set about jiggling the shaker to and fro like a musician playing the maracas before filling two glasses, dropping in slices of lemon, and handing them to the guests.

The Martini was so strong that it took Rosa's breath away but Mrs Ross sipped hers without a tremor and said in her most refined voice, 'Delicious.'

Uncle Joe was very much in charge. 'I flew up from London this afternoon and we're going back to New York tomorrow,' he announced.

Rosa looked at Mary Lou who was smiling sweetly, but she caught Rosa's quizzical look and explained, 'Uncle Joe's told me everything he found out about Jake. He's married after all, and he did steal money. He'll probably go to jail.'

'He's a crook. Mary Lou believed everything he said but I don't blame her because she's not a worldly girl. She's led a very sheltered life,' added Uncle Joe.

'I was conned,' chirped Mary Lou happily. Jake was the past as far as she was concerned. A future of more suitable men and shopping trips to Saks beckoned for her. She'd had a lucky escape.

Rosa wanted to laugh, but managed to keep her face straight. She was pretty sure that Mary Lou and Jake had shared a bed but Mrs Neil would never tell for she was as closed as a clam on the subject, and Mrs Ross would not broach such an indelicate subject with Rosa, who smiled at Mary Lou and said, 'You'll have to put it all down to experience.'

An impish gleam came into Mary Lou's eyes as she dimpled and replied, 'I sure will.'

Uncle Joe's Martinis softened them all up and soon they were chatting like old friends. He sat down beside Rosa and detailed Jake's crimes to her. They were a series of petty larcenies, and Jake had sensed a huge opportunity when he bumped into Mary Lou in the family firm's office.

'He must have thought his lucky day had come but I guess it's the family's fault. We're very private people, you'll never find our names in the gossip columns, because we deliberately lead quiet lives. Mary Lou didn't know anything about the world when that guy hit on her. She was fresh out of school and fell for his stories about growing up in the slums and wanting to better himself,' said the uncle.

He also said that the stories about the vastness of Mary Lou's fortune were exaggerated. 'Mary Lou's not in the Barbara Hutton class, but she's not poor and it's my job to make sure she doesn't get exploited like that poor woman,' said Uncle Joe, who obviously took his guardian role very seriously.

'You know I'm a journalist, don't you?' Rosa warned him.

He nodded and said, 'Sure I do.'

So Rosa continued, 'You see, I'd like to write an end to the runaway couple story and use some of the things you're telling me. I'll not say too much about what Jake's done in the past because we can't prejudice any trial he might have to go through, but I'll show you're not the wicked uncle Jake said you were.'

'Go ahead. It'll be nice to be presented in a better light,' he said with a laugh and she warmed to him because he really was a very attractive man. Life was going on again.

Next evening, returning from an amateur performance of *An Inspector Calls* at the Y.M.C.A, during which half of the scenery fell down on top of the cast, Rosa was stopped in the hall of her digs by Mrs Ross, who said excitedly, 'The doctor phoned ten minutes ago. He's at Waverley Station and wants you to pick him up.'

'He'll have got a taxi by now,' said Rosa.

'No, I said you'd be home by ten o'clock and he said he'd wait in the station till then. He's so keen to see you,' said Mrs Ross.

Rosa looked at her watch. It was nine fifty, so off she went to fetch him.

Roddy, in uniform, was waiting by the bookstall. For the first time in their acquaintance, she thought he looked very glamorous. When he got into the car, he leaned over and kissed her. She kissed him back.

'Are you going to marry me?' he asked.

'Perhaps,' she said.

She dropped him at his mother's, refusing to go in too but promising to pick him up early next morning, which was her day off. Driving home, she tried to understand herself. Why was she dithering? She could easily convince herself it was right to marry Roddy; she was ready for marriage and he would make the ideal husband. Most people would think she was lucky to have found him. Besides, everything was changing at the office. Soon she would have no real friends left there.

She liked Roddy a lot, but was not swept off her feet and still longed for a mad, headlong infatuation, the kind of magical love that filled the church on her father's wedding day. Did people have to wait till middle age before they found perfect love?

She knew she'd behaved churlishly by refusing to go in to see Roddy's mother and only pecking his cheek in farewell but she resolved that tomorrow she would go out of her way to be charming, and make his leave as enjoyable as possible.

The next day dawned in a blaze of sunlight. Dressed in a pink cotton dress and white sandals she was transformed into a conventional young lady as she drove to Morningside to pick him up.

His mother was presiding over a loaded breakfast table and Rosa could tell that today she approved of her son's girlfriend's clothes, if not of the girl herself. Mrs Barton was suspicious about Rosa's strange job and her background was too unconventional for her to feel comfortable with – a father who invented things that never seemed to work, was alien to her. For her son's sake, however, she made great efforts to be cordial.

'Where are you going today?' she asked as they headed for the door.

Rosa looked at Roddy and said, 'It's such a lovely day, I thought we might go to the Borders, to the place where I grew up.'

'I'd love that. Is this your way of introducing me to your past?' he asked.

'I suppose it is. Our cottage is called Catslackburn and I love everything about it. My father's not there right now because he's in France, but Eckie, our neighbour, is always around and he's a sort of unofficial grandfather to me. If you come up to his exacting standards, you'll have a great advantage. Father accepts Eckie's advice on everything.'

'My goodness, what a responsibility for me,' joked Roddy. He was a good passenger, never carping about the way she drove, about her fondness for speed, or the route she chose, as The Basher would have done. He sat back comfortably in the front seat, arms crossed over his chest, and did not smoke. All her male colleagues, except Charles, smoked heavily. Compared to them, Roddy was a paragon and it struck her that she might find it hard to live up to his standards.

The Border countryside looked lovely, with its vistas of rolling hills, deep beech woods, and slow running, glittering burns where she knew fish lurked in secret pools the colour of China tea. Her heart melted with love and longing as it always did when she drove into the secret land, and she gave her passenger a running commentary as they drove along. 'This is Stow, there's a lovely old ruined pack horse bridge over the river here on the right-hand side . . . I won't go into Galashiels because it's full of tweed mills and not very pretty, but I'll take you over the hill to Clovenfords. There's a Victorian vinery there that sells gorgeous black grapes and they'll be ripening now. We'll stop to buy a bunch. Eckie loves them.'

After buying the grapes, they drove through Selkirk, then up the narrow valley that led to St Mary's Loch. Here Rosa fell silent; her feeling for the country here was too overwhelming for words. The sheep-cropped hills and scrubby thickets of rowans, elders, wild rose bushes and hazel trees, made her want to weep with love. She knew what it was like to go gathering rosehips and brambles through those woods; and to search for early morning mushrooms in the fields.

'When I die I want to be buried up here,' she said softly to herself, forgetting about Roddy.

'I'll remember,' he said.

They were both solemn as she steered the car up the rutted track that led to the cottage. In the yard no other cars were parked and there was no sign of Jess, the dog. The windows were shuttered and the door barred. It looked as if no one had been there for years.

Roddy looked at her with his eyebrows raised in enquiry, but she only smiled and tooted the horn. In a few moments, a black and white thunderbolt came dashing round the corner and Jess threw herself at the car door. She knew the new arrival was Rosa even before she got out of the car.

The dog was followed by Eckie, dressed, as in all weathers, in baggy old flannels tucked into Wellington boots, woolly jersey and a flat cap. His wrinkled face twitched into a smile when he saw Rosa. 'The dug kent it was you, lass, she must hae smelt ye,' he said. Roddy was not sure if that was meant to be a joke.

Rosa introduced them to each other and when he shook hands with the old man, Roddy noted the roughness of Eckie's palm, hardened by a lifetime of outdoor work.

Eckie rarely smiled at strangers, so he only nodded and said, 'Oh aye, a freend o' Rosa's, are ye? The boss is away in France. He sent me a postcard frae some place called Saint Tropez.' He pronounced it to rhyme with 'trapeze' but neither of them dared to correct him.

'I got one too. They seem to be having a good time,' said Rosa.

'And why not,' said Eckie loyally. She handed him the luscious-looking bunch of black grapes, as big as marbles, nestling on a white cardboard plate and he accepted them with muted pleasure, saying, 'Oh, grand.'

Then he looked round at the shuttered cottage and said, 'Are ye goin' in? I've been keepin' an eye on the place. The letters are on the kitchen table. Hae ye got yer key?'

She nodded, jingling a ring of keys of different sizes. 'Come in with us, Eckie, and have a beer. It's very hot,' she said.

He needed no persuading. 'I dinna fancy beer but if there's

a wee nip goin' I widnae say no,' he admitted, following them to the front door. It was obvious that he wanted a closer look at Roddy.

The sitting room smelt fusty, so she opened the window, remembering the terrible night when Boyle came crashing through it feet first, determined to kill her. Eckie had saved her life but she hoped he would not mention that adventure. It still made her shake to talk about it.

The ancient fridge was purring away in the scullery, and, as she expected, there was a shelf of beer bottles gently frosting inside it. She fished out two lagers and poured the golden liquid into glasses while Eckie, who knew the house and all its contents better than she did, searched in the wall cupboard for a bottle of malt whisky. She handed him a glass and he poured out a modest measure.

'Do you want some water with that?' Roddy asked, getting up to fill a glass from the tap, but Eckie shook his head. 'It's a sin to spoil guid whisky wi' water. It's the water that kills folk, ye ken,' he said.

'I bet that's a prescription you didn't know,' laughed Rosa, and turning to Eckie she said, 'Roddy's a doctor.'

Eckie looked at him from under lowered grey brows. 'Weel, weel, a medical man are ye? I'm eighty-five and I've never consulted yin o' you lads in my life. I think that's why I've lasted so long.'

Rosa, vastly amused, said, 'You're never going to die. We'll have to shoot you, Eckie.'

He loved being teased. 'In that case I hope your aim's improved since the last time you were near a gun,' he said. The fond way he looked at her was a secret sign that he had no intention of talking about the Boyle adventure. It was Eckie's expertize with a gun that had stopped the murderer in his tracks.

She wondered what he made of Roddy because his opinion was very important to her.

They sat outside side by side on a rickety wooden bench under the kitchen window, eating grapes in the sun. With a sigh Rosa leant her head back against the rough stone wall

207

and closed her eyes, luxuriating in the heat given off by the multi-coloured boulders that long ago had been gathered from a nearby stream to build the house.

Roddy was leaning forward with his chin resting on his fists, staring around. 'This is a very peaceful place. It has tremendous atmosphere,' he said to Eckie.

'Aye, it's aye been like this. If the house likes the folk that live in it, it looks after them. Old wives used to believe in brownies. Hae ye ever heard o' brownies?' asked the old man.

Roddy shook his head. 'No, I'm a city man, I'm afraid.'

'Ah weel, ye canna help that. A brownie's a kind o'goblin chap. He does the heavy work in a hoose and guards the fire at night, if he likes you, but ye've got to treat him weel. When I was a laddie we aye put out a saucer o' cream every night for our brownie.'

Rosa opened her eyes. 'You never told me that before, Eckie,' she said.

'And I bet you do it still,' said Roddy with sharp perception.

'If I mind, but sometimes I think the dog gets it first,' said Eckie.

They all laughed, and Rosa stood up stretching her arms towards the sky. 'I'm going for a walk. Coming, Roddy?' She did not ask Eckie because he did not consider aimless walking worthwhile. During his working life as a shepherd he trudged fifteen or twenty miles a day, seven days a week, and in all weathers, over the local hills.

They headed for a hill behind the cottages and were both breathless when they flopped on to soft, sheep-cropped turf at the top. She pointed out Eckie's cottage, snuggling in a hidden hollow behind her father's, and over on the horizon the silver glitter of the water of St Mary's Loch.

'It's like fairyland. No wonder the people who live here believe in goblins,' he said.

Rosa was filled with affection for him, glad that he understood. Impulsively she leaned towards him and kissed him full on the mouth. He gasped and clutched her to him, fervently kissing her back. They lay a long time on the grass, and she let him run his hands over her, but when he tried to roll on top of her, she pushed him away.

'No, no,' she said.

He stopped and leaned on one arm looking at her. 'What are you afraid of?' he asked.

'I don't know. I just don't want that. I'm not ready. It's – it's too final somehow.' She'd heard Lawrie talking about 'cock teasers' who led men on and then refused to 'come up with the goods'. She hoped she was not one of them. Or could she be suffering from some sort of sexual hang-up. Was she frigid? Lawrie, the chief source of sexual information for her and Patricia, had been most scathing about frigid women. According to him they were beyond help or sympathy.

Roddy stood up, brushing grass from his trouser legs. 'Let's go back,' he said with dignity, holding out his hand.

She took it and rose too without speaking because she did not know what to say. Should she apologize? Should she pretend nothing had happened? Should she attempt to explain? The trouble was she did not know why she was acting as she did. Kissing him was very pleasant – but that was as far as she wanted it to go.

They were constrained during the walk back to the cottage where they found Eckie sitting on the bench in the setting sun with a pot of tea and a packet of ginger biscuits on a tray beside him.

'I saw ye comin' doon the hill so I put the kettle on. Are ye goin' back tae Edinburry or are ye spending the night here? Ye'd better put a fire on if ye are,' he said.

Rosa shook her head. 'We're going back, Eckie.' The last thing she wanted was the embarrassment of sleeping in her single bed when Roddy would obviously prefer them to climb together into the big double in the front bedroom where he would have to sleep alone.

Roddy said nothing.

Before they left, Eckie went back to his cottage and returned with two combs of honey from his bees. He kept four hives in the overgrown garden behind his house and it was a special honour to be given honey by him. As he handed a comb to Roddy he said, 'Now that's something you doctors dinna ken aboot – honey. It cures everything from rheumatics to ulcers. Ye dinna need your penny-cillin if you hae heather honey and there's naethin' better than a spoonfu' o' it in a glass of whisky for cheerin' ye up.'

Smiling, Roddy accepted it. 'I do need cheering up sometimes,' he said.

During the drive back to the city, she was awkward but he was wonderfully tactful and talked easily about Cyprus, its pretty villages and the archaeological sites he'd visited there. He said nothing about E.O.K.A. terrorists, and she felt he thought that to tell her about them would only worry her. *He doesn't realize that would interest me most of all*, she thought.

But she played her part and listened to him with interest, asking lots of questions, but inside she was distracted, resenting him relegating her to a woman's world where a female's only concerns were looking nice and nurturing her family.

At his mother's flat, he turned in his seat and asked, 'Will you be able to arrange some more days off?'

She nodded. 'I might.'

'In that case, would you like to come to London with me? My plane leaves from there on Sunday and I'd like to spend the rest of my leave with you – but not in Edinburgh. It would be good for us to go somewhere different and really enjoy ourselves. We can go to the theatre and visit some exhibitions. Will you come? If you like we can book into separate hotels . . .' he said, making her realize that he had been aware of her reluctance to spend the night with him in the cottage.

'That sounds wonderful,' she said. She had only been twice to London and it was like Mecca to her. Her greatest ambition was to work in Fleet Street and she'd walked along it three or four times on each visit, breathing in the heady smell of paper and printers' ink, staring in at the reception halls of big newspaper offices and imagining what it would be like to work there.

Roddy was pleased and surprised by her eager acceptance of his proposition. 'Good. I'll buy the train tickets. The afternoon train will be best because I'll be able to take my mother out for lunch – she likes to have me on her own for a little while before I go away. Meet me at the station at three o'clock. It'll be too late for the theatre when we get to London tomorrow but we can go to something on Saturday night,' he said.

She woke early next morning and knew without a shadow of doubt what she must do. Her life had reached a point where decisions had to be made; she could not go on playing games any longer.

Dressing quickly, she let herself out of the house and ran to the nearest phone box for she did not want Mrs Ross to overhear what she said. Her heart was beating fast as she dialled Roddy's mother's number. She hoped he would be the one to answer the phone, and he was.

In a rush she said, 'Roddy, it's Rosa. I've phoned to tell you that I can't go to London, much as I'd like to. I can't marry you either because I'm not in love with you, and I'd be cheating you if I did. I'm very sorry.'

His voice was calm and measured as he replied, 'Rosa, you are upset because of what happened with your friend. I'm not trying to rush you, and I quite understand if you don't want to go to London, but I'm not going to disappear from your life yet.'

She was distraught. 'I'm sorry, but you must. You make me feel guilty, even your reasonableness about this makes me guilty. I shouldn't keep you dangling because *I don't love you* and I never will. Please believe me. Goodbye.'

Then she hung up, knowing that she'd never see him again.

Twenty-Six

As summer faded into autumn, gossip and speculation about Patricia's death faded too.

The high blue skies of early October were replaced by grey clouds and drifting rain. The gloom of the weather depressed Rosa and she tried to divert herself from sad thoughts by concentrating on her work, finishing the MP series, which attracted a good deal of congratulatory interest, and then launching into a similar one about young Scottish artists. The galleries of the New Town were a good source of information and she was able to browse among works on show, picking out the most interesting. It soothed her to look at pictures, to examine the blending of colour, draughtmanship and brush work, to try to pick out artists who would become big names.

She began making new contacts, some of which might in time become friends, and her inner misery softened a little. Her father and Jean were in France, happily doing up their new home in Provence; Great Aunt Fanny was slowly fading away in her bungalow at Corstorphine; Roddy was back in Cyprus, but no longer writing or telephoning, much to Mrs Ross's disappointment; and the office seemed dull without ebullient Mike or sly but stimulating Lawrie. Sometimes Rosa looked around at her colleagues and was gripped by the fear that if she did not stir herself soon, she would end up like Harriet or Hilda, or even worse, like poor old Fanny.

To her surprise, Charles Rutland phoned her up one day and invited her to afternoon tea in Jenner's upstairs tea room. She still felt guarded about him, but he could be amusing when he chose and so she accepted his invitation.

The hushed ambience of the luxury store's tea room suited him very well. It was packed with conservatively dressed, very respectable older ladies who sipped from thin china cups with their little fingers politely sticking out.

As he rose in reputation among the journalistic hierarchy, Charles seemed to have become more old-maidish than ever. She saw with amusement that he surreptitiously sucked a Rennies tablet when he thought she was not looking, but in fact his skin had a glossy sheen and the whites of his eyes glittered like egg shells with health.

He gloried in gossip, and had some choice items to pass on: who was sleeping with who; whose wife was driven to lesbianism because of the failings of her spouse; who was confined in the drying-out wards of the Royal Edinburgh Hospital.

It distracted Rosa from her overwhelming gloom to sit with him. He had persuaded the waitress to give them one of the best tables in a window with a view of the Scott Monument on the other side of the road. The monument was a favourite place for suicides and Rosa deliberately chose to sit in a chair with its back to the window because she dreaded seeing someone leap over the parapet.

Remembering Jack's belief that some journalists had the power to make newsworthy things happen, she feared that the combination of herself and Charles might cause some terrible sort of upset. Scott Monument suicides always seemed to choose the middle of the day, when Princes Street, and Jenner's cafe, were crowded, for their terrible gestures of despair. That train of thought took Rosa back to Patricia. *Did she deliberately throw herself down the stairs?* she wondered.

She looked at the owlish young man sitting opposite her and wondered why he wanted to see her, for they had never been close. Eventually, after indulging in chit-chat, he got to the point. He wanted to talk about Patricia, and was anxious to go over what Rosa said at the inquest about her friend always drinking black coffee.

'I wonder why she went out to buy milk on the afternoon

213

she died. Was it because she was making tea for Hugh and Maitland Crewe, I wonder?' he said.

'I doubt it. Knowing Patricia, if they wanted tea, she'd probably tell them to make it themselves. Besides, it was a very hot day, so they were probably drinking beer or something cold,' Rosa replied.

Charles nodded slowly. 'Yes, I'd forgotten. It was a hot day, wasn't it? But I saw Hugh at Blackie House when her body was being carried out, and he was wearing a thick polo neck sweater in spite of the heat. I remember pulling at his sleeve. I thought it odd at the time . . .'

Rosa snorted. 'He's a cold piece of work. I think he pushed her – maybe by accident, maybe not. Oh, I shouldn't have said that. He's warned me that he'll sue me for slander if I do. Forget it, please.'

He did not say whether or not he shared her suspicions, but he reassured her, 'I've forgotten already.'

'I didn't know you were at Blackie House the afternoon she died,' said Rosa curiously.

He nodded. 'I was in the courtyard when they brought her out. Ned Ingram sent me up to her flat to find out why she hadn't turned up for an appointment at five o'clock.'

'How did Hugh behave?' Rosa asked.

'He seemed upset, but in control of himself,' said Charles.

'Did you see Maitland Crewe, too?' she asked.

'Not then.'

'I met him at the Royal Scottish Academy the other day and he was really going for the free wine, swigging it back like a man in the desert . He didn't used to drink like that. I wonder if Patricia's death has affected him,' said Rosa.

'I see him sometimes. He doesn't seem too bad to me,' Charles told her lightly and changed the conversation to a rumour that Jack was on the verge of resigning his editorship of the *Dispatch*.

She stared at him in horror and said, 'If he goes, I won't be able to stand Edinburgh. The paper would be too boring for words without him.'

'Then my advice is to start collecting your cuttings and

writing off for another job,' he said with the air of a man who had organized his own future prospects to his own satisfaction.

Her old dislike of him came back. *You smug so and so*, she thought.

He did not invite her out again and it was a surprise to see him next in the Press Club with Hugh and Maitland Crewe. She was in the lounge, looking through the serving hatch, when she saw the three of them standing together and looking very companionable. *My God, I hope he really has forgotten what I said about Maling*, she thought.

Before she left, she asked the steward if Charles had become a Press Club regular. He nodded. 'Yes, he comes in quite a lot these days with Mr Maling and Mr Crewe.'

So much for loyalty to Patricia, thought Rosa. If she bumped into Maling these days, she ignored him – and he ignored her.

What she did not know was that Charles had seen her peeping through the serving hatch into the Press Club bar – women were not allowed in there, and a good thing too, according to Hugh.

It was a pity, he thought, that he could not tell her that he had a good reason for socializing with Maling and his friend. He was avid for information because Patricia's death obsessed him and the coroner's verdict had not stopped his speculations or satisfied his curiosity.

She had become a dream figure for him, the ideal woman. Never again would he meet anyone like her – so beautiful, glamorous or sharp-witted. Like an Arthurian knight, he took up the cause of avenging her because something told him there was an unsolved mystery about her death.

If she did fall accidentally, he wanted to know why she was in such a hurry that she lost her footing. If the fall was not accidental, did she throw herself downstairs? Why do something like that? Was it to draw attention to her unhappiness? If a deliberate fall was not the explanation, was Rosa right to suspect she had been pushed?

Every time Charles sat drinking with Hugh, he studied the

other man's face, weighed up every word he said, speculated about what might be passing, unspoken, through his mind.

Maitland Crewe was another object of his scrutiny. The man was cracking up. Shamelessly, Charles pushed his way into their acquaintance, though Maling tried to rebuff him, and when they met up, Crewe had usually been drinking already. By the time he was on to his second pint, he began slurring his words and staggering when he tried to stand up.

He was a lachrymose drunk, often bursting into tears. One night, drunker than usual, he began groaning, 'It's awful, it's awful', and Maling became extremely exasperated with him. In fact, he seemed apprehensive as he hurriedly propelled his friend out of the club and into a taxi, berating him as they went, 'If Sonya's giving you trouble, kick the bitch out. It's your house, isn't it? I don't know why you put up with her. She's forever on your neck.'

After he despatched Crewe home, he came back and said to Charles, 'He's desperate because his wife's sleeping with that friend of his who works in the Lyceum Theatre.'

Charles had met the friend. 'But I thought he was queer,' he said.

'That's just an alibi!' snorted Hugh.

The next time they met in the Press Club, Hugh began giving his friend Maitland a lecture. 'You've got to sort yourself out. You've not gone hill walking or bird watching for weeks, have you? And your work's slipping. If you don't come up with another feature soon, the Beeb'll fire you,' he said.

Crewe nodded miserably. 'I know. I've been thinking about that. This Sunday I'm going to walk along the shore at Cramond and do some recording. Do you want to come? You could act the part of an interested spectator and I could feed you information about the birds.'

'I'd like to do that,' interrupted Charles eagerly.

Hugh Maling glared at him. 'I'll come too,' he said. It was obvious he did not want someone else taking over his friend.

The walk was pleasant. Crewe was sober and very

216

informative and said that Charles, playing the spectator, had a good radio voice and would come over well.

'I've made up my mind that next weekend I'll do the piece about the peregrines at Loch Skeen. It'll soon be winter and when the weather gets bad, it's hard walking up there, so I have to record it now. Do either of you want to come?' he said as they were parting that evening.

Again, when Charles accepted, so, grudgingly, did Hugh, who said, 'Have you any idea how hard it is walking over the Dumfriesshire hills, Rutland?'

'I'm not a weakling and I'm used to walking,' was the reply.

'Pavement pounding maybe. This is different. Have you any walking gear – boots, things like that?'

'We don't need hiking boots for Loch Skeen. Wellingtons do well enough. We'll walk a circuit of the loch and that's only seven miles. On a fine day, it's really little more than a stroll and if the weather's bad, we won't go,' Crewe told them.

Though inwardly he dreaded taking such intensive exercise, Charles made himself look eager. 'That'll be wonderful. I hope it's a good day!' he enthused.

Twenty-Seven

Ned Ingram was a close friend of Leo Fairley, with whom he often dined in the Cafe Royal.

They were sitting at the Oyster Bar when Ned told Leo that Charles Rutland was trying hard to take Patricia's place in the office, though he had not yet found a worthwhile story to get his teeth into.

Leo sipped his wine and shook his head. 'You'll have to watch that guy. He's dodgy,' he said.

'He writes well,' said Ned cautiously.

'Yeah, he has a good style, but you know and I know that he doesn't draw the line between fact and fiction. He can't stop himself gilding the lily. Even if a story is good, he dresses it up. It's like being a kleptomaniac – he's driven to overstep the mark. That could get him – and you – into trouble,' said Leo.

Ned demurred, 'I've warned him about that and I think he's taken the message on board. You just don't like him. Do you feel he's young blood elbowing you out?'

'Not a bit. It's only that I believe in journalistic integrity and he's never heard of it. I've been taking the trouble to check up on some of his *scoops* and several of them are phonies. Remember the one about a wolf escaping from the zoo? That caused a hell of a to-do but the keepers are pretty sure that no animal ever got out that day. They are very fed up about it. And what about the bowler-hatted beggars? Nobody but him ever laid eyes on one, did they? Take my advice, read all his copy very carefully and ask for proof and pictures.'

Leo was serious and, though Ned laughed, the conversation stuck in his mind.

Charles was well aware of his new boss's reservations and went out of his way to be obliging and pleasant while inwardly yearning for an opportunity to make Ned's eyes light up with admiration. He wanted more good stories for his cuttings book because he intended to move on eventually, but not yet. He had unfinished business with Hugh Maling and would stay around till that was concluded to his satisfaction.

Three days before the planned walk round Loch Skeen, a glue factory in Fountainbridge went up in flames. It made such a spectacular conflagration that even the latest bulletin from the Suez Canal was driven off the front pages. Fire engines from all over the city went clanging towards the leaping flames and thick black column of smoke that rose over the tenement roofs to the west of the Old Town.

Charles went to cover the story, but when he wheedled his way past the cordon of police who were holding spectators back from the factory buildings, he found reporters from all the other papers there as well.

Friendly, disingenuous Pat was covering the story for the *Dispatch* and hurried over to say, 'It's not as bad as it looks. All the workers and people living round about are safe. The fire brigade's getting it under control.'

That's a pity, thought Charles. His eye fell on a group of women in overalls who were huddling from the rain in a doorway opposite him, staring at the burning building and chattering among themselves.

Pat said, 'I'm going back to the office now because Jack wants a piece for the last edition.'

Hunching his shoulders inside his raincoat, and stubbing out his cigarette end with the toe of his shoe, he prepared to leave. Charles hastened him on his way by saying, 'There's nothing much here for me either. I'll go back as well in a couple of minutes.'

As soon as Pat was out of sight, he went over to the women, turning on his little boy charm and asking if they'd had a very frightening experience.

They were phlegmatic. All that worried them was that

219

they'd had to leave their shopping bags and handbags inside the factory when the fire broke out.

'I had a pound o'mince in my bag. It'll be a burnt offering by noo. God knows what I'll gie my man for his tea the night,' said a very fat woman.

Her friend, a thin little scrap with a kindly face and spectacles, said, 'Buy him fish and chips, Nellie. Isn't it a mercy that Kitty died last month? It would've been awfy if she got caught in the fire, wouldn't it?'

'You and that cat! Can ye no' stop talking aboot it. The thing's deed, Ina. It died of auld age. Maybe if the insurance pays up the boss'll get anither yin for ye to cuddle,' said Nellie roughly.

Charles succeeded in ingratiating himself with them so successfully that they were happy to tell him their names, addresses, and even ages, but not until after the usual jocular challenge, 'Hoo auld de ye think I am then, laddie?'

By this time he'd learned to deduct at least ten years from any estimate and that softened them up even more. When he went back to his office, they waved him off cheerfully.

He knew it was an unexciting story. It would be lucky to make the next day's paper at all. He could not help himself. The old imp perched on his shoulder whispering in his ear. When he sat down to type, his fingers flew over the keys and another wonderful piece of fiction emerged:

> At the factory fire, an animal lover, Mrs Ina Ballantine, 41, of 14 Lauriston Place, risked her life to rush back into the flames and rescue Kitty, the factory cat.
>
> The police and the fire brigade warned her against trying to save it but she would not listen to them. Hearing it mewing pitifully from an upstairs window, she fought her way out of a policeman's grasp and rushed up the burning stairs to save the animal. When a fireman pulled them both out through a window, Mrs Ballantine's clothes were singed but the cat was safe.
>
> She took it home and gave it a supper of sardines.

*   *   *

220

When Ned read this story, he gasped, 'That's good!'

He ran his eye over it again. Charles had put in the woman's name and address. It had to be true.

'We need a picture of this cat with the woman that saved it. Tell the picture desk to send someone to Lauriston Place now,' he said.

A surge of fear ran through Charles as he remembered Ned's warning against making things up. He'd never get another good job if the *Express* fired him. 'Let me warn her that we're coming,' he said quickly. 'She's bound to be a bit shocked after all that excitement. She might have needed medical attention.'

Ned clasped his hands. 'That's even better. We'll get her with bandages on feeding the cat.'

Charles was struggling into his coat and trying to look enthusiastic. 'I'll go to warn her now. Give me time to soften her up. Tell the photographer to follow me in half an hour,' he said.

Ned agreed. There was no heavy pressure of time on the *Express* as there was on the *Dispatch* because *Express* stories need not be filed until late evening. 'All right, off you go,' he told Charles, who was thinking fast.

Lauriston Place was not his first stop. Instead he went straight to the little pet shop in Fleshmarket Close. Fortunately it was still open, so he rushed in and said to the proprietor, 'Have you any cats for sale?'

'I've kittens but nae cats,' was the reply.

'Give me a kitten then. The biggest one you have.'

The man reached into a basket in the window and hauled out a black and white kitten that opened it mouth and gave an indignant miaow.

Charles did not ask its name or its sex. 'How much?' he asked grabbing his wallet out of his inner pocket.

'Two pound,' said the man, because he saw this was a sucker customer. Kittens usually sold for five bob each.

Charles passed over the money and was given his kitten in a thick brown paper carrier. 'Watch it doesn't claw its way oot. You'd best put it under your jacket and button it in,' said the pet shop man.

With a struggling, fighting kitten inside his jacket, Charles ran all the way to Lauriston Place. To his relief, Mrs Ballantine was alone when he got there. Opening the door to him, she smiled in recognition and then jumped back in surprise as he reached inside his coat to haul out a spitting, struggling black and white scrap of feline fury.

'I brought you a cat, Mrs Ballantine,' he gasped. His chest felt as if it had been flayed by the bloody animal's claws ripping through his shirt.

'That's awfy kind o' ye,' she said, stepping back cautiously.

'You haven't got one already, have you?' he asked.

She shook her head. 'No, my man doesnae like them, but I do and that's why I made sic a fuss o' the old cat at work.'

'Well, here's another one to fuss over,' said Charles, stepping inside her door.

She took the cat with reluctance. 'I dinna ken if I can keep it. My man, ye see . . .'

He decided to come clean. 'Mrs Ballantine, please take it. My career depends on you taking it. I've written a story about you taking the factory cat home with you and if you haven't got a cat when our photographer turns up, I'll be fired!' he gasped.

This astonished her. 'Oh, I dinna ken,' she demurred.

He put the cat on the seat of a chair and clasped her hands. 'Mrs Ballantine, I'm not joking. I will be fired if you don't take this cat. I'm only starting my career with the *Express* and my wife and child will be destitute if I lose my job. Please help us!'

'Oh my goodness! You're sure all I have to do is take your cat?' she quavered. She was a kind woman.

He still hung on to her hands, shaking them up and down slightly as he spoke, 'Yes, take it and call it Kitty. I said it was the cat from the factory, you see. The one you liked. A photographer from my paper is coming now to take a picture of you with it.'

She stared into his pleading brown eyes. He looked so distressed and genuine that she gave in. 'Oh, all right. If my husband doesnae like it, I'll gie it to the wee lassie next door.'

This time the tears in his eyes were genuine. 'Mrs Ballantine, you are a saint. You've saved my life,' he said.

When the photographer arrived, he did not hang around or make conversation apart from saying to Mrs Ballantine, 'Look up, please. Give us a smile.'

When he left, Charles shook her hand and thanked her profusely for her help. Then he too went away, leaving her with the cat.

His story appeared next day beside a touching photograph of Mrs Ballantine cuddling the cat, and he got a big byline.

When he read the story, Leo Fairley was furious and phoned his friend Ned to say, 'I was at that bloody fire and I never saw any woman running in to rescue a cat.'

Ned sighed. 'Come on, Leo. We have a photograph of her with it for God's sake!'

Leo was not satisfied. 'Don't make too much of it. I'm following this up, Ned,' he warned.

Because the international news was so depressing, with slaughter going on in Hungary and a war in Suez, newspaper readers seized on a happy story with relief.

Mrs Ina Ballantine became a heroine, and dignitaries of the R.S.P.C.A. turned up at her house to congratulate her, but the heroine of the hour kept on saying, 'I dinna deserve a' this.'

'Of course you do. You're too modest,' gushed a large lady who was head of a local Kindness to Animals committee that intended to put Mrs Ballantine up for an award.

Leo Fairley lurked at the back of the gathering. 'Where's the cat then?' he asked loudly. Fortunately Mr Ballantine had not insisted that his wife give the animal away and it was sleeping in a basket by the gas fire. Leo lifted it up and said, 'It's not very old, is it? What do you call it?'

Mrs Ballantine, who was wishing she'd never been inveigled into this, looked shifty and said its name was Kitty. Leo cuddled the cat. 'Do you mind if I take it to let a friend see it?' he asked innocently.

She said she didn't mind at all, and even loaned him a zip up shopping bag to carry it in. He rushed round to a local vet's surgery, thrusting the kitten under the nose of the vet, who he knew because they often drank in the same hostelry. 'How old is this and what sex is it?' he asked.

The vet examined the struggling cat and said, 'It's about eight weeks old and it's a male.'

When Leo bore his burden back to Lauriston Place, he said, 'Mrs Ballantine, you did not save this cat from a fire, did you? You've been telling lies!'

She burst into tears. 'Oh dear, it wasnae me. It was that other laddie. The one who said he'd lose his job if I didnae tak' the cat. He said he has a wife and a bairn. Oh, I'm awfy sorry. I didnae mean all this tae happen. I dinna even want the cat!'

Delighted, Leo clapped her on the shoulder. 'I'm not going to make trouble for you but you're quite right to tell the truth. Here's a tenner for your trouble, and don't you worry.'

Next morning, the *Daily Mail* scooped the *Express* with a full page spread under the headline '**The Great Pretender**' written by Leo. First of all he demolished the rescued cat story, telling of Ina Ballantine's tearful rebuttal of Charles' fabrication, and then went on to disprove several other of Rutland's stories, including the bowler-hatted beggars and the escapee from the zoo.

'This man is a disgrace to journalism. He's the sort of journalist that gives our profession a bad name. He takes away credibility from anything people read in newspapers. What happened to ethics?' declaimed Leo.

Ned Ingram, very trim in a dark blue suit, a white shirt and a painful-looking boiled collar, was sitting at his desk with folded hands on top of a copy of the *Daily Mail* when Charles turned up for work.

'Have you see the *Mail*, Mr Rutland?' he asked, throwing the paper at Charles.

'Not yet,' said Charles.

'Page seven will interest you,' said Ned.

Charles turned to the relevant page and read for a bit. His face was drawn when he finished and he looked at Ned without saying anything. They stared at each other in silence for what seemed an age.

'Do you want to write a reply?' asked Ned.

'I could try,' said Charles.

'On second thoughts, don't bother. You're fired. And let me tell you something else, Mr Rutland. Because of this, you will never find a job on a decent newspaper again. I have contacts everywhere and I'll put the word round so don't waste paper writing letters of application.' Ned was coldly furious.

Twenty-Eight

It was arranged that unless the weather was very bad, Hugh, Maitland and Charles would meet at the arch into Lady Stair's Close at nine o'clock on Saturday morning. By 'very bad', Crewe meant torrential rain.

In the morning, it was raining, but only a typical Edinburgh drizzle. Charles dressed quickly putting on three layers of sweater, a waterproof coat, a cloth cap and new thick-soled, lace-up boots with ridged soles which he had bought the previous day from the sports shop in Princes Street.

He left home at eight o'clock. Edinburgh's air was redolent of hops and yeast because the breweries were working flat out. The smell that hung everywhere was so strong, he felt that if he breathed in deeply it would go to his head.

For the last half mile, he ran, clomping in the heavy boots. It was important to be on time for the rendezvous because he feared if he was late, Hugh Maling would go without him. He was eager to go for several reasons; it would take his mind off worrying about what was going to happen to him and where he would find work, but, more importantly, he was determined to find out exactly what had happened to Patricia before he had to leave Edinburgh and this could be his last chance.

He was right that Maling was reluctant to let him share the outing. Though he arrived at the meeting point ten minutes before the deadline, Crewe's snub-nosed black Ford, was waiting in the roadway with its engine idling.

Maling, looking thunderous, was in the passenger seat. 'Get in!' he snapped.

'I'm not late,' protested Charles as he climbed into the car.

Crewe looked over his shoulder at the back seat passenger and said, 'Hugh wanted me to go without you, but I insisted on waiting.' His eyes were glistening brightly and Charles wondered whether he was excited or drunk.

As they drove out of Edinburgh towards Penicuik and Peebles, Crewe talked enthusiastically about their destination. 'It's high in the hills above a waterfall called the Grey Mare's Tail between Selkirk and Moffat. The loch is three quarters of a mile long and it's a wonderful place for naturalists because peregrines breed on a hill called the Dragon's Snout and a big herd of feral goats have roamed around there since time began. We'll see them, I'm sure. I'm really looking forward to making this programme.'

Charles said little and did not tell his companions that Ned Ingram had fired him the previous day. If they did not know already, they'd soon find out. He made some encouraging noises to please Crewe, but Maling sat grim-faced and silent, staring out of the window. It was obvious he was sulking – why had he come?

As they passed through Peebles and took the hilly road to the Yarrow Valley, Crewe's mood changed and he lost patience with his front seat companion.

'You're not happy about this, are you? Do you want me to leave you at the Gordon Arms Hotel and pick you up on the way back? Don't you feel up to a bit of exercise?'

Maling glared at him and said, 'I'm fitter than you are. Drink's softening you up.'

Crewe shrugged. 'Maybe I have a reason to drink. A long walk will clear my head, I hope.'

'It'll take more than a seven-mile walk to do that.'

'You could be right. What do you think I need? A father confessor?'

Maling turned his head and looked out of the window. His mouth had a sour, downward turn and he looked angry. 'That's up to you,' he snapped.

They drove past the Gordon Arms Hotel that stood bleakly

on an isolated crossroads, and from there the road snaked along the north shore of St Mary's Loch. The water was utterly smooth and looked like burnished silver. At the end of the loch there was a little inn, standing a short way off the road.

'That's Tibbieshiels. We'll have a meal there after our walk. They serve a great mixed grill and the beer's good,' said Maitland Crewe, who seemed to have cheered up again.

The Grey Mare's Tail, an immensely high waterfall of rushing white foam, took Charles's breath away. It was the sort of dramatic cataract he imagined would only be found in Scandinavia or Switzerland.

Crewe parked the car in a lay-by beside a humpback stone bridge, and said, 'Right, we're here. All out!'

The rain had stopped and there were a few patches of pale blue in the sky. Crewe sniffed the air and said, 'It's going to stay dry but it'll be windy and cold. Wrap up well.'

Charles had taken the precaution of bringing a woollen muffler, winding it round his neck and ears. Clapping his gloved hands together, he began to feel excited by this manly expedition though it was something in which he had never imagined taking part. He stamped his feet in the heavy boots and noticed that, while Crewe had boots like his but more battered, Maling was wearing heavy Wellingtons.

They set off in single file, climbing a steep path beside the tumbling water that Crewe said was called the Tail Burn. He was bent to one side by the weight of the heavy Uher recording machine that swung from his right shoulder. 'Stay on the path. It'll be slippery after all the rain. Going up isn't too bad, but you have to be very careful coming back down this bit because it's the dangerous part. Quite a few people have been killed here,' he called back to the other two as they climbed the steepest slope. On their left, far below, the waterfall stormed and raged through a rocky canyon.

Charles thought Maitland's remark wasn't particularly tactful, but Maling did not seem to notice, only bent his head and marched on behind Crewe. Charles brought up the rear and was puffing and breathless when they finally reached the flat ground far above the road.

Maling looked back at him and laughed. 'Are you going to make it or do you want to drop out now?' he jeered.

Crewe stopped and put his Uher on the ground. 'We'll take a stop to let you catch your breath,' he said. Then he reached into his pocket and brought out a half bottle of whisky wrapped in a bandanna. He opened it and took a long swig before passing it to Charles. 'Have some,' he said. He was smiling and cheerful.

Charles shook his head. Maling too refused when it was offered to him, but sneered as he said, 'I don't need Dutch courage.' The look he gave Crewe was like the stare of a man about to take part in a duel, and Charles felt the atmosphere between them spark as if it was infused with electricity.

The path followed the burn to the head of a long loch. Near its shore there was an small island on which one tall silver birch tree was growing. Crewe pointed at it and said, 'That's the only tree you'll see up here and it's survived because it's on an island. The sheep and goats that graze these hills eat every sapling before it grows into a tree.'

He produced a microphone and held it out to Charles. 'Tell me what it's like,' he said as he turned on the recorder.

Charles looked around. 'It's like the landscape of the moon and there's nothing growing except grass and one tree, not even any heather . . . It's awe-inspiring. I feel as if I'm on the roof of the world. What are those mounds all over the moor? Has there been quarrying up here at one time?'

Crewe, enjoying himself, leaned over and spoke into the mike, 'No, they're called moraines and they are heaps of gravel deposited from a glacier that swept through here at the end of the Ice Age.'

Then he switched the mike off and said, 'That was good. We'll do some more at the other end of the loch.'

They walked for half an hour without speaking, heads down against a strong wind. At the far end of the loch, they huddled with their backs against a bank of earth and Charles, prompted by Crewe, described the Deacon's Snout and the slowly circling falcons that soared around it. He was genuinely impressed and did not need to force himself to sound enthusiastic.

Maling sat silent, eating sandwiches from a packet he produced from his pocket. Then, without explanation, he got to his feet and walked off, heading away from the path. Crewe switched off the machine and watched him go. There was a strange expression on his face when he brought out his whisky again and drank it down. Charles watched most of it disappear. The effect it had on Crewe was unexpected – instead of cheering him up, this time it made him morose.

He leaned towards Charles and said, 'Listen. I want you to do something for me. Don't let Maling walk next to me on the way down the hill.'

Charles stared. 'What do you mean?'

'What I say. Don't let him walk behind me. Keep between us. He's in a strange mood. I shouldn't have brought him here. He's capable of it, you know, he did it to her.'

Charles caught his breath. 'Capable of what?'

'Capable of shoving me off the path. It was when I told you both about the people who've fallen down into the gorge that I realized. All it takes is a little push. With a fingertip even. He knows that. I should have kept my mouth shut. He thinks I've brought him here deliberately to remind him.'

'Remind him of Patricia, you mean?'

'Remind him of shoving her down the stairs. He's scared of me because I know what happened. He'll not be happy till he's rid of me one way or another,' said Crewe.

Charles wished the whisky was being offered round again, but Crewe was drinking it himself and was not for sharing now. 'What happened?' Charles persisted.

The other man looked wildly at him. 'She ran along the hall and opened the front door when she found us in bed. He ran after her. He thought she was going to shout to the neighbours – but *she* grabbed hold of *him* and tried to push him out into the landing. She shouted that he was to get out of her house and take me with him.'

'You were in bed?' repeated Charles astonished.

230

'We used to sometimes, but not often and never since . . .' Crewe's face looked ravaged.

'What happened next?' It was essential not to allow Crewe to stop speaking now.

He shrugged. 'They struggled. She lost her balance. She was on the edge of the stairs. She fell. She didn't have time to shout. He says he didn't push her, and maybe he didn't, but if I told what I saw he'd be up for manslaughter, if not for murder. He had hold of her . . . When we went down to see if she was still alive, her eyes were wide open in surprise. I don't think I'll ever forget it.'

Charles put his head between his hands and gasped, 'That's hellish. She was so young and lovely.'

Crewe nodded. 'Yes, she was. She still looked lovely lying at the foot of the stairs.'

'What did you do when you realized she was dead?' Charles wanted to know.

'We got dressed. He put on a big sweater because she'd scratched his chest with her long fingernails. He told me what to say and then he phoned 999 for an ambulance. He's kept his eye on me ever since because he's afraid that I'll tell somebody. Where is he anyway?'

Charles stood up and looked round at the empty land that now had taken on a look of sinister isolation. 'He's over there, looking around,' he said.

'I don't trust him. He's up to something. Remember and keep between us. He'll not try anything on with you here,' said Crewe.

Charles was not so sure. Somehow he must arrange it so that he was last in line when they came to the dangerous part of the walk.

For the first part of the return walk, he was in the middle of the single file and the path was nowhere broad enough for them to walk abreast. Crewe strode ahead, outdistancing them. He was by far the fittest in spite of Maling's jibes about his drinking, and it was obvious that he was trying to lose them.

By making strenuous efforts, he succeeded in putting

231

about twenty-five yards between him and Charles, who found it impossible to keep up because his heart was pounding and his breath rasping in his lungs. When a terrible stitch bent him double, he was forced to stop, and bent forward in the middle of the path with his hands on his knees and his head hanging down. Through bleary eyes, he saw Crewe's figure far in front and panic seized him. 'All it takes is a little push . . .' The words rang through his brain.

A little push, a gentle shove, a tap on the shoulder – who was to push first? Why not him? His suspicions about Patricia were confirmed and even if Maling hadn't deliberately pushed her, he was responsible for her death. He deserved to die.

Gasping and choking, he heard Maling coming up behind him. 'All puffed out?' he scoffed.

Charles nodded. 'You go on. I'll follow,' he managed to say and stepped back from the path. It was made of loose gravel and the fringing grass was wet and slippery.

Maling passed him, but though he was not prepared to admit it, he too was tired and was walking fairly slowly now. With a huge effort of will, Charles stepped behind him and kept up to his pace.

'I don't want to be left behind,' he managed to say.

Maling did not turn his head but a laugh drifted back over his shoulder. The wind had risen even more and any words were swept away into infinity.

Keep up, keep up, keep up! Charles chanted the words inside his head. He must stay close to Maling, close enough to reach out and touch him.

By this time they were descending the hill and the path narrowed even more. Beneath his boots bits of gravel crunched and tiny stones fell away into the void on his left-hand side. It was essential not to stare down, to keep his eyes on his feet, to plant each one carefully. The sound of rushing water filled his ears but he did not look down into it.

Crewe was in front, out of reach and moving fast and,

though Maling seemed to be making an effort to catch up with him, he had too big a lead. Charles lifted his head and saw Maling's waterproof jacket filling his vision. They were at the narrowest and most dangerous part of the path. It was now or never.

He opened his mouth and shouted with the full force of his lungs, 'PATRICIA!'

Maling's stride faltered. Charles took an extra big step, remembering to put his foot down very firmly. With his left arm extended he leaned forward and pushed at the other man's shoulder. 'PATRICIA!' he shouted again.

Maling was turning his head, his mouth open to ask a question. Taken by surprise, the shove disoriented him and his rubber-booted foot slipped. Charles stopped dead as Maling tumbled sideways and disappeared over the slippery slope. The fingers of his hands were clenching horribly in an effort to find a hold but there was nothing, not even a sprig of heather. Propelled by his own weight, he disappeared over the canyon edge without uttering a sound.

Charles knelt on the crumbling gravel and stared into the void. All he saw was a surging torrent of water far below. Hugh Maling's body had disappeared. He shouted, but nothing and nobody heard him except a few startled birds and three grey-black goats on the top of a hill that raised their heads in surprise.

Twenty-Nine

The general reaction to Hugh Maling's death was incredulity.

It seemed too much of a coincidence for him also to be killed in a fall only a few weeks after his wife. Newspaper reports made a great deal of the similarity between the accidents, and Leo Fairley wrote that the 'fickle finger of fate' had picked out the couple.

An accident inquiry was held but it was only a token. The police and everyone else agreed that Hugh's death was definitely an accident. The path where he fell was notoriously dangerous and he was wearing rubber boots with worn soles.

Charles Rutland gave his testimony in tears and was assured by the coroner that he was in no way to blame.

Maitland Crewe told the hearing that he had been walking some distance in front of Hugh, and that Charles was a good bit farther on behind him. After the hearing, Crewe's wife Sonya signed him into an alcohol drying-out establishment near Peebles where he languished for six weeks. When he came out, they emigrated to America.

After the inquiry, Charles Rutland disappeared. Though the press waited for him outside the court building, he simply vanished, for he had been shown out of a side door by a sympathetic policeman. He did not say goodbye to any of his ex-colleagues, but packed up his possessions and checked out of Mayfield Road without leaving a forwarding address.

On her twenty-fourth birthday in November, Rosa was still on the *Dispatch*, and so was Jack. Both, however, were restless and anxious to make changes in their lives. Rosa spent her days in a dreamlike state and sometimes found it difficult to accept that so much had happened in such a short time.

Great-aunt Fanny died soon after Patricia and Maling's violent deaths. She was found in her armchair with her spectacles on her nose and the *Scotsman* on her lap, looking as if she'd fallen asleep. She left Rosa her bungalow and a letter advising her to sell it and use the money for foreign travel. 'I have always wished I was more adventurous myself,' the old lady wrote.

All the people who had been close to Rosa were gone: her father and Jean were in another country; Roddy was out of her life forever; Hugh Maling and Patricia were dead. The loss of Patricia was the most difficult to accept and every time Rosa walked up the High Street, she half expected to bump into her friend.

To her it seemed fit retribution for Maling to die the way he did, but she wished she'd been able to question Charles Rutland about the accident for she remembered his anger and anguish about Patricia's death and wondered if there was another untold story that she would never hear.

The money from Fanny's bungalow was a responsibility. She could almost sense it lying in her bank, jingling away like a constant reminder that she ought to be doing something adventurous. But she was in limbo, getting up in the morning, going to the office, and churning out copy that she knew was uninspired. Jack did not seem to care any more because he was sunk in the same state of indifference as she was.

When he leaned in characteristic pose on his table and surveyed his staff, he found it hard to summon up any feelings for them, but one afternoon he beckoned to Rosa and said, 'Have you thought about looking for another job? It's time you moved on.'

She shrugged. 'I don't know if I want to stay in journalism.'

'Something else in mind?' he asked.

'Not really,' she said.

'If you like, I'll give you a letter of introduction to a friend of mine on the *Mirror*,' he said.

She was surprised, because she genuinely did not think she was ready for the big time. 'I don't know if I could keep up the pace in Fleet Street,' she said.

'Don't be a wimp. You should try,' said Jack. 'Let me know if you want a letter. I'm not going to waste my time writing it if you'll not use it. In the meantime, what about doing some work? I need some features. Any ideas?'

She remembered some information she'd picked up when visiting a New Town art gallery. 'I heard about an artist living near Eyemouth who's been commissioned to paint a twelve-foot wide scene of the Battle of Minden,' she said.

Jack was startled out of his apathy. 'Twelve feet. Like a bloody Michaelangelo! The battle of what?'

'Minden. It's in Germany. In 1759 during the Seven Years' War, the British and Prussians defeated the French and Austrians there. To this day the British regiments involved wear red roses in their hats on Minden Day, August 1st. The King's Own Scottish Borderers were at the battle and this big picture's being painted for their mess.'

Jack liked stories with a historical angle. 'Red roses! That sounds great. Go down to see the guy. Take a photographer. I need five hundred words and two good pictures,' he said.

The Basher was alone in the photography department and she had not seen him for some time. 'Jack wants a photo feature on a painter in Eyemouth,' she said.

'When?' he asked, as terse as ever.

'As soon as possible.'

'Tomorrow?' he said and she nodded.

The next morning was crisp and bright with frost shimmering on the grass. The air tasted like chilled champagne and had an invigorating effect on her.

On the A1 heading south past Dunbar and North Berwick, her spirits rose and she began to feel there might be some reason for living after all. The Basher was sitting silently staring out of the window and she smiled when she remembered his dance routine down the Fleshmarket Close steps.

'Done any dancing recently?' she asked.

He looked surprised. 'Me? Dancing? Not much. I used to go to the Palais but I've given that up.'

She looked at him with curiosity. 'What *do* you do?' she asked.

'This and that. I walk a lot and take pictures. I play football. I go to the theatre. I play the saxophone . . .'

She laughed. 'You play the saxophone! I'd never have believed it. Are you any good?'

'Not bad. I'm in a band. I like music.'

'You're a dark horse,' she said.

He laughed as he replied, 'Maybe.'

'Where do you live?' she asked, going on with her inquisition. He had always been the most reticent of her colleagues and she knew little about him.

'I have a flat in Danube Street,' he told her.

She grinned and said, 'An interesting street.' The most famous brothel in Edinburgh was there. He said nothing and because he offered no more information, she persisted, 'Do you live on your own?'

'Yeah.'

Unlike some of the other bachelors she knew, he was always very clean, and his shirts looked freshly laundered as if he came from a home with a careful mother. 'Where do your family live?' she asked.

'I don't know.' He was lighting a cigarette and squinting as he held the match to its end.

'Want one?' he asked and she shook her head. She was not going to let him divert her. 'You don't know where your family are? Did you run away or something?'

He drew on the cigarette and turned to look straight at her, as he said, 'I'm a Barnardo's boy. As far as I know my mother was an Irish girl who came to Edinburgh to have me and left me in the orphanage.'

She felt impertinent. 'I'm sorry. I shouldn't have been so nosy,' she said.

237

'It doesn't matter. Being given away means that there's nothing holding you back and nobody expecting anything from you. It's a kind of an advantage,' he said.

'I'm sorry,' she said again lamely.

'Forget it,' he replied and they drove along in silence for a while till he asked, 'Where exactly are we going?'

She had a note of the painter's address stuck on the shelf behind the steering wheel and passed it to him. 'To there. The painter is doing an amazing battle scene – twelve feet wide,' she said.

He folded the paper and put it in his pocket. 'I know where that is. It's near an estate with famous gardens that I was sent down to photograph last year.'

The artist, a shock-haired young man in a blue smock, was cordial and happy to co-operate with them, posing for pictures before his cottage and in his studio where there were several canvases propped against a table.

The Minden scene was roughed out on an enormous spread of white canvas pinned along a wall. There were battling men and dying horses, officers with their swords held high and Frenchmen bleeding to death beneath their horses' hooves. You could almost hear the cries of the dying and the clashing of arms.

The painter's wife gave the visitors a lunch of bread and cheese with glasses of beer and they were cheerful when they drove away.

As they headed back towards Edinburgh, The Basher suddenly said, 'It's a pity to waste a day like this. There won't be many more like it before winter sets in. Jack doesn't expect us back till late. What about driving to St Abbs?'

St Abbs was a picturesque fishing village in two parts, half of it clustering beneath a steep cliff around the tiny harbour, with the other half perched on top of a cliff, staring out to sea. When they got there, Rosa bought two bars of Cadbury's milk chocolate in the post office and gave one to The Basher.

'Beer always makes me want to eat something sweet after it,' she explained.

He put his bar in his pocket but said, 'Me too. Thanks.'

They drove out of the village to a grass-topped cliff that jutted into the sea. Hundreds of sea birds were roosting in crevices in the rock face. When they got out of the car, a brisk wind set Rosa's hair flying about her face and made her laugh out loud for the first time in ages.

'What a glorious day,' she cried and set off at a run along the cliff edge.

The Basher took his time following and when she looked back, she saw that he was aiming his camera at her. She waved and grinned. Life seemed liveable again.

They walked for a couple of miles before she sank down on a flat boulder and stared out across an expanse of pale green sea. A small trawler, like a child's bath toy, was slowly crossing the horizon and she said, 'I've always wanted to travel. I'd like to go to China.'

'What's stopping you?' asked The Basher, who settled himself beside her.

'Cowardice,' she said.

He grinned, reached into his pocket and brought out his bar of chocolate. 'Cheer up. Chocolate might help. I bet you've eaten all yours by now,' he said, giving it to her.

She accepted it eagerly. 'I can't resist chocolate. Thanks.'

When she looked at him lolling beside her, something happened. It was if she froze. Her heart seemed to stop beating and she could not take her eyes off his face. For the first time she realized that, in spite of the crooked nose, he was very good looking and amazingly like her hero Burt Lancaster. Why had she not noticed that before?

Like someone in a trance, she stared at him and he stared back, transfixed too. Her heart began thudding fast again, and, very slowly, as if drawn by some magical force, they leaned together and closed their eyes. Very gently their lips met. They did not speak, only put their arms round each other, kissing over and over again. A spirit of sheer light heartedness filled Rosa and she felt as if a string orchestra was playing inside her head.

There was no time, no place, nothing except this glorious

nearness. All her gloom miraculously disappeared. What mattered was the here and now and she was not going to waste any worries about yesterday or tomorrow.

A long time later – how long? She had no idea – they separated and stared at each other, looking as guilty as children caught stealing in a sweet shop. Neither of them knew what to say.

The Basher spoke first. 'If Jack or Gil hear about this, they'll rib the life out of me. They were bad enough about the photograph I took of you for the MP profiles.'

'It was very flattering,' she said.

'Yeah, Jack said a photographer influences his pictures. If he fancies the woman he's photographing he makes her look wonderful. Gil said the same thing. They had a good laugh at my expense,' he explained.

She held on to his hand when she got to her feet. 'Did you? Do you?' she asked.

'Yes,' he said simply.

'But you're always so rude to me – and you like blondes,' she exclaimed.

'You're the one that's rude,' he protested, 'and I've grown out of blondes. Anyway you were involved with that car salesman, and then Mike told me you had some Army doctor in tow . . .'

She laid her head against his chest. 'That's all past. I feel the same about you and I think I have done for ages but never realized it till now. You're such an awkward so and so.'

They drove back to town leaning against each other and talking about everything that came into their heads: Rosa's father and his inventions; and The Basher's plans to leave Edinburgh and wander the world taking photographs.

'I sold the pictures I took of the cathedral at Santiago del Compostella in Spain to National Geographic and they've said they'll use anything else I send them. If you come with me and do the words, we could sell features all over the world,' he said.

'We'll argue,' she reminded him, but she thought it sounded a good idea..

'I'm sure we will, but that won't put me off,' he told her with a laugh.

His flat in Danube Street was in a basement opposite the famous brothel. When they parked the car, they could hardly restrain themselves from embracing before they were inside his front door. Walking blindly, lips locked, they stumbled into the bedroom and fell on to his neatly made bed where they stayed till next morning.

When she woke, Rosa had trouble remembering where she was and how she got there.

'Oh my God, Mrs Ross!' she exclaimed, sitting up at the same time as The Basher came through the bedroom door with two steaming cups of tea.

'Who's she?' he asked, putting the cups down on a bedside table.

'My landlady. She'll think I've had an accident,' said Rosa.

'Ring her up and explain,' he suggested.

'Explain what? That I've spent the night with a man I've been fighting with for the past year?'

'I'll tell her if you like,' he said.

'You would too,' she replied, then sobered a little and asked, 'What do you want me to call you? The Basher is a sort of joke name, isn't it?'

'My name's Robert but I don't like it because it reminds me of the orphanage. The chaps in the football team call me Mac,' he told her.

She shook her head. 'I don't like that either. The Basher it stays then.'

Tea forgotten they fell back into bed, and it was eleven o'clock before they realized they should have been at work three hours ago.

When they finally dressed, they went to the office and resigned.

Jack looked at them in obvious amusement. 'My God, it took you two some time,' he said.

Mrs Ross was frosty when Rosa presented herself in Northumberland Street that night.

'And where have you been, madam?' she asked.

'I spent the night with a friend,' said Rosa cravenly, and before her landlady could give her notice, she rushed on, 'I'm giving up my room, Mrs Ross. I've been very happy here but it's time to move on.'

'And where are you going?' asked Mrs Ross more gently, for she was sorry to lose Rosa.

'I thought I might go travelling – with my friend,' Rosa explained.

'I hope she's a responsible girl,' said Mrs Ross.

Rosa decided to tell the truth. 'It's not a girl. It's a man. It's the photographer who took the pictures of Mary Lou at Prestwick – do you remember him?'

'You mean the one who kicked the dog?' Mrs Ross was shocked. She obviously thought Rosa had taken leave of her senses.

'Well, it *was* biting him,' said Rosa.

Mrs Ross held up her hand and said in a despairing voice, 'I do hope you know what you're doing!'

'Not really, but it's tremendous fun,' said Rosa with a laugh.

Epilogue

Thirteen years later, a couple sat, companionably argu-
ing, in the bar of the Algonquin Hotel in New York
after lunching with Mary Lou and her husband, a Wall Street
broker called Malcolm Coates III.

Rosa was teasing The Basher about flirting with their
hostess. 'You've always liked blondes,' she said. Though
he protested that she imagined the whole thing, he was glad
she was still jealous.

From the topic of Mary Lou, they went on to discuss
whether they should go to the Cloisters Museum by bus
or taxi. Rosa liked buses because they passed through bits
of the city that visitors normally avoided; and she could get
into conversation with other passengers en route. The Basher
preferred taxis because they were more direct and he did not
have to talk to strangers.

Suddenly a huge man in a pale blue seersucker suit, that
was draped round his big frame like a deflated barrage
balloon, bore down on them with his hand held out and
crying, 'It's The Basher! And Rosa!'

They looked up in surprise and it took a few seconds
before they recognized the imposing figure leaning over
them was Mike, though he was hardly changed except for
having expanded vastly in girth.

'Hey, what are you doing here? On a story?' he said,
sharp-eyed, and Rosa laughed because it was obvious he
still worried in case someone was scooping him.

'Mike! How wonderful to see you. Are you still on the
Enquirer?' she asked.

He nodded proudly. 'I'm head of the New York bureau

now. I've seen your bylines – Makepeace and McIvor – on lots of big pieces over the years. You're top liners, but in Edinburgh we never thought you'd get it together.'

'Neither did we,' admitted Rosa. She smiled at The Basher when she said it and he grinned back.

Mike looked from one to the other and asked, 'Married?'

'Yes, but only last year. My father thought it was time we did the right thing. What about you?' Rosa replied.

He shrugged. 'Twice – and divorced both times. I'm doing it again soon. Hey, it's great to see you,' he said, pulling out a chair and settling himself at their table, where, for the next hour they reminisced and exchanged information.

Though he lived so far from home, Mike maintained contact with a lot of old friends. He knew about Maling's death, of course, but he also told them that Tony was minister of a Church of Scotland parish in Argyll; Pat was on the London *Evening Standard*; Lawrie was Public Relations officer for a firm of bookmakers; and Clive, another serial marrier, was living in tax exile in the Channel Islands. He'd sold a television company a crime serial and was writing the episodes under a pseudonym.

'He doesn't use his own name because he's afraid his ex-wives will hit him for more money. Gil's still in the business, on the staff of the *Mail* in Paris, but Jack died last year in a car accident.'

That news, which they had not yet heard, saddened them and they toasted their old editor's memory in dry martinis, which seemed most appropriate given his liking for gin.

When they cheered up again, Rosa provided Mike with some information she had picked up during her last visit home to see her father and Jean.

'Harriet died. She collapsed in the office. Etta said she fell off her chair "like a budgie off its perch". She was over seventy, apparently, though she told everybody she was fifty-nine,' she said.

Mike laughed. 'All those free beauty creams must have worked,' he said and added, 'How's Etta?'

'She left the Cockburn. Now she runs the bar of the Wee

Windaes in the High Street, but she still knows everything that happens in Edinburgh's newspapers,' Rosa told him and added, 'She brought me up to date on Hilda too. Remember her? She married a banker and sits on the bench as a J.P.'

Mike laughed and said, 'God help any High Street drunk who comes up in front of her. I don't suppose you know what happened to that lying toad Rutland? He vanished off the scene when the *Express* fired him, didn't he?'

They shook their heads, but the mention of his name could still make Rosa feel uneasy, even after so many years.

'All I know is that after the inquiry into Hugh Maling's death, he vanished and no one's heard of him since,' she said.

From New York, Makepeace and McIvor flew to Los Angeles where they were commissioned to do a piece for a prestigious architectural magazine about period houses associated with famous 1930s film stars.

Over breakfast in their hotel room, Rosa, who read local newspapers wherever she went, was leafing through the *Los Angeles Times* show business section when she cried out in surprise, 'Here's a coincidence for you. Look at this.'

The Basher got up and leaned over her shoulder, sniffing appreciatively because he loved the way she smelt, a mixture of musk and vanilla.

'Let's go back to bed,' he suggested.

She shook her head. 'No, in a minute. Look at this. Doesn't that remind you of somebody?'

He sighed and took the magazine. Page seventeen was headed by an obviously snatched shot of a very thin, neurotic-looking man, turning round from a supermarket trolley, and staring in owlish surprise from behind an enormous pair of horn-rimmed spectacles.

'Amateur. A snatched shot and under exposed,' he said.

'Not that. Look at the man,' she told him.

He read the caption beneath the picture: 'Reclusive thriller writer Lancelot Learmonth has just signed a million dollar contract for his blockbuster novel *Killing For Pleasure*.

245

Sculnik will film it with Marlon Brando or Richard Burton in the starring role. The stars are fighting for the part.'

'Lucky bastard,' said The Basher and handed the magazine back to his wife.

'But *look* at him! Don't you recognize him? It's Charles Rutland,' she exclaimed.

He took back the paper and examined the picture more closely before he said, 'Hey, you're right. Those spaniel eyes give him away.'

She stood up to lean on him and read out bits of the article aloud. 'Learmonth is paranoid about his privacy. No one knows for certain if he is married and he lives in seclusion on a vast estate in the hills behind Los Angeles, in the Lake Arrowhead area. He never gives interviews and has threatened to shoot intruders on his property. He's made a fortune from his thrillers and has written ten. Each one's been a best-seller, but this one's the biggest yet.'

They looked at each other in amazement till Rosa said, 'So, he put his imagination to good use after all.'

'Do you want to do a piece about him?' her husband asked.

She shook her head. 'Oh no. I don't want to see him ever again if I can help it. I've always felt that he had a hand in Maling's death though I've no grounds for the suspicion. Anyway, he's not our kind of story but let's phone Mike and tip him off that the best-selling writer Lancelot Learmonth is "that toad Rutland". He'll track him down. Can you imagine what'll happen when they meet?'

The Basher laughed and said, 'Our Mike won't be put off by a threat to shoot him. We'll read all about it in the *Enquirer* soon. Pass me the phone.'